MORE TALES
OF
ZORRO

RUBÉN
PROCOPIO

First MOONSTONE Edition 2011
MORE TALES OF ZORRO

Published by Moonstone
© 2011 Zorro Productions, Inc. All Rights Reserved
Zorro ®
Produced under license

ISBN 10 digit: 1-933075-53-4   13 digit: 978-1-933076-53-9

Edited by Richard Dean Starr

Cover Illustration by
Douglas Klauba (Softcover Trade Edition)
Erik Enervold (Limited Hardcover Edition)
Cover Design Erik Enervold
Cover Concept & Art Direction by Richard Dean Starr

Interior Illustrations by Rubén Procopio

Interior Layout and Design
David Paul Greenawalt

Book Design & Prepress by
Erik Enervold/Simian Brothers Creative

Printed in USA

Published by Moonstone
582 Torrence Ave
Calumet City, IL 6040
www.moonstonebooks.com

This book is dedicated to

Matthew Baugh, Joe Gentile and Douglas Klauba...
friends and caballeros, all.

*"Great things are done
when men and mountains meet."*
- William Blake

Acknowledgements:

Completing a project like More Tales of Zorro presents a host of significant challenges. Therefore I must extend my most heartfelt thanks and gratitude to the following individuals without whom this book would not have been possible. As always, any omissions are unintentional and entirely the fault of the editor:

Matthew Baugh, a man of remarkable generosity and character, and a true and loyal friend; Author Erin "E. R." Bower, my friend, co-worker, and first writing protégé, for whom I have tremendous respect and affection; Mel Cotran, for friendship past and future; Sandra Curtis of Zorro Productions, Inc., for her remarkable intellect, good humor, and steadfast support; Henry Darrow, a gentleman and a fine actor whom I hope to meet in person one day; Kathy Gentile, for her uncommon support and kind nature; John Gertz, also of Zorro Productions, Inc., for allowing me to continue to play in Zorro's world; Jim Harrington, who knows why and (I hope) always will; Lee and Pat Hartz, who continue to be two of the kindest people I've ever known; Mark Headley, who proves every day that there really are a few good, loyal folks in Hollywood; Greg Litster of SafeChecks.com, for my dream home--and more importantly, his friendship and wise counsel; Fantasy master Tim Powers, who continues to teach me lessons that began more than two decades ago; Lili Stewart, who helps me to grow and feel welcome in more ways than I could have ever imagined; Rubén Procopio of Masked Avenger Studios, for his generosity, patience, and amazing artwork; Kristine Remick, for all the reasons under the sun and quite a few more; and last but not least, Ephraim Woods, with my eternal gratitude for your empathy, your generosity, and your wisdom.

Introduction

BY HENRY DARROW

Zorro has been my hero for a long time. I remember seeing the Tyrone Power version of The Mark of Zorro as a boy and loving it. The other kids and I would break up fruit crates and make swords out of the pieces so we could pretend to be Zorro. I had no idea then that I would be the first Hispanic actor to play him, or that I would be the only actor in three different productions of his story.

I had been thinking about Zorro when Moonstone approached me to write this introduction because I'm in the process of putting together my autobiography. I plan to say a lot about him there too. Of all the roles I've played, Zorro has been one of the most significant, and the most fun.

My first chance to play Zorro came in 1981, when Lou Scheimer was doing an animated series for CBS. I was pretty well known at the time. I'd played a lot of roles, including Manolito Montoya on The High Chaparral (1967-1971) and Lt. Manny Quinlan on Harry O (1974). Originally, they had wanted Fernando Lamas for the part, but he couldn't do it, so I stepped in.

The New Adventures of Zorro was the first voice-acting I'd ever done so it was a very different experience. I was never in the studio at the same time as the other actors; in fact, I didn't even find out who many of them were until after the show ended. I remember that Don Diamond was the voice of Sgt. Gonzales on our show and he had been Corporal Reyes on the Disney Zorro series years before.

The other thing that was different about voice-acting was that I didn't get to play off the other actors. It's natural for me to use a lot of intonation in acting, but I had to un-learn that. I'd say something like, "Buenas días, señorita, ¿Qué tal?" and Lou said it sounded too sexy. All of us had to use a flat intonation and that worked pretty well when they edited it all together.

Lou did a lot of things to take Zorro back to his roots. Instead of borrowing the names of the supporting characters from the Disney series, we had Captain Ramón and Sgt. González from the original novel by Johnston Mc-

Culley. He also changed a few things. Zorro was still Don Diego de la Vega, but instead of Diego's mute servant, Bernardo, we had a young helper named Miguel, who had his own costume and mask.

After that series ended, my next connection came when I auditioned for Zorro and Son at CBS. They wanted to do something with Zorro and Disney still had all the sets and props from their series. The idea was that I played the original Zorro who had gotten middle-aged and was training my son, played by Paul Regina, as my replacement. At the audition I climbed up on the desk and nearly fell off.

"That's exactly what we want," they said.

It was a good idea for a show, but they could never decide what direction they wanted to go. Some scenes were like a regular comedy, where the running gag was that Zorro couldn't do all the athletic stunts any longer, and then they would do something wild. A character would say, "The walls have ears," then they would cut to the wall and there were ears growing out of it.

It only lasted for a few episodes, but it was a lot of fun to work on, and there was some nice nostalgia for me. They altered Guy Williams' old costume for me to wear, but they had me use the black hat and gloves I'd had on High Chaparral. I also got to work with a lot of the same stuntmen who had been on Chaparral, and the cast and crew were great.

In 1990, New World created a new Zorro series for syndication. I auditioned for the role of Zorro's father, Don Alejandro. As it worked out I got a call to do the daytime drama Santa Barbara and the role went to Ephram Zimbalist Jr. I met him a few years later and he was a great guy; a very generous and gracious man. They were filming in Spain and Ephram didn't like living outside the United States at his age, so after a year he left. By that time my stint on Santa Barbara had ended so, when they called me again, I said yes.

The whole thing was set up on a farm fifteen miles outside of Madrid. Sadly, you can't see any of the sets any longer. When we left the farmer took everything down and there's no trace we were ever there. Working in Europe had some great advantages though. Duncan Regehr, who played Zorro, traveled the continent, and my wife and I followed his example. We visited some wonderful places, though I regret that we never made it to Barcelona.

Aside from some name changes, the characters were mostly the same, and we had a great cast. Our director, Ray Austin, was just a delight to work with. I was Don Alejandro, of course, and I played the role a little differently than Ephram had; I made him a bit more forceful. Duncan was Zorro and Don Diego; he was a tall, athletic guy who looked every inch the part. Our main villains were both Brits. Michael Tylo was the evil alcalde Ramon in the first two seasons. He was a villain in the Iago vein; really cruel and vicious. When he left, John Hertzler came in and his character, DeSoto, was more the comedic, blustering villain. Another person who was wonderful to work with was Jimmy Victor, who played the bumbling Sgt. Mendoza. Then, the lovely Patrice Martinez played Victoria, the female lead.

In the first version of the show, the character of Victoria had been the aristocratic daughter of one of the Dons. The producers liked Patrice, but not the character. They changed her into a feisty tavern owner with a passion for justice. She was probably the first female character in any version that really held her own with Zorro.

That was my last official involvement with the character; at least it was until now. It's great to see that Zorro, who will see his one-hundredth year in 2019, is still going strong. I'm glad to have had my part in his legend, and I'm glad for the role he's played in my life. It's wonderful to see him reappear in More Tales of Zorro and I hope and trust his adventures will continue to bring the same delight to new audiences that they have always brought to me.

Henry Darrow was born Enrique Tomás Delgado in New York City, on September 15, 1933. His "show business" debut was made at age 8, when he played a woodcutter in a school play. Henry was in his third year at the University when, for the first time, the Puerto Rican government authorized scholarships to acting schools. Only one was offered to a resident of Puerto Rico, and through hard work and determination, Henry became that one. He was soon on his way to Southern California and the Pasadena Playhouse–pursuing the career he'd begun at age 8. After graduating with a Bachelor of Arts degree in Theater Arts, he kept busy collecting film credits and acting experience in 12 feature films and 75 television series before he was chosen for what is probably his best-known role: Manolito Montoya on the TV series, "The High Chaparral". Throughout his career, Henry has appeared in some five hundred episodes of soap operas, mini-series, sit-coms, and dramas, along with numerous stage plays. He is the first Latino actor to have portrayed "Zorro" in two different television series, as well as providing the voice for a cartoon version of the masked hero. He won a "Bambi" Award–the German version of an "Emmy"–for "The High Chaparral", and a Daytime "Emmy" Award for his role on "Santa Barbara". Henry lives in North Carolina with his wife of many years, Lauren Levian, an actress/screenwriter.

FOREWORD

BY RICHARD DEAN STAR

It is the summer of 1977 and I am nine years-old.

At movie theaters, fans are still lining up to see a science fiction movie that opened in May and immediately shattered box-office records. My favorite t-shirt, with fanciful artwork showing a pair of robots and a squadron of spaceships rising toward an artificial moon, is testament to the enormous popularity of this cultural phenomenon.

Nonetheless, a film called Star Wars is the last thing I'm thinking about.

On this hot, Southern California day, I am balanced on a branch inside an enormous avocado tree, using my trusty sword to battle a pair of Spanish soldiers who are determined to run me through with their blades and send me plunging to the leaf-strewn ground below.

The thought most prevalent in my mind is not my impending doom, however, but the sheer awesomeness of my swordsmanship.

One of them jabs his blade toward my chest and I parry easily, pausing to sweep my black, silk-lined cape out of the way in a gesture more theatric than practical.

Just then, I hear a woman calling for me from beyond the giant tree's shadowy embrace. Could it be someone in need? A damsel in distress, perhaps, who seeks the assistance of the one and only Zorro?

Distracted by the female voice, the Spanish soldiers let down their guard for just a moment. I use this opportunity to slice a large, mocking Z across the closest man's chest, then push him back into the soldier behind him. They tangle together and tumble, screaming, off the branch and out of sight.

Another victory for the legendary Fox!

Then I hear the voice again, louder this time. And rather insistent. Hardly the tone a fair lady might use when summoning her champion.

I navigate down the limb to where the massive trunk rises up before splitting off into various smaller branches. From here the ground is just a few feet away. I clamper down easily and my polished boots dig into the soft layer of old leaves that conceal the earth below. A rich aroma rises up--the scent of the old, dead leaves that feed the roots of the tree.

On that day, and for all the days of my life, it will remain the smell of summer.

As I duck out from beneath the low-hanging branches, I find myself standing in bright sunlight. Dust motes float in the air, and across the sprawling one-acre yard, scattered dandelions stand frozen in the hot, dry air.

I glance down, and I am not surprised to see that my elegant boots have become simple tennis shoes--and dirty ones at that. I reach up and pull off my cape--only now it is nothing more than an old towel. And my mask? A tattered rag with two holes cut out for the eyes.

No hat, of course, because my parents won't spring for one.

But that's okay. My imagination has assembled a wardrobe grander than anything that they could have bought for me at White Front or the local Toys R' Us. And that includes my sword—which, alas, has reverted to its original identity as a simple bamboo stake.

The voice sounds again, edging from insistence into frustration. I shield my eyes from the sun and squint toward the front of the enormous property where my grandmother's house is located. My mom is standing by the side door, hands planted on her hips in a posture I know all too well.

So much for a damsel in distress.

"Coming!" I cry and jog toward the house.

Reality, it seems, has trumped imagination.

Even at nine years old, however, I know that I have the power to summon my alter-ego whenever the occasion presents itself. And in the interim, I can enjoy the adventures of Zorro on TV and sleep well at night, dreaming of righting wrongs before I ride my faithful steed, Toronado, off into the sunset.

Once I'm in the house, I roll the towel around the bamboo stake and then tuck my homemade mask in one end of the package before stowing the whole thing away in the guest room closet. The Wonderful World of Disney is just starting out in the living room. If I'm lucky, maybe they'll play one of the old Zorro episodes.

Either way, it doesn't matter, because I know that Zorro—at least, my nine year-old version of him—will ride again next Sunday.

I can hardly wait.

Looking back, it seems hard to believe that it has been more than thirty-three years since I last enjoyed the privilege of "playing" the legendary Fox. Oddly, I've never felt inclined to dress up as Zorro for Halloween, although there were certainly were—and still are—costumes a whole lot more realistic than a bamboo stake or an old towel!

Perhaps it's because I've long felt that those memories of my childhood were precious, and that if I tried to replace them with a fleeting, holiday fantasy for adults it would somehow dilute the wonder of those long-lost summer days.

One thing I am sure of: as a child, I never dreamed that I would someday have the opportunity to make a lasting contribution to the real world of Zorro. Or that I would eventually meet, and come to admire, two of his most stalwart defenders: author Sandra Curtis and John Gertz of Zorro Productions, Inc. I cannot fully express my gratitude to them and to Joe Gentile of Moonstone Books for the privilege of working with this incredible character and his world.

As a child, I wanted nothing less than to be the Fox. When you read these stories I know that you, too, will be transported once again to those days of action, adventure, and romance in Old California. And maybe, if you're lucky, when you go to sleep at night you'll dream of being astride Toronado or battling your own cadre of Spanish soldiers.

I know that for me, it's a journey I hope to make again.

- Richard Dean Starr
Starchase
Los Angeles, California
June, 2010

LETTER FROM GUADALAJARA
THE STORY OF CAPITÁN MONASTARIO

BY KEITH R.A. DECANDIDO

Capitán Enriqué Sanchez Monastario loathed Spring.

One of the few things he liked about his assignment to this appalling desert wasteland of Alta California was that, he imagined, he could escape his twin weaknesses to damp and pollen. However, he did not reckon with the settlement's wealthier denizens (of which he was one, of course) having large gardens filled with flowers both local and transplanted from the motherland.

And so for one week out of every year, generally around late March, the flowers would bloom, the landscape would grow pretty, and Monastario was not permitted to breathe.

The pounding in his head was only made worse by the arrival of his second, Sergeant Garcia. "Er, Capitán?"

"What is it, Sergeant?"

"Er, well, you see, Capitán—the mail has arrived."

Glancing out the window of his well-appointed office, Monastario saw that the sun was at its zenith. "It is midday, Sergeant."

"Yes, sir."

"Correct me if I'm wrong, but the mail always arrives at midday on Wednesday, yes?"

"Well, yes, sir, but—"

Monastario let out a long sigh that quickly modulated into a snarl. "Sergeant, at present I feel as if my skull has been filled end to end with gunpowder, waiting only a lit fuse that it might explode. The mere act of inhalation causes me misery on a scale that would make a leper weep. You would therefore be well to explain, and quickly, why you have gone to the effort of carrying your corpulent form all the way to my office simply to inform me that an event that happens at this time every week has, in fact, happened at this

17

time *this* week."

Garcia shifted his great weight back and forth from one foot to the other, an action that made the rotund officer look as if he'd teeter over at any minute. "Ah, well, sir, you see, there are two letters here for you that I thought required your immediate attention. One is from General de la Nueva in Santa Barbara."

Another verbal skewering of the sergeant died on Monastario's lips. De la Nueva was the one whose signature adorned the bottom of orders that sent him to the Pueblo of Los Angeles almost a year ago—and was also the recipient of the letter Monastario had sent to Santa Barbara a fortnight ago. "And the other?" he asked, rubbing his temples in a failed attempt to get them to stop throbbing.

"There is no name, but it comes from Guadalajara."

Monastario's hands dropped to his desk, and he looked up at Garcia. "Guadalajara..." He shook his head, an action he immediately regretted, and asked, "Sergeant, is the J in the city name adorned with an unusual flourish, and is it dotted with an X?"

As Monastario watched, Garcia's face took on several expressions at once, no doubt borne of the confusion engendered both by the capitán's asking of the question, and of the fact that the answer was apparently "yes."

"How did you know, Capitán?"

Returning to the rubbing of his temples, Monastario said, "Read me the letter from the general."

"Sir?"

"The request was clear, was it not, Sergeant?"

"Yes, sir, but—"

"You haven't lost your facility for Spanish in the past minute, have you?"

"No, sir, but—"

"Then read the letter, if you please."

"But, sir—I am not fit to see such documents!"

Monastario smiled bitterly. "Please, Sergeant, do not sell yourself short. The list of things for which you are not fit is a lengthy one, and one I would be happy to enumerate in detail were I in better health. In fact, I would grant 'being a sergeant' primacy on that list. Nonetheless, I am currently suffering from pain in my head that would stop a bull in its tracks, and attempting to decipher the general's secretary's hand will only exacerbate an already miserable situation. I therefore, as your commanding officer, hereby give you leave to read the general's letter aloud to me."

Garcia cleared his throat several times before finally saying, "Yes, sir, of course, sir." Fumbling with the envelope with his pudgy fingers—to the point where Monastario was tempted to loan the sergeant his own dagger, and only didn't for fear of Garcia slicing open a vein and making a mess in his office—Garcia eventually managed to tear it open and liberate the one-page item inside.

Unfolding the paper, he opened his mouth to speak, but Monastario, recalling Garcia's literal-minded tendencies, quickly said, "Skip to the important part, please, Sergeant."

Hesitating, Garcia said, "So you don't wish me to inquire as to your health?"

Monastario snorted, an action that felt as if it expanded his nose to the size of Garcia. He spit some phlegm into the spittoon next to his desk, and then said, "Correct."

Again, Garcia cleared his throat. "'Regarding your request for a transfer, Capitán, I'm afraid that approving the request is, of course, out of the question, and I am surprised that you would even have the effrontery to ask.'" This time Garcia's clearing of the throat had nothing to do with preparing to speak. "Is the capitán sure that—"

"Go on," Monastario said through clenched teeth.

"But, sir, I don't think it's right that I should see this—"

Slamming a fist on his wooden desk, Monastario bellowed, "Sergeant, the only consideration I have ever given to what you *think* is to comment on the extreme rarity of such an event. Go *on*."

"Yes, sir. 'You were told the conditions under which your term at your current post would end. Those conditions have yet to be met. Until they are, you shall remain assigned there. The subject is closed.' Er, then he wishes you well, signs it, and, ah, and whatnot."

"I see." Monastario leaned back in his chair.

Garcia stammered. "I'm, ah—I'm sorry sir."

"Well, Sergeant, I must thank you—after all, my life is a quagmire of misery, and my one hope has just been dashed. But that's all right, because Sergeant Demetrio López Garcia has pity for me! That makes *everything* better!"

19

"Sir—"

Cutting off yet another pathetic exhortation, the capitán said, "Set that, and the other letter, on my desk."

"Er, uh—yes, sir."

As Garcia moved to do so, Monastario added, "Unless King Ferdinand himself enters the compound, I am *not* to be disturbed for the rest of the day."

"Yes, sir. Uh—what about Zorro?"

"What *about* Zorro?"

"What if *he* enters the compound? Should I disturb you, then?"

Giving Garcia as foul-tempered a look as he could manage—which was quite considerable at present—Monastario said, "Not then, either. If Zorro comes today, he can have me."

After Garcia's hasty departure, Monastario slowly rose to his feet. His reaction to the flowers made him somewhat dizzy, so he had to steady his stance for a moment before continuing to the ornate wooden cabinet.

Like virtually everything in this office, it was scarred with the triple-sword-slash pattern in the shape of a letter Z that the Fox tended to leave behind before departing a room. There were so many of those scars among the furnishings that Monastario barely noticed them anymore.

Fishing a key from his uniform pocket, he unlocked the small door on the cabinet's bottom left-most corner, swinging it open to reveal a cubbyhole that could hold far more than its actual contents: a thick-bottomed clear bottle of an equally clear liquid that sat alone in the center of the cubbyhole.

He had yet to crack open the Tequila since he brought it here from his last post.

But he suspected he would need to imbibe some—if not all—of it before he worked up the strength to actually read the second letter.

Monastario took a glass from the sideboard where he kept the drinks he was willing to share with the superior officers, Dons, high-ranking priests, and others of equal or greater station who visited his office and then poured himself some of the Mexican liquor.

The memories prompted by the lovely, intense odor that emanated from the bottle were almost palpable…

…you're eight years old, riding with your older brothers Pablo and Juan, your older sister María Esperanza, and Mother and Father to a dinner party. The carriage passes a building that looks horribly damaged.

Ever inquisitive, you ask, "What happened to that building?"

Pablo looks down on you, as Pablo always does to everyone except for Father. "It burned, stupid!"

Out of habit more than rebuke, Mother says, "Pablo, don't speak to Quiqué that way!"

Father adds, "That house belonged to the del Gados. Both the owner and his two sons died in the fire, which is why it still stands empty a year later."

"I don't understand," you say honestly.

"Of *course* you don't," Pablo says.

"Shut *up*, Pablo!" Juan says.

"*You* shut up, Juancito!"

You ignore your brothers and look out the carriage window again. You see children wearing too little clothing and covered in too much dirt. They seem to be searching for something in the building. "Why are those children there?"

Father sighs. "Who knows why the peasants do as they do? Perhaps they think they can find money there."

"Peasants don't have money?"

"No, stupid," Pablo says, expectedly.

"God is very careful, Quiqué," Father says before anyone can castigate Pablo again. "He only gives money to those who are able to handle it. People who are born poor are born such because God knows that money would cause them evil."

"I see," you say, even though you really don't…

…you sneak out to the building a week later. It's easy: the house staff is too busy trying to break up Pablo and Juan's endless quarrelling, and to cater to María Esperanza's every whim, so no one ever pays attention to the littlest one.

When you arrive, there are three young boys there again. You're not sure if they're the same ones, but they look similar enough. They are wearing clothes that are in just *dreadful* condition, their hair is a mess, they're filthy, some of them have no shoes, and they're all so—so *skinny*. You're appalled.

"Who are you?" one of them asks.

"My name is Enriqué. What's yours?"

Another one cuts off the first one. "We're not supposed to talk to you."

This confuses you. "Why not?"

"You're one of the upper classes. If we talk to you, we'll get whipped."

"That's crazy!" you say, meaning it. "Why are you in this building? You could get hurt!"

"If we're lucky we'll find some money—or something we can sell. If we do, then we can eat today."

You gulp in shock at that. Eat "today"? Your eight years has never contained a day that didn't have *at least* three meals. "All you need is money in order to eat?"

"Yes," the boy says slowly.

Reaching into your pocket, you pull out some coins. You're not sure how much—sums were never your strong suit—but it's an amount you can spare easily.

The boys' eyes all go wide. You realize that they've never seen this much money before. "Go ahead," you say as they hesitate. "Take it. You need it more than I do."

Eventually, they grab hungrily at the coins…

…you make regular trips to the house after that. Each time you go, you bring more coins. Each time you go, there are more boys. You can't bring enough coins for everyone.

They start to get angry.

One time, you go, and you've only been able to scrape together a small pile of coins—but there are a dozen boys at the burned-out building, and one of them is bigger than Father.

The big one says, "That's all you got?"

"I—I'm sorry, I just—"

Turning to another boy, the big one says, "You said he had money."

"He does. He's probably holding out on us."

"Filthy traitor, leading us on!"

"Yeah, just like all the other rich people—trying to make us look stupid!"

Before you know what's happening, the boys are all yelling at you, and the big one starts to hit you. In eight years of life, your only direct experience with violence has been the occasional spanking as a baby—until now. The boy hits you and there's blood and the pain is just *awful*…

…Father is yelling at you while the doctor treats your injuries. "What were you *thinking*, Quiqué? Did I not *tell* you that God wishes the peasants to be poor? If He wished otherwise, He would have made them be born of our class."

"I'm—I'm sorry, Father."

"Your heart was in the right place, Quiqué, but you cannot simply *give* to the poor. If you do, they will only ask for more until you have nothing—and then they turn on you like the beasts they are."

"It wasn't all of them," you insist. After all, the first three boys were nice. "It was just the one!"

After the doctor is done, Father takes you into the city to find the boy in question. It's not as difficult as you think at first, since this boy is so much bigger than the others, and he makes no effort to hide himself.

When the soldiers seize him at Father's orders, the large boy does not deny what he has done. "He provoked me!" the large boy insists. "I was just defending myself!"

You watch the boy get whipped fifty times, see him break down into tears by the tenth lash, and you enjoy watching him suffer as you did…

…you revel in the melodious laugh of Marisela de los Santos as you walk through her family's beautiful garden in Guadalajara. You're even willing to suffer the stuffing-up of your nose that results from being among the blooming flowers, only so you can hear that laugh again.

"I must return to the house," she says, clutching the parasol that shields her porcelain features from the violence of the sun. "Thank you, Quiqué, for the company."

You kiss her white-gloved hand the way your tutors instructed you, and then watch her navigate slowly through the garden back to the house, casting several glances behind her.

"That's a fine form you cut in that uniform, Quiqué," comes a voice from behind you.

You wince as you turn to face Pablo. At seventeen, only two people call you "Quiqué." From Marisela it's an endearment; from Pablo, it's an unsubtle reminder of which of you is Father's eldest, and therefore his heir.

As the third son, your only option is the military, where you are placed in the officer corps immediately. Your training will begin soon, but you already have been issued the uniform of a cadet.

The compliment on how you look in that uniform is a rare one from Pablo, so you thank him. Of course, such an occasion often precedes a favor.

"I was wondering, Quiqué, what you think of Señorita de los Santos as a wife?"

Your eyes go wide; your stomach starts to churn like mad. There is nothing, *nothing* that would please you more than to make this angel yours.

But before you can reply, Pablo continues: "I can think of no one better suited to be my bride, can you?"

And then you realize—*this* is why the Monastarios and the de los Santoses have spent so much time together of late. The intention was to merge the families' fortunes through a union between Father's oldest son and the de los Santos's only daughter.

Marisela will never be yours…

…Padre Esteban has been very generous in allowing you to see Marisela in the days leading up to the wedding. It is difficult to arrange meetings—she is awash in preparations for marriage to Pablo, and you are enmeshed in officer training—but with the help of the priest, you are able to steal precious time with your lady love.

You try to thank the priest, but he insists on no payment. "It is enough," he says, "to see two young people who adore each other be allowed to express themselves as God intends."

But one day, you arrive to find, not only Esteban, but Pablo and Father— and Governor-Intendant Roque Abarca himself! You make a half-hearted attempt to explain your presence at the mission, knowing that the truth will result in punishment of some sort. Possibly death.

Somehow, they believe you when you say you have a private message for the priest from a friend of his stationed at the training camp, and you are able to steal a moment.

"What is happening?" you ask.

"What do you mean?" Esteban asks.

"Why did you not get word to me that I could not visit Marisela?"

Esteban draws himself up to his full height. "My good man, are you insinuating that I would allow you to see Señorita de los Santos, a woman affianced to your *brother*, in secret? I am a man of *God*, sir!"

Glancing behind to make sure that no one comes running at the sound of Esteban's bellowing, you whisper, "Please! You said that we should be allowed—"

"The only thing I will allow, sir, is your departure from my church. And never set foot here again, if you know what is good for you."

As you leave, you hear the priest apologize to the governor and your family, and then he asks the governor what, precisely, the arrangements for the delivery of the gold will *be*...

...your career proceeds at the pace of a snail. Padre Esteban is Bishop Esteban now, and he has the governor's ear. So does Pablo, who inherited Father's lands and titles upon the latter's death, and proceeded to invest and increase his power, soon becoming Don Pablo Sanchez Monastario.

You don't know for sure, of course, but so many promotions are blocked, and so many opportunities are given to lesser officers—lesser in skill, lesser in breeding—that you cannot believe that there isn't an invisible hand or two guiding your misery.

Especially since you are the consummate soldier. Every order you are given, you follow to the letter. Every commander you are assigned to, you pledge your loyalty to, and that loyalty is rewarded every time. Every rule, every regulation, you follow religiously, even such comparatively inconsequential minutiae as grooming. Your commendations pile up to as great a height as your turned-down promotions.

Don Pablo never speaks to you again after that day at the church, leading you to believe that Esteban's outraged words *did* carry to the front as you feared.

Only one thing keeps you sane. Once a year, in springtime, when the flowers bloom, you receive a letter from the former de los Santos estate—now one of many Monastario holdings—in Guadalajara.

The first year, the letter comes with a box that contains a bottle of liquor from a city called Tequila, not far from Guadalajara. You swear not to drink it until the proper occasion presents itself.

And then you are invited to share a meal with General de la Nueva.

"We have a problem in Los Angeles," he explains while devouring a bloody steak with his gloved hands. "An outlaw who continues to defy the King's law. He styles himself the Fox."

You are stunned. "Zorro? I thought him a legend, like the Weeping Woman or the Seven Cities of Gold."

"Rest assured, Capitán, he is real. And your job is to stop him. He has already brought disgrace to both the military and the governor's office. You will be made military commander of the pueblo and its outlying territories, but those duties will be secondary to this: Zorro must be stopped at *all* costs, by *any* means."

"I will report immediately," you say without hesitation. From what you've heard, Zorro is a blight upon Spain, a creature who defies the rightful dictates of law—both God's and man's. True, you'd not believed those stories, but neither do you doubt the general's word. Besides, if you are the one to stop the Fox, perhaps that would finally allow you to come out from under the thumb of your brother and the bishop.

And so you proceed at first light to your new post...

"Wake *up!*"

Letting out a gasp, Monastario lifted his head from the desk. Instinctively, his hand reached for his sword.

Even as his hand closed over the hilt, the weapon still lodged in the scabbard attached to his belt, the capitán realized that Zorro was in his office—and that he'd been asleep for some time.

He quickly looked about the office. It had grown dark—Garcia had disobeyed orders long enough to have the lanterns in the office lit, which Monastario was willing to forgive—and most of the Tequila was gone. His headache was even worse. And drool was dripping from the corner of his mouth.

"Whatever it is you want, Zorro," Monastario said blearily as he wiped the drool with the back of his glove, "may we please proceed ahead to the part where you make me look a fool, deface my furniture, and leave via the window?"

"Why have you done this, Capitán?"

"Done *what?*"

"Do not pretend ignorance!" the outlaw shouted.

"I am not *pretending*, sir!" Monastario shouted right back. "I have been alone in this room since midday—as Garcia is my witness." He knew that, for reasons passing understanding, Zorro trusted the fat sergeant's word, even though the Fox tormented Garcia as much as he did anyone and everyone in authority.

Zorro seemed to consider this. "Perhaps you are innocent."

"Hah!" Monastario rose unsteadily to his feet, resting his hands on the surface of his desk to hold himself upright. "What do you know of innocent and guilty, Zorro? Those are terms of law, and you have placed yourself outside it."

"Perhaps, but I do so for the greater good."

"Whose greater good, I wonder? Do you know that a military commander of a settlement of this size usually has three times the manpower? I do not, because of you. My superiors view it as a waste of resources. And yet, in addition to having to clean up *your* messes, I must also perform my usual duties."

"Such as making yourself richer?"

Monastario did not take the bait. "Such as preserving the security of the pueblo. Such as maintaining order in the settlement. It was my soldiers who fixed the bridge that was destroyed in those rains last month."

"And the Dons who paid for it."

Now Monastario did take the bait. "Your sarcasm notwithstanding, sir, our superiors in fact *do* encourage us to make ourselves richer. However, they do discourage us from using our own capital to finance endeavors of the state. If the military's own funds cannot provide—as indeed they could not last month—then we look outside. That is what the Dons are for."

Finally, the capitán felt confident enough in his stability—if not his sobriety—to stand upright without help from the desk. "But then," he continued, "you know that. You *are* one of the Dons. Oh," he added quickly, "I do not know which, but it was clear from the first weeks after I arrived that you were one of them."

"Why do you say that?"

"I've seen you smile, sir," Monastario said. "Only a man of breeding and station has such fine teeth. For that matter, only a well-fed man could do what you do so skillfully, and your well-cared-for mustache is one that is primarily seen on the upper classes. Also? The only part of you I can see is your smirk—and only a Don smirks *quite* like that." The capitán did not add that Don Pablo had the same smirk.

"You are perhaps smarter than I gave you credit for, Capitán," Zorro said with a small bow.

"I could hardly be stupider than *you* give me credit for, sir."

"Then I must ask you, Capitán—how can you perform the acts you perform? Surely a man of your intelligence knows that what you do is wrong."

Monastario shook his head. "What *I* do is wrong? By whose standard? You see, I am a soldier—my *duty* is to follow the orders of my superiors. If I shirk that duty, *then* what I do is wrong."

"Even if those orders are immoral?"

Now Monastario leaned his head back and roared with laughter—loud enough that it made his own headache worse, but he no longer cared.

"I amuse you, Capitán?"

"Very much so, actually," he said, getting himself under control. "Do you know what my primary orders *are* at this post? To stop *you*. All other matters are secondary, including protection of and security for the settlement. The *only* right thing for me to do, sir, is stop you by any means necessary. You see, Zorro, while anonymity frees you, my rank shackles me. I can do naught but follow the orders I am given, for if I do not, my fate will well and truly be sealed."

"No matter how many peasants or men of God get in the way of you following those instructions?"

Again Monastario laughed, but it was a bitter one. "Believe me when I tell you that the welfare of vermin is *not* listed among my responsibilities."

"The peasants are human beings, created in God's image like everyone else, and they do not deserve—"

Monastario interrupted. "More proof that you are a Don, sir. Only a Don could be *that* ignorant. I know peasants quite well, Zorro, and they deserve neither consideration nor compassion. And I'd sooner give it to *them* than any so-called men of God."

"It is ironic," Zorro said, shaking his head with apparent pity—an emotion that Monastario no more wanted from the Fox than he did from Garcia.

"What is?"

Zorro stared at Monastario. The capitán supposed it might have been an intense stare, but the mask that covered the top of the Fox's face served its purpose well, reducing the effectiveness of the outlaw's glare. But then, if Monastario could see Zorro's eyes clearly enough for the glower to have full effect, he would also see enough of his eyes to perhaps identify him.

"You see, Capitán," Zorro said, "I had retired. Capitán Ramon was dead, the governor had returned to Spain in disgrace. Zorro was no more. I only came back out of retirement because of *your* arrival."

A multitude of emotions washed over Monastario, breaking on his mind like so many waves. Anger, laughter, amazement, bitterness… General de la Nueva mentioned nothing about Zorro retiring—but then, how does anyone know for sure that a mysterious, anonymous figure who only appears for brief intervals is gone?

"I cannot leave until you are gone, yet my being gone is the only way to be rid of you." Monastario snatched the thick glass that had the last sip of Tequila. "God, it seems, has a greater sense of humor than even I imagined." He slugged down the last of his drink. It burned as it travelled down his throat. "Enough. I would like to go to bed. Kindly leave."

The capitán could see one of Zorro's eyebrows rise from the motion on his mask. "You will not try to thwart me?"

"Not today. Consider it a gift."

"What is the occasion, Capitán?"

"An anniversary." Monastario sat back down in his chair.

Holding up his rapier, Zorro said, "Very well, Capitán. Until next time."

Zorro cast about the office for several moments. Monastario was used to this—he was looking for something to leave his mark upon.

But after a moment, he looked back at the capitán.

Then he put the rapier's tip to his own forehead in salute. "Good night!"

And, for the first time since his arrival in this sand-choked hole of hell, Monastario saw the Fox leave his office without defacing a single item.

Once Zorro was gone, Monastario looked down at his desk.

The letter from the general had been dampened by Monastario's drool, causing a blot upon General de la Nueva's signature.

Monastario found that he could live with that.

He took hold of the envelope and held it to his nose, wondering what he would smell were his nose functioning properly. As he did so, he imagined that he heard a melodious laugh.

Reaching for his belt, he unholstered the dagger he'd been issued. Gently, he sliced open the envelope and took the letter out from inside it.

As always, it was three pages long. Marisela never wrote more or less than that.

As always, it began with the words, "Dear Quiqué."

And for one hour on one day in the Spring, Capitán Enriqué Sanchez Monastario knew joy.

ZORRO
AND THE BRUJA

By Matthew Baugh

Zorro laughed.

The black-clad horseman rode full-tilt into the night, a dozen lancers, Don Rafael Montero in the lead, following close behind.

"Steady, Toronado," Zorro whispered. "I know you want to outrace them, but that would spoil the little surprise I have planned."

The stallion nickered as if understanding his rider's words.

They neared a point where the path ran parallel to a stream lined with cottonwoods. As they entered the stand, the big trees shielded them from the soldiers' eyes. Pulling the reins, Zorro brought the stallion to a stop. The gleam of water was almost impossible to see on the shadowed path, but the masked rider had been expecting it. He turned his mount and guided him into a camouflaged blind.

A moment later the ground shook with the pounding hooves of a dozen horses. The lancers charged past, never seeing a thing. Montero was in front with his sword drawn. He was still moving at full tilt when he came to the mud slick that Zorro had created by damming the stream earlier that evening.

Montero's horse scrambled in an effort to stay on its feet, then fell, sending him into the shallow water. Behind them other horses went down or lost their riders on the slippery trailbank.

Zorro trotted Toronado out of the blind, laughing.

"You should be more careful on your night rides, Don Rafael!" he called.

Montero struggled to his feet, his face and uniform coated with mud. He aimed a pistol at the masked man and pulled the trigger, but the weapon failed to discharge.

"Wet powder?" Zorro asked. "That's just as well. I doubt you could hit me at thirty yards on a night like this anyway. Now, if you will pardon me, I have another engagement."

He wheeled Toronado around and raced into the night. By the time the troop had remounted, he was gone.

Z

Zorro didn't see anyone in the graveyard. That was a good thing. He had worried that there might be parents keeping vigil on this, the last night in October, the night when the angelitos, the souls of deceased children, slipped into the land of the living for a visit.

He left Toronado at the edge of the graveyard afield and moved through the markers until he found the tombstone he wanted. It was made of fine marble, engraved with the words,

L⬤LITA DE LA VEGA
1798-1817
BEL⬤VED WIFE

Zorro crossed himself and knelt by the marker. He pulled a single rose from his shirt, and laid it on the grave.

"You'll like this, mi corazón," he whispered. "You always loved it when I brought you roses to wear in your hair."

"Four years since I lost you, he said. "Four years and still I must ride as El Zorro. I tried to set Don Tomás free tonight, but Montero is as cunning as..." he paused and chuckled. "He is nearly as cunning as a fox. I will have to find a new plan to get past him."

He shook his head.

"It is always someone. When I came home from Spain it was your cousin who was exploiting the people. I chased him away only to face that pig, Esteban. Then it was Monastario, Ramon, De Soto, each time a new face with the same schemes. I sometimes worry that my poor pueblo is cursed.

Zorro removed a gauntlet to press his fingers to the stone; they traced the letters of his late wife's name.

"There is something else," he said. "I've met someone—Esperanza

Berríos—I think you would like her." He paused, a trace of a smile played on his lips. "If you didn't claw her eyes out you would like her, that is.

"I've thought that perhaps it is time for me to marry again, but she is so gentle...so delicate. You understood what I did as Zorro, but I am not sure that she...

He heard a noise and paused. Someone else was moving among the tombstones. He rose, one hand resting lightly on the hilt of his sword.

He could make out two shapes in the darkness, one small and the other very large; a man and a woman. They stood close to one another, speaking in soft voices.

"Buenas noches," Zorro said.

"Who is it?" the woman's voice asked, then with greater urgency. "Whoever you are, help me!"

The big man growled something and grabbed for her. Zorro leapt forward as the two struggled. He saw the flash of a blade in the moonlight; then the man had a long knife with a wavy edge held to the woman's throat. Zorro lashed out with his whip, snaring the knife-hand. He flicked his wrist and the blade spun away into the darkness.

"Take her then!" the man cried. A powerful shove sent the woman sprawling into Zorro's arms. The attacker turned and fled. When the Fox tried to follow, the woman clung to him.

"Don't leave me!" she pleaded. "I think he cut me." She swooned, and he lowered her to the ground.

He gave the fleeing man a last glance. As much as he wanted to pursue, the victim came first. He looked her over, but saw only a small nick at the hinge of her jaw.

The woman began to stir and Zorro noticed that she was very attractive. He wondered who she was. Her eyes opened, a startling blue against her olive complexion.

"You... you are El Zorro?" she said.

He flashed a grin.

"There is nothing to fear, señorita. The man is gone."

"Gracias!" She shook her head, as if trying to clear it. "Who was he?"

"I wondered the same thing," Zorro said. "What were you doing here, so late at night?"

"I am a curandera," she said. "I use herbs to heal the sick. There is a kind of mushroom that can only be found growing near graves. If it is picked on the eve of El Día de los Muertos, it can cure many ailments. That man must have seen me and decided to..."

She shuddered and drew her shawl tighter around her.

"I should see you safely home," Zorro said.

"God bless you." She smiled warmly. "But there is a reward on your head. I would not put you at risk, especially when there is no need."

She nodded across the graveyard to the Mission of San Gabriel Arcángel.

"I will ask Fray Felipe to send one of his neophytes to escort me."

"As you wish, señorita." Zorro stood and whistled for Toronado. A moment later the great horse appeared out of the darkness.

The woman watched until he was out of sight, a smirk on her lips. When she was certain he was too far to hear, she gave an ululating whistle, like the call of some exotic bird. A moment later, a big form moved through the gravestones to join her.

"You played your part well," she said. "He thought you meant to harm me."

"I can understand the use of such a ruse if the soldiers had found us," the big man said. "I do not understand why it is necessary to deceive a common bandido. I could simply have killed him for you."

"Are you questioning me, Julio?" The woman's voice was gentle, but the expression in her blue eyes made the brute cringe.

"Of... of course not, Doña Inez."

She offered him the beneficent smile of a forgiving monarch.

"Come, help me search the graveyard. I want to know what he was doing here."

As silently as the hot wind from the ocean, the two began to move through the stones. After a few moments, the woman found a single fresh rose.

"Lolita de la Vega," she read. "Why does the famous Zorro bring you flowers? Could it be..."

This time the smile that came to the woman's lips was one of triumph.

Don Diego de la Vega and Esperanza Berríos strolled through the plaza, arm in arm; her duena, Mirabel, trailed behind, discretely out of earshot. A group of children dressed in wooden skull-masks ran up to them.

"Calaverita señor, por favor," one of the boys cried.

Diego chuckled and gave small coins to each of them.

"Here are your gifts, little ones. Now, go and frighten someone else."

The children rushed away, gloating over their treasure.

"Do you suppose they'll use it wisely?" Esperanza asked.

"I'm sure they'll spend it on calaveras de azucar," he replied.

Esperanza smiled. "Was that what you did at their age?"

He nodded. He had loved the little sugar candies made to resemble skulls. He had also enjoyed wearing the skull-shaped calacas. Diego had always been fond of masks.

"You have strange customs here in California," Esperanza said with a smile.

"The skeletons?" He said. "Fray Felipe tells me it is an old Indian idea that has mixed with our Christian ways. They say that the barrier between the worlds of the living and the dead is thinnest on these three nights. The spirits of the dead, the angelitos, sometimes come to visit the living."

"It's a charming superstition," she replied. "So much better than real life."

He heard the change in her voice.

"You're thinking of Don Tomás?"

"I know that he spoke out against Rafael's new taxes," she said, "but treason? I can't believe that such a good man is to be executed."

"Governor Montero is very harsh."

"I know that you don't like him, but Rafael is no monster." She hesitated, then tightened her grip and spoke quietly. "I know that he would govern more wisely if he had someone by his side to temper his moods."

He stopped walking and stared at her as the implication settled in.

"Esperanza! Surely you don't mean..."

"I'm sorry, Diego. I wish I'd known a better way to tell you."

"But, this is not... you can't..."

"Can you think of another way?" She smiled sadly and shook her head.

Diego caught her by the shoulders, at a loss for words. He ached to tell her his secret, that he was the masked avenger who would defeat Montero. He wanted to promise her that she didn't have to do anything, because he was Zorro.

She gazed at him for a moment, tears brimming in her eyes, waiting for something.

He didn't say a word.

Esperanza turned and hurried away, Mirabel trailing in her wake.

Diego cursed himself for not telling her his secret. Perhaps the truth would be too hard for her to handle, but would it really be worse than marriage to that animal, Montero? Still, he found that he could not make himself go after her. The power of his secret held him in place as surely as if he had been if he was bolted to the ground.

"Señor de la Vega?"

A boy of ten or eleven approached Diego, his dark face somber.

"Sí," Diego answered gloomily. "Do you want a calaverita young man?"

The boy ignored the copper coin he produced.

"Doña Inez sent me to find you," he said. "Please follow me."

"Who is Doña Inez?"

The boy didn't answer. After a moment Diego shrugged.

"Very well, show me the way?"

The boy led him to a house on the edge of the plaza. They walked through a dark corridor, finally coming to a small sitting room. Diego's eyes widened. The woman at the table was the one Zorro had helped last night.

"Thank you, Ysidro," the woman said.

The boy bowed and backed out of the room. Diego looked around. There were cabalistic symbols painted on the walls. A crystal ball rested in the center of the table.

"Don Diego," the woman said, "welcome to my home."

"Gracias, Doña Inez." He nodded to the crystal ball. "Have you brought me here to tell my fortune?"

She smiled enigmatically.

"I understand why you might scoff. I assure you, my powers are real. I summoned you because of a vision. Something terrible will happen tonight, an injustice that will claim innocent lives."

Diego felt his throat go dry.

"But why tell me? Surely this is a matter for the authorities."

"Last night the man they call El Zorro saved my life," Doña Inez said. "I prayed to the spirits, hoping to find a way to repay him. They told me that I was to carry my message to Don Diego de la Vega."

"But I have no connection to Zorro."

Doña Inez seemed unperturbed.

"I do not understand the wisdom of the spirits. I merely obey."

"Very well," Diego said. "I suppose it won't hurt to hear this message."

Doña Inez took out a slender chain. A golden charm worked with strange letters hung from it. Diego recognized some of the markings as Egyptian hieroglyphs. He raised an eyebrow in curiosity. He wondered if it was one of the thousands of items that had been plundered when Napoleon had conquered Egypt more than twenty years earlier.

"The Talisman of Byagoona is my link to the other side," she explained, closing her eyes. The air in the room was still, yet the candles flickered and the golden talisman seemed to shine as if lit from within with eldritch light.

Diego hid a smile. He had learned about effects like these when he was a youth and Galileo Tempesta taught him the magician's art. This woman's set of illusions might be different, but they worked on the same principles.

Doña Inez's eyes snapped open.

"This evening there will be a crime in la taberna," she said. "I see a box of coins. I see a knife and three swords. I see blood on the floor."

"If this is true, it is clearly a matter for the authorities."

"No, señor. There were no soldiers in my vision. If you notify them you will only delay things. One evening when there are no soldiers the tragedy will unfold, just as I have seen."

"You're saying that only Zorro can stop it?"

She nodded.

"But I have no way to pass this message to him."

"Perhaps," Doña Inez said, "but I have done as the spirits have told me. The rest is out of my hands."

The sliver of a moon cast the faintest light across the plaza, making it easy for Zorro to move unseen. The only activity he could see in the plaza was that of three men staggering along. They wore the skull-like calacas and one carried a nearly empty bottle of wine pulque. Zorro knew that everyone else must be at the Mass mass for All Saints.

He slipped behind the taberna to peer through the window. The place was empty except for Guillermo, the barman, and Sergeant Garcia. Zorro grinned. The portly soldier had fallen asleep at his table, an empty wine bottle and mug in front of him.

The front door burst open, catching Zorro by surprise. The three skull-masked men entered, brandishing weapons. They spoke loudly enough for him to hear them through the glass.

"The money, old man!"

Zorro moved to the back door. It was bolted but a powerful kick took care of that. He stepped inside, sword ready.

"Zorro!" Garcia cried, relief evident on his face.

The robbers turned to face him. Two; two raised their swords. The third, a big man, grabbed a fistful of Garcia's hair and held a long knife with a wavy blade to his throat.

"Drop the sword, Señor Zorro," he growled. "The whip also."

Zorro let his rapier fall to the floor. As he reached for his whip he palmed a small knife in his left hand. With a sudden movement he sent the tiny weapon speeding across the room. It pierced the big man's hand. He howled and dropped his knife, a long weapon with a wavy edge.

Zorro recovered his rapier and advanced to advance on the swordsmen. They came at him together with a fierce series of cuts and thrusts. He deflected the attacks but found himself pushed back. The men were talented fencers; more than that, they had clearly practiced combining their efforts against a single foe.

Zorro grinned, relishing the challenge.

"Two on one, eh? Señores," he said over the ringing blades, "It seems that you like to make up your own rules. Well, so do I."

With a deft motion, he pulled off his stiff-brimmed hat and flung it in the face of the shorter swordsman.

The taller man attacked with a lunge, but Zorro the fox parried and, with a quick riposte, wounded his sword arm. The robber He dropped the weapon and retreated.

Seeing his comrade disarmed, the short man lunged with a ferocious cut to the head. Zorro's grin widened as he side-stepped, and a well-placed shove sent the swordsman crashing across a table.

The big man ran out the door, followed by Garcia's outraged bellows. Zorro didn't pursue him, choosing instead to make certain the two he'd beaten were disarmed. That done, he pulled off their carved masks.

"Do you recognize either of these men?" he asked.

"No, I do not," Garcia said, and old Guillermo shook his head.

"I leave them in your custody, Sergeant," Zorro said.

"Señor Zorro," Garcia said. "I am grateful for your help, but it is my duty to arrest you."

"You can try," Zorro replied, "but if you chase me these criminals are sure to escape."

Garcia thought about that as Zorro slipped out the back.

"An excellent point," he called after him.

Doña Inez sat in a darkened room. Her window offered an unobstructed view of home was across the plaza from the taberna on the far side of the plaza and had an unobstructed view. Governor Rafael Montero collapsed the spyglass he carried and placed it in his jacket.

"I am impressed," he said. "When you told me that you could predict where Zorro would appear, I didn't believe you."

"You believe in my powers now?" she asked.

"I am not a superstitious man," said Montero replied, "but I believe in results. You claim you can deliver him to me?"

"Follow my instructions and Zorro will walk into a cell by himself."

"If you can do that, you'll be well rewarded."

"Good!" she replied. "Now you must leave, Don Rafael, and quickly. I am expecting company."

Zorro entered the house of Doña Inez through a balcony. He was only mildly surprised to find her waiting for him in her sitting room. The candles blazed, their light twinkling off the golden talisman she wore.

"Buenas noches," he said.

"Buenas noches, Zorro."

"Your vision saved the lives of two people tonight. I am grateful."

"It was nothing compared to what you did for me," she said with a smile. "But there is something more I can offer."

"What is it?"

"The spirits have told me that you are concerned about the fate of young Don Tomás Alcazar. With their help he can be saved."

"I have already tried and failed," Zorro said. "How can your spirits help?"

"Tomorrow is the great procession to the graveyard," she said. "When everyone is there, Fray Felipe will say the mass of All Souls. Many of the soldiers will be in attendance."

"True," Zorro said, "but the cárcel will still be well guarded."

"There will only be three guards you must pass to reach Don Tómas' cell," she replied. "I shall cast a spell on these men. You will have no difficulty coming and going."

"Forgive me, señorita," Zorro said. "How can I be certain you are telling the truth? I have spoken to the peones since I met you. Some say that you are a great healer, but others say you are a bruja... a witch."

"You must trust in the spirits," she said. "Without their help there will be no way to rescue Don Tomás."

Z

Esperanza sat on the edge of her bed watching the slender crescent moon rise. She'd tried to sleep but the voices in her head gave her no peace.

My daughter, you are of age. Her father's voice said. You have two suitors, either of whom would make an admirable match. I will not tell you who to choose, but a choice must be made.

Ah, corazón, your gentle spirit soothes me. This voice belonged to Rafael, so harsh with others, but never with her. With you by my side I'd be a different man.

Esperanza! The voice had shifted to Diego's shocked tones. Surely you don't mean...

"I don't want to," she whispered.

There had been a time when she had dreamed of becoming the wife of the great Governor Montero. He was so strong, so commanding, yet he could be so tender. But as his actions had grown harsher she'd found it harder to turn a blind eye. She discovered that she preferred a kinder, more compassionate sort of man, like Diego.

She wondered for a moment what it would be like to have a husband who combined the best of both of her suitors; someone bold and dashing who cared for the people... someone like Zorro.

She smiled at the thought. Surely every girl in the pueblo had dreamed of him at least once, but romantic daydreams weren't going to solve her problems tonight. An innocent man was slated for execution and even El Zorro hadn't been able to save him.

But perhaps she could.

Lighting a candle she took out quill and paper and began to write.

My Dearest Rafael...

Don Diego sat at the great wooden desk in the caverns beneath the de la Vega hacienda, staring at nothing. Bernardo entered the cave and signaled that Toronado was saddled and ready. When Diego answered with an absent nod, a look of concern crossed the mute man's features. Bernardo moved closer, his dark fingers dancing with a rapid series of questions in the sign language they shared.

"You're right," Diego said. "I don't trust Doña Inez, and her claims of spirits and supernatural powers, but that's not what's bothering me. It's Esperanza; she intends to marry Montero."

Bernardo held up his hands in a gesture of frustration.

"I know," Diego replied, repeating the ideas his friend had suggested so often. "Marry the girl and trust her with Zorro's secret, but I can't do that. She is too gentle to accept the kind of life I must lead."

Dark fingers moved in a series of dismissive moves.

"No," Diego said. "As practical as that seems, I cannot give her up either. I have given her my heart and cannot take it back. What must I do?"

Bernardo's lips formed an ironic smile and he brought his hands together in the position of prayer.

Diego chuckled. "Maybe I do need a sign from Heaven," he said.

"Unfortunately, those seem in short supply these days. For tonight I must focus on the miracle of freeing Don Tómas. The situation with Esperanza will certainly wait until another day."

Z

Montero's eyes widened as he read the note.

My Dearest Rafael,

I have thought about your most gracious offer of marriage and it fills me with a joy that I cannot describe. Please meet me at the Mission this evening after the Mass of All Souls and I will give you my answer.

With my deepest affection,

Esperanza.

This was truly a night of wonders, he thought. It was as if Heaven was answering all his deepest desires at once. The woman he adored had all but promised that she would be his, and the trap that he and the bruja had prepared for his greatest enemy could not fail.

That thought brought a frown to his handsome features. Most of the off-duty soldiers would be attending the procession and the mass that followed. That would be the logical time for Zorro to strike. If he went to meet his beloved he might miss the outlaw's capture.

"Montez!" he called and a moment later his aide stepped in his office.

"Sí, Señor Governor?"

"Fetch the woman, Doña Inez. I want to see her right away."

Si, señor."

Montero sat quietly as he waited, measuring his options. Others might allow their emotions to carry them away, but he had risen to power by discipline and patience. He had two opportunities this evening but, by deploying things just right, he could fulfill them both.

He was feeling very sure of himself as the bruja entered, flanked by her two familiars, the hulking Julio and the strange child, Ysidro.

"All is in readiness?" he asked.

"Of course," the woman replied said with a bold smile. "The plan is foolproof, Don Rafael. There is no way for Zorro to escape our trap."

"I'm glad to have your assurance on that, for there is pressing business that takes me away this evening."

"An affair of the heart, perhaps?"

"An affair that is no concern of yours."

Montero managed to keep his tone even though the woman's guesses were eerily accurate. He imagined that she had honed her powers of observation through years of bilking gullible caballeros and superstitious peasants.

"Of course, señor," she said. "And what is it you require of me?"

"You are responsible for the success of the plan," he said. "If I return to find the Fox in a cage, you will have your reward, and more. But if he has slipped through your fingers, I will be very unhappy."

"There is no need to worry," the bruja replied. "The spirits have guaranteed our success."

The sun had set and the crescent moon had yet to rise when Esperanza appeared at the gate of the presidio. She strode confidently to where Sergeant Garcia stood guard.

"Can I help you, señorita?" the big man asked, somewhat bashfully.

"Sí," she replied with a gracious smile. "Could you take me to Don Rafael? He is expecting me."

Garcia's expression shifted to one of confusion.

"But, the Governor is at the mass of All Souls, señorita."

"How odd. He specifically asked me to meet him here. I can show you the letter."

She produced a folded piece of paper but Garcia waved it away.

"Please, señorita,; there is no need for such things. I will escort you to the Governor's office. I am certain he will be back very soon."

Once Garcia led her across the Predidio's courtyard and opened the door to Montero's richly furnished office.

"If you need anything, señorita, please call for me," Garcia said with an ingratiating smile.

"Thank you, Sergeant," she replied.

When he had left her in the room, Esperanza took a deep breath. So far things were going better than expected. The handwriting on the letter—carefully forged using the many love letters he had sent—was a convincing copy of Montero's. Just the same, she was glad it had not needed to stand up to inspection.

She rummaged through the desk until she found a ring with a dozen keys. Now came the difficult part, getting to Don Tómas' cell without being suspected.

With a silent prayer to St. Dismas and the Blessed Virgin, she slipped out the door.

Z

The presidio walls had never offered a serious challenge to Zorro. Standing in his stirrups, he cast his whip to snare a viga projection on the wall. He climbed to the projecting beam and peered over the wall. Doña Inez was right; there seemed only to be a skeleton staff on duty. He slipped over the scaled the wall and made his way to the entrance of the cárcel.

Two guards stood by the barred gate, leaning on their muskets; he could hear them snoring. Zorro stepped past the men, wondering how Doña Inez had accomplished this. Most likely, he thought, she had found a way to slip them a sleeping potion.

Inside, he found that most of the cells were empty. Montero often let out petty criminals when he had prisoners he considered important.

The jailor was asleep at his desk. Zorro took his key ring and moved to the rear of the cellblock. A slender figure in a shirt and riding pants lay on a narrow cot in the cell.

"Don Tomás!" His whisper was urgent. "Wake up! It's time to leave this place."

The figure stirred but didn't rouse. Zorro opened the door and moved inside. He grabbed the sleeper's shoulder and gave it a firm shake. As he did, he noticed that the arm was too slender, even for a boy of 18.

The figure turned to him, and he saw that it was a woman dressed as an elderly man. Doña Inez's lovely face greeted him with a triumphant smile.

"What is this?" he cried.

She dipped her hand into a small pouch at her waist. She blew a handful of white powder into his face. He held his breath, but not before a bitterness filled his nostrils and he staggered back.

"What have you done to me?"

"The drug won't kill you," the woman said. "It will only make you sleep for a few hours. This is the true use for those mushrooms I told you of."

"Bruja!" Zorro said, "You'll pay for this!"

He clutched at her but caught only her pouch, pulling it free without any strength. She shoved him with a slender hand, and he collapsed. As he stumbled to his feet she backed out of the cell and pushed the door shut, turning the key.

"You must be very strong, Zorro," Doña Inez said. "Most men would be sleeping by now but you are merely drowsy. No matter, in your condition you will not be able to resist the soldiers. Soon we shall all see your true face... Don Diego de la Vega.

"Santa Maria!" Sergeant Garcia said. "I didn't believe you could do it."

"You should learn to have faith in the spirits," Doña Inez replied.

"What have you done to Zorro?" Don Tomás demanded. The old man was shackled, and two soldiers stood by him, one on either side.

"He is not hurt, señor," Garcia said, then turned to the bruja with an anxious expression. "He isn't hurt, is he, Doña Inez?"

Zorro heard the voices, but they seemed to be coming from a distance. He had been ready for treachery but had still not been able to fully block the attack. His senses were so confused that he knew a fight with the guards was out of the question.

Fortunately, he had not come away from his scuffle with the woman empty handed.

"Take off his mask, Sergeant," Doña Inez said.

"Sí, señorita." Zorro felt a stab of affection as he heard the reluctance in the big man's voice. It almost made him regret what he had to do.

As Garcia's fingers touched his face, Zorro sprang up and swung the pouch he had taken from the bruja in a wide arc. The white powder spread over her, Garcia, the guards, and even Don Tómas. With the exception of Doña Inez, everyone the dust touched sank to the ground, asleep. The bruja seemed to have some resistance to her own potion, however. She stumbled out of the cell, banging the door shut behind her.

Zorro reached for her through the bars, but she backed away, laughing drunkenly.

"Very clever, Zorro," she said in a slurred voice. "But you will find

I am cleverer still. Before you can free yourself, I will return with more guards."

She turned and staggered toward the door while Zorro hunted for the keys he had dropped.

Making as little noise as possible, Esperanza moved toward the cár-cel. It puzzled her that there was only a pair of soldiers in sight. They were on duty at the main gate and easy to avoid. The jailor was not at his desk and the room was dark; she paused at the desk to light a candle.

To her surprise, the door leading to the cells was unlocked. She promised herself she would say a novena for St. Dismas' help if this rescue actually worked, then she stepped through.

Inside she saw half a dozen soldiers lying on the floor while Zorro knelt in a locked cell. Strangest of all, a woman dressed in men's riding clothes stared at her with terror-filled eyes.

"Let me past, Spirit, stay back," the strange woman said. "In the name of he who is called Faceless, and the All-Seeing Eye, and the Chaos that Crawls, I command you, begone!"

Esperanza grabbed her by the shoulders. She didn't understand what was happening but knew that she couldn't risk anyone raising an alarm.

"Release me," the woman said, but her feeble struggles didn't match the fire in her voice. Esperanza held on as the struggles slackened and finally stopped."It's alright, señorita," Esperanza said, taking a step forward. "I will not harm you."

The woman gave a frightened bleat and cringed against the far wall.

Garcia had fallen on his belly and Zorro rolled him over in the hope of finding the keys underneath. In his present state it was a herculean task, and proved to be a futile one as well. As he levered the big soldier onto his back, Zorro saw the key ring out of reach on the other side of the bars. He then heard a scuffle and turned his attention to the door. It was a struggle for Zorro to extricate them. As the the keys came free, he looked up and froze.

Someone had entered the room, a woman of unearthly beauty who seemed to his disoriented brain to be clothed in a gown of light. She woman held the struggling said something to Doña Inez as easily as if she was a child. Then the bruja went limp and the angelic newcomer lowered her gently to the floor—her voice was too quiet for him to make out the words—and the bruja recoiled in fear.

The vision turned to look at him and a glorious smile lit her face.

"Madre de dios," he whispered. "Can it be my Lolita?"

She crossed to him and her face resolved itself into that of Esperanza Berríos. He realized that the powder was still distorting his perceptions and wondered if this new vision was any more real than the last.

"Zorro," she said in a voice full of wonder. I should have known you would come. But what has happened?" She gestured at the fallen soldiers. "Are they dead?"

"No," he replied, "they are only... bewitched."

"And what of you? You do not look well."

He grinned at that. "I came expecting treachery, señorita. Perhaps I did not guard against it quite as well as I could have, but I will be fine. But what are you doing here?"

As Esperanza explained her plan to help Don Tómas, the masked man felt a glow of admiration fill him. He had never seen this side of the gentle and refined young woman.

"So tell me, my brave one," he said when she had finished speaking. "What do we do now?"

"You are in no shape to carry Don Tómas over the wall," she said. "Is there enough left of the bruja's powder to use on the gate guards?"

He checked the pouch. "Just enough, I think. Very thoughtful of Doña Inez to have provided for our escape."

"Perhaps you should get the recipe from her?"

"No," Zorro said with a grin. "Where would be the fun in that?"

His gaze drifted to the sleeping woman.

"But you do give me an idea, señorita."

Don Rafael Montero returned late, and in a foul mood. He could stomach a long mass when he had to, but the thought that he had been deceived by the woman he desired made him furious. When he saw the sleeping sentries, anger melted away in alarm.

"Search the presidio," he shouted to his escort. "Rouse the garrison and check the cells!"

Within minutes the place was frantic with activity as groggy soldiers searched for signs of what had happened. They found Garcia and his men sleeping in the cells and splashed water on them, however, but there was no sign of the prisoner, Don Tómas.

They found Esperanza sound asleep in the jailor's office. Montero roused her more gently than he had the soldiers.

"Mi corazon," he said. "What has happened here?"

"Rafael?" she blinked groggily. "Where have you been?"

"I was at the mass of All Souls. Your letter asked me to meet you there."

"My letter?" Esperanza let a look of confusion cloud her face. "Rafael, I sent no letter. I came here because of your letter."

Montero barely restrained an angry oath. "This must be the work of that devil, Zorro!" he said.

"Zorro, yes," Esperanza's eyes brightened and she leaned closer. "But this time he was not alone. There is something I must tell you Rafael."

Z

Doña Inez opened her eyes to find herself in a cottonwood grove. She could see the night sky, and hear the trickling of a stream nearby.

"Did you rest well?" said a man's voice.

With a gasp the bruja sat up to see a tall figure all in black standing a few feet from her. The slender blade in his hand glistened silver in the faint light of stars and crescent moon.

"Zorro!"

"At your service, señorita."

"What have you done?"

"I have done the very opposite of what you attempted to do," he replied in a pleasant tone. "Where you would have locked me in a cell, I give you freedom. I suggest that you use it to get out of Alta California."

"You cannot threaten me. I know your secret."

"Your spirits told you, no doubt," he replied in a mocking tone.

"My wits," she said. "I figured it out that night in the graveyard."

Zorro chuckled.

"You think I am bluffing?" she asked.

"I think you will have a hard time selling your theories to Montero. Right about now he is hearing from an unimpeachable source about how you helped me to rescue Don Tómas."

She was speechless as she considered this. After a moment he spoke again in a more serious tone.

"Zorro does not make war on women, however deserving they may be. The governor is another matter. He doesn't like to be cheated of an execution, and one prisoner on the gibbet is much the same as another to him."

"It seems I have no choice in the matter," she said. "Very well, you have my word."

Suddenly Zorro lunged at her, his blade striking with lightning quickness. She heard the rip of cloth and her hands went to her belly. He had made three quick slashes in the form of a 'Z' in the fabric of her dress without breaking the skin.

"Something to remember me by, in case you're ever tempted to forget," he said.

After Doña Inez hurried away down the path, Bernardo emerged from the trees. He led Toronado and a mule, which carried the still sleeping Don Tómas on its back.

The small man's hands moved in a question.

"Perhaps I am being foolish in letting her go," Zorro replied. "I do have a bad habit of underestimating women. Take Esperanza; I would never have guessed that such a delicate flower could be so brave and clever; that she had such depths."

Bernardo cocked his head to one side and spelled out another question.

"You want to know if I got my sign from heaven?"

Did you get your sign from Heaven?

Zorro grinned as he remembered the vision of Esperanza entering the cárcel, wreathed in light.

"Perhaps I did," he said.

THE CURSE OF LA BREA

By Johnny D. Boggs

Toledo iron against Damascus steel. *Espada ropera* attacks a heavily jeweled rapier. *Soldado* against *Caballero*. *Mano a mano*.

Dress sword thrusts. Rapier parries. Back, back, back, till Don Diego de la Vega presses against the adobe wall. Beaten. He starts to smile, begins to lower his rapier, then sees something in his opponent's face, something beyond malevolence in those dark eyes, and he knows he has made a mistake. He tries to grip the hilt, defend himself once more, but the dress sword dashes forward, the blade piercing Diego's heart, and he hears the loud laughter of Adán Castillo as he dies ...

And wakes to the mocking yips of coyotes.

His right hand throbbing, Diego threw off the blanket, careful not to wake the beautiful Lolita, his young wife, sleeping beside him. He rose from bed, waiting for the song of the coyotes to fade into the coming dawn. Yet as soon as the coyotes stopped, a new noise cried out–the ringing of the Mission of San Gabriel Arcángel's bells. Lolita stirred, but did not wake, and Diego sighed. There had been another death. Another gruesome murder. Another addition to the Curse of La Brea. His hand ached, and he reached for the tincture on the table near his bed, yet stopped, recalling the dream.

A moment later, when the pealing ceased, Bernardo stood at his door.

"I have heard the bells," he told the mute Indian. "Another death?"

Bernardo's head bobbed.

"Like the others."

Another somber nod.

"There will be no more deaths," Diego said, and began unwrapping the thick linen bandage that covered his hand. "Zorro will put a stop to this curse."

Bernardo stood beside him now, his face hard, reaching down to stop Diego, trying to sign a warning, a plea, but Diego smiled. "It is all right, my loyal companion. I should have acted sooner, but did not know, did not think the Curse of La Brea would strike again. Like this. And I did not understand everything until just now."

Bernardo's grip tightened.

"I will be fine," Diego said. "Come. We must waste no more time."

He dropped the linen on the floor, gingerly flexing his fingers, and turned to kiss the sleeping Lolita goodbye before...

As the two men disappeared into the last of night, Diego remembered.

Z

It began as a celebration. Of wine and *paella*, of songs and stories.

Adán Castillo had arrived in Alto California, and his first stop was at the Hacienda de la Vega.

"It has been much too long, *amigo*," Adán Castillo said, kissing Don Diego de la Vega's cheeks, and holding him back at arm's length.

"Much," Diego said.

"You trained with my son in Spain," Diego's father said softly.

"*Sí*, Don Alejandro." A rich smile spread across Castillo's face, and he laughed. "Great days, were they not, Diego?"

"But of course. You are quite the dashing soldier, *teniente*."

The lieutenant stretched to show off his expensive uniform. "And you the bold *caballero*."

"Not so bold," Don Alejandro said with a sigh, and Castillo turned to look back at the solid man, heavier, shorter than Diego, with his hair turning gray. Don Alejandro smiled. "My son prefers poetry over the rapier."

"Indeed?" Castillo arched his eyebrows as he stared at Diego. It was true. Diego wore no sword, even though most *caballeros* in California would. "What would *El Maestro* say of this, Diego?"

Instead of answering, Diego offered Castillo a glass of wine. They were on their second when Lolita descended the staircase. Immediately, all three men in the room rose, as Diego introduced his new wife to his old friend. Castillo bowed graciously, kissed Lolita's hand, and, as she sat, he whispered to his friend, "You were always the lucky one, *amigo*."

"What brings you from Spain to California?" Don Alejandro asked.

"To oversee the land of my late uncle," Castillo replied as he settled in the leather chair. He sipped his wine. "I did not wish to leave Spain, but this was an opportunity that I could not let slip through my grasp."

"Where is this land?" Diego asked.

"La Brea."

"La Brea!" Lolita cried.

"You do not approve?" Castillo grinned.

"Have you seen this land?" Don Alejandro asked.

Castillo shook his head, and finished his wine. "But I know of it. Of its pools of tar. And the bubbling gas, and the stench of the land. And, yes, I have heard the stories of the curse, that tragedy befalls whoever owns, or tries to own, this worthless land."

"Not so worthless," Diego said practically. "Indians have used the tar for centuries to mend their canoes. Many from the pueblo go to La Brea to tar the roofs of their homes."

"Perhaps I should open a business," Castillo said.

"The curse is superstition, of course," Diego said.

"Of course," Castillo interrupted.

"My father knows the story," Diego said.

Don Alejandro nodded. "There is not much of a story to tell. It happened when I first settled in California. One man tried to make his home at La Brea, and we pulled his body from one of those pits. Years later, another came, an accident claimed his life."

"Two deaths in thirty years," Diego said. "That is not such a curse."

"Be that as it may, I am glad to be here," Castillo said, slapping his hands, and reaching for his wine. "I do not believe in the curse of La Brea, either." He drained the glass, and stood. "Now, I must go, to offer my services at The Presidio. After all ..." He winked at Diego at patted the sheathed sword. "I am still a soldier."

"You seem distracted, my husband," Lolita said as she brushed her hair in the bedchambers that evening. "Do you fear for your friend, because of this curse?"

He stood on the balcony, overlooking the hills, the wind whipping the moonlit mustard grass into waves like an ocean in storm. "I fear Adán," he said.

She stopped brushing.

"You fear no one," she said.

He shrugged. "I fear his return. For the people of the Pueblo of Los Angeles. For you. For my father." He let out a sigh, and moved toward the wine. He needed to tell her of Spain.

Yes, Diego and young Adán had been friends in Barcelona. An instructor would have found it difficult to tell who spent more time with the gypsies, or in the taverns, or, for that matter, who was master of the rapier. Perhaps that was why Diego was so surprised when their fencing instructor had brought Diego into La Justica, the secret society sworn to fight for the rights of the oppressed.

"Adán knows more than I," Diego told Maestro Manuel Escalante. "His steel is always true."

"But not his heart," Escalante said. "The heart is what matters when one seeks justice for those in need. The heart and the head. And remember our creed: Never spill innocent blood."

That blood was spilled four nights later when Castillo returned to the hacienda. After dining on roasted beef and flavorful wine, laughing at their boasts, Castillo rose and walked to the wall, unsheathing the rapier mounted beside a pair of silver-inlaid flintlock pistols. He balanced the ceremonial weapon, made a few experimental slashes, then walked back to the table where Diego, his wife, and his father waited, wondering.

"Rise, Don Diego," Castillo said lightly, and when Diego had obeyed, Castillo tossed him the rapier.

"Our blades should cross," Castillo said as he drew the old dress sword. "As we practiced under the watchful eye of Maestro Escalante."

"I am much out of practice," Diego said.

"Bah. It is good. Else you will grow fat from wine and beef." The steel of his sword tapped the center of the brilliant rapier.

"We wear no protection," Diego said. "And this is no sword to wield in combat. It is ceremonial."

"As is mine. Not that I believe in ceremony. Or protection."

Castillo tapped Diego's weapon again, only harder.

"*En garde*," the Spaniard said in mocking French, and moved into the stance.

Toledo iron against Damascus steel. *Espada ropera* attacked a heavily jeweled rapier. *Soldado* against *Caballero. Mano a mano.*

They dueled across the courtyard, both men sweating underneath the summer sun, Diego on the defensive, backing, holding back his ability, hiding his skills, but putting up enough of a fight.

"You have grown weak," Castillo said.

Diego grinned, thrust, fell back. The steel rang loudly, but not as demanding as Don Alejandro's shouts of instructions to both men.

"Your father's voice gives me a headache," Castillo said.

Diego retreated. *Adán is right*, he thought. *This has gone on long enough.* He backed to the wall, let Castillo pin him there, and then, with his rapier held against the wall, above his head, Diego announced his defeat, and as he lowered his sword, he saw the *espada ropera* dart forward, the blade stabbing through the jeweled German hit of the rapier, and into the center of Diego's hand.

Lolita screamed.

Diego followed Bernardo into the San Gabriel Mission, holding his heavily bandaged right hand in his left, crossing himself as they moved through the mission, and into Fray Felipe's quarters.

The big, booming Franciscan in the poor brown robe and knotted rope belt, turned, looking suddenly old and tired. His stare locked on Diego's hand. Diego didn't appear to notice. He was looking at the dead body lying on Felipe's bed.

"I am sorry, my son," the fray said.

Diego stepped closer. Bernardo closed the door.

"His body was dumped in front of La Taberna at some time during the night," Fray Felipe said.

The body of Adán Castillo. At least, Diego thought it was Castillo for the dead man wore the expensive Spanish clothes of Castillo. He wore Castillo's boots, although sword and scabbard were missing, yet his flesh was mangled, coated with tar, then burned.

"The Curse of La Brea," Diego said.

"The Curse of Capistrano," Fray Felipe said, "or so is the word from Sergeant Garcia. They say this is the work of Zorro."

"No doubt," Diego said. A "Z" had been slashed deep into the dead man's chest. The mark of Zorro. Diego looked at the fray. "And what do you say?"

"I know better, my son."

Diego nodded. "I have not seen Adán since this accident." He lifted his injured hand.

"Accident?" Fray Felipe grunted in disgust. "Deliberate, from what I hear."

"He apologized," Diego said, shrugging, "vowed to make things right, then departed for the pueblo and La Brea. That was a week ago."

"You will avenge his death?" Felipe asked.

Diego looked at his hand, and walked out without another word.

The bells rang from the mission the following night. The Pueblo of Los Angeles and much of California had enjoyed a wonderful peace since Zorro had killed the brutal *Capitán* Pasquale. Now, after a second man had been brutally murdered, his body coated with tar, then burned, a savage "Z" carved into his chest. A soldier screamed at the people on the streets, "This is your hero! This is the work of your protector! Zorro is a killer of all, not just soldiers. He kills peasants. He is a monster."

When a white-haired farmer dared speak up against such slander, the soldier reached for his sword.

"*Señor*, please," Diego said, stepping between the soldier and the old man. He raised his wounded hand. "I cannot look at another blade. My hand throbs at the mere thought of such a sight."

At that point, Sergeant Garcia appeared, sweating, panting from exertion, asking the soldier to sheathe his blade. He wiped his brow, turned to Diego, and seeing the poet's injured hand, laughed. "My good friend, Don Diego, I heard about your accident, but it serves you right. You should lift only books, not blades."

"It is true," Diego said.

"Your hand heals, does it not?"

"*Sí*. The blade went right through the lifeline."

"The lifeline! And you live still?"

Diego shrugged. "Fray Felipe thinks it will leave no scar, not one that will be easily noticed, but it hurts. And what pains me most is that it is hard to grip ..." He winked. "A goblet of the best wine."

"Perhaps, I should grip one for you, Don Diego," Sergeant Garcia said.

"Then I would insist on buying a goblet for you."

"It is a shame this villain Zorro had to slay your friend from Spain," Sergeant Garcia said after his third goblet. "He could have replaced *el capitán*. It would only have been right."

Diego fanned himself, drinking wine with his left hand. "I had assumed they would make you *capitán*, if not *alcalde*, if not governor."

"You amuse me." Garcia rocked so hard with laughter he almost spilled the wine he poured.

"Where was the latest wretched man, so foully murdered, found?" Diego asked.

"Like the *teniente*," Garcia answered. "In front of La Taberna."

"Do we know his name?"

"Please, Don Diego. You spoil my thirst. No more talk about this matter. We could not tell who that poor soul was. We would not have been able to say it was *Teniente* Castillo if not for his clothes, and the money he carried. You would think the killer would have stolen that money, no?"

"*Sí*. You are wise beyond your years, Sergeant. This was not the work of a bandit like Zorro."

Wine poured onto the front of Garcia's uniform. "Why do you say this?" He tried to wipe his blouse with a cloth, but only stained the garment more. "You saw the mark. It must have been Zorro."

Diego was staring at the ceiling. He hadn't heard the sergeant. Suddenly, he leaned forward. "Why did you say it would have been right for Adán to have replaced *Capitán* Pasquale?"

"You do not know? The late *teniente* ..." Garcia stopped refilling his goblet long enough to cross himself. "He was the nephew of *Capitán* Pasquale. He told me that he sailed from Spain as soon as word reached him of his uncle's murder at the hands of this fiend Zorro."

"Esteban?" Diego leaned back. "Esteban Pasquale owned La Brea?"

The sergeant shrugged. "No one owns La Brea. Who would want to own such a foul place? And with such a curse. But *el capitán* had said he would like that place. He called it a fitting Hell. And said there could be much wealth to be found there."

"Selling tar to the Indians, the people of the pueblo," Diego said.

Garcia shrugged. "The family hoped for a grant from the king," he said.

Diego rose, dropping a handful of coins on the table. "Such talk exhausts me, Sergeant. I must return to the hacienda. I pray there will be no more terrible murders."

But the next night, the bells rang again.

"You swine!" Fray Felipe's voice boomed. Hands bound, he turned, showing no fear despite the heavy blade a man in a black mask pointed at his throat.

"Turn," the man demanded, and when the father refused to obey, the masked figure thrust the blade forward. Felipe fell back, and tumbled down the hill.

The sun was scorching. A strange odor permeated the air. Felipe struggled to his feet, turned again to face the man in the mask.

"You will answer to God for all you have wrought." He stood straighter, not sweating despite the heat, not blinking, not moving, refusing to show any fear.

"No," a new voice said. "He will answer to me."

Both heads turned as Zorro walked easily, his black cape flowing as if the man in black had summoned the wind.

"The Curse of Capistrano," the other masked man said. "I am the Curse of La Brea. I hoped you would come. Yet I was beginning to suspect this great fox to be a coward."

"Zorro is no coward!" But, now, Fray Felipe showed fear. As Zorro walked between two small black pools, the Franciscan stared at Zorro's gloved right hand, while beads of sweat appeared on the *padre's* face.

"The people of California are hard to persuade," the Curse of La Brea said. "Three men dead in as many nights, all bearing the mark of Zorro, but they still defend him. Therefore I decided if this fat man of God were to be found, then the truth of Zorro would be revealed. The people would rise up against him. But this is better. Killing you gives me much pleasure."

"Is that what you think, Castillo?"

The masked man stepped back, straightening, then whipping off the silk mask that covered his face, revealing the angry glare of Adán Castillo.

"How did you know?"

Zorro did not answer. He drew his sword.

"You are left-handed?" Castillo wet his lips.

Again, Zorro didn't answer. Now, he charged.

Toledo iron against a Gypsy alloy of iron and silver. *Espada ropera* attacks a Spanish rapier. *Asesino* against *Caballero*. Madman against Justice. Coyote against Fox.

Thrust. Parry. Back. Forward. Metals clashed. The black pools slowly bubbled. The two swordsmen moved back and forth, feet as lithe as the best dancers, neither man slowing, despite the oppressive heat, until, suddenly, Castillo stopped his attack. Zorro wiped his brow.

"You can't win," said Castillo, trying to catch his breath. "Even if you kill me, which you cannot, they will still blame Zorro for those deaths."

Zorro grinned. "You forget the Franciscan."

Castillo turned savagely. "I should have killed him first." He leaped over a pool, ran for Felipe, but Zorro, like a cat, blocked his charge. Their swords crossed, but now Zorro was using his right hand, driving Castillo back.

"What I want to know," Zorro said, "is why?"

"Why? You murdered my uncle, you rascal!"

"Why pretend to be dead?"

Thrust. Parry. Back. Forward. And suddenly, a wild, desperate slash from Castillo that cut nothing but the heavy air as Zorro ducked. The momentum of the unwise attack turned Castillo around, and Zorro kicked him, laughing, as the crazed man fell to the grass.

"You were taught by Maestro Escalante?" Zorro asked mockingly, stepping back to let Castillo pick up the sword he had dropped.

"How do you know of Escalante?" Castillo demanded.

Zorro answered with a wink.

"I will kill you," Castillo said. "Like I killed the others."

Castillo attacked. Zorro fell back, deflecting Castillo's blade, using his left hand now, flexing his right.

"I think I see now," Zorro said. "Adán Castillo had to die. Because the next ship from Spain will likely bring word that he is a fugitive. Maestro Escalante always said you were not worth the hours he spent teaching you. That you would shed innocent blood."

Castillo hacked. Rose. Wiped his brow. Thrust the blade. "How do you know what happened with that merchant in Madrid?"

"I didn't." Zorro parried, moved the rapier to his right hand. "Until now."

Zorro moved forward. "You murdered three men. Four if you count the merchant from Madrid."

"And you will be the fifth," Castillo said. "And that arrogant fray the sixth."

Backing up, backing up. Then sinking. Yelling.

Zorro lowered his sword, stepping back, leaned his head back, and laughed. "*Señor*, your reputation, I am afraid, has been *tar*-nished."

Castillo sank past his ankles in the bubbling mass of midnight. He started to raise the sword, but Zorro stepped forward like lightning, thrusting his blade, pulling back as Castillo dropped his weapon and himself into the tar pit. The *espada ropera* sank beneath the pond. Castillo reached for it, screamed as he withdrew black-coated hands.

"I will kill you for this!"

"*¡Alto!*" came another voice, and Sergeant Garcia charged–or as close as a man of the sergeant's weight could charge–out of the brush, followed by a squadron of soldiers.

A musket ball sliced over Zorro's black hat. Zorro ducked, the blade made a final move, and Zorro was running, leaping over one bubbling pit, his cape flying, Adán Castillo screaming, and then the highwayman was gone.

"After him!" Sergeant Garcia ordered. "Two of you help Fray Felipe. The rest of you, quickly, after Zorro. Don't let Zorro escape." The soldiers ran, careful to avoid the black pits, while Garcia sheathed his sword, and walked to the screaming Castillo.

"Get me out of here, Sergeant!" Castillo roared. "Get me to a doctor. Zorro tried to murder me."

"He left his mark, it is true," Garcia said, staring as blood gushed from the "Z" carved into the center of Castillo's forehead. Angrily, the lieutenant slapped tar over the wound. "Help me out of this pit, or I will see that you spend the rest of your life in El Diablo Prison!"

Garcia stood silently. Two soldiers untied Fray Felipe's hands and led him to their sergeant.

"I received a note that I could catch Zorro at La Brea this afternoon," Garcia said absently.

"I left no note!" Castillo yelled. "Get me out of here before I sink to my death."

Fray Felipe sighed. "Did you hear everything?"

"I heard enough."

"Sergeant! I am a lieutenant!"

"You are a murderer," Sergeant Garcia said, and suddenly he laughed. "Look at him, good Fray. He has done half the work for us. All we need now are some feathers!"

Fray Felipe shook his head. "Alas," he said somberly, "it will be a rope, not feathers, for this monster."

The sergeant's laughter died, and he nodded. "*Sí.*"

The two men looked up as the exhausted soldiers returned. "Zorro has escaped, Sergeant," one of them said.

"It is so," Garcia said. "The Curse of Capistrano has eluded me again, but I have stopped the Curse of La Brea, and he is much worse than that sly black fox. That is not such a bad trade, do you not think so, *Padre*?"

PIKE'S PEAK

BY ALAN DEAN FOSTER

"Dear me! Americans? Those uncouth creatures who dwell on the Atlantic coast and live on raw meat and corn kernels like the wild Indians?" Lifting an exquisite lace handkerchief to his nostrils, the effete young aristocrat swayed perceptibly.

Comandante General Salcedo eyed the guest with a mixture of alarm and disgust. "You're not going to faint, are you, Don Diego?"

Placing the back of his right hand dramatically against his forehead, de la Vega steadied himself with a visible effort. "I am all right, Comandante. Thank you for your concern. It was the overwhelming thought and ghastly vision that for a moment had me reeling. In the interest of science and anthropology, I should very much like to meet the leader of this group of noisome invaders."

Salcedo lifted his wine glass, swirled the dark contents, and took a swallow before continuing. Visiting Chihuahua on business from distant Los Angeles, this young gentleman was the sort of pampered fop the General could not stand. But he was a guest at the Alcalde's ball, and he had connections. For the sake of propriety, Salcedo would tolerate him.

It would be amusing to observe such a confrontation as the young man had requested. Placed face to face with the coarse, trail-toughened Americans, this de la Vega would probably go weak in the knees.

"I've been interrogating the Lieutenant in question for some two weeks. He's little older than you, Don Diego. His name is Pike, and he insisted from the time he and his men were first taken into custody in northern New Spain and brought to Santa Fe that they were on a 'scientific' expedition." The General let out a derisive snort. "As if the observations they were making and the charts they were drawing up had no military value." He set his glass aside. The quartet on the rostrum was playing Haydn. "I tell you, Don Diego, new as their country may be, these Americans have criminal designs on the territory of New Spain! As a loyal subject of the Crown, I am sure you can appreciate the situation."

"Indeed, Comandante. And the trouble is not only with these Americans. Why, where I live in Los Angeles the priests and local people have begun to agitate for 'independence' from the motherland. It is all so very tiresome."

"Tiresome—yes." Salcedo shook his head. Plainly, this wastrel neither knew nor cared anything for the details of the politics that were roiling both the Old and New Worlds. "Regardless, Don Diego, as a guest I am afraid I cannot allow you to visit this Lt. Pike." He smiled disdainfully. "I would not wish you to suffer an attack of some sort for which I would be held responsible. Besides, tomorrow at mid-morning I am going to have him taken out and shot."

The younger man looked horrified. "Shot? For making charts? Won't that enrage his deranged fellow countrymen?"

Salcedo waved dismissively. "He is the leader of an unauthorized military expedition into Spanish territory. That is enough to condemn him as a spy. By the time anyone in Mexico City learns of it, the useful deed will be done and the government will have no choice but to acquiesce to it. His death will be a lesson both to his men and to the upstart country from which he hails."

"You have my admiration, Comandante. Your resolve does you credit." His attention drawn to a discussion involving giggling young ladies as well as equally overdressed young men, he excused himself effusively and wandered off to join in a conversation better fitted to his refined tastes.

Salcedo did not lament his departure. What a fate lay in store for the Empire of Spain, he told himself disgustedly, if that is the sort of creature it must one day rely upon.

The attack came out of nowhere. No, the corporal realized. It came out of the night.

Clad entirely in black, the upper half of his face masked, cape swirling, and an Andalusian style flat-brimmed hat perched firmly atop his head, the nimble figure seemed to the terrified soldier to have fallen from the moon—when in actuality it had only been from the edge of the tiled roof. Of more immediate interest to the guard than the interloper's ensemble was the luminous rapier whose tip now hovered motionless barely a centimeter from the center of the corporal's throat.

"What—what is it you want, señor? Please, I have a family, and…."

"Control yourself." The stranger's voice was firm and it was plain that he was in complete command of the situation. The corporal hoped the man's command over his weapon was equally as unshakable. "You will take me to the American officer—now!"

The soldier swallowed, having barely enough room between throat and the tip of the rapier to do so without nicking himself. "There are other guards, I cannot…."

"How many?" The black-clad visitant was looking around intently. At this hour of the morning, with the half moon still high and the sun hours from making an appearance, the area around the city square was empty.

"I don't know, it varies according to the whims of the Captain of the Guard and also…."

"…according to how many of the men are drunk, gambling, or both." Sharp metal pricked the corporal's throat. "Take me there now!"

Reaching out, the interloper put a gloved hand on the corporal's shoulder, spun him around, and set him in motion with a sharp shove to the back. As they walked, the soldier tried to engage his captor in conversation in the hopes it might be overheard.

"I am wearing a sword, señor. I also have a knife. Don't you want to disarm me?" They started up the torch-lit stairs to the second floor where the American officer was being held separate from his troops.

There was a hint of mirth in the stranger's reply. "I think you are already disarmed. Be calm, do as I say, and no harm will befall you." The soldier lurched forward from the force of a second shove.

As soon as they reached the corridor outside the rooms where the American officer was being held prisoner and the corporal heard the voices of his comrades, his instinct was to cry out. That he did not do so was a tribute to those limited but undeniable qualities of intelligence that his captor had perhaps generously attributed to him. Martinez, Calavdos, del Verde, and Sergeant Lobo were playing cards, but they were not drunk. As white-faced prisoner and concealed captor reached the top of the stairs, Calvados turned in his chair to frown at his colleague.

"Hoy, Torres, what are you doing here? You're supposed to be on door duty and...."

The soldier's eyes widened as he caught a glimpse of the dark figure behind the corporal. "Madre de Dios!" Rising, he kicked aside his chair and lunged for the sword that was propped up nearby.

Throwing Torres aside, the interloper charged and knocked the soldier aside before he could reach for his weapon.

In seconds chaos filled the corridor. While Torres huddled on the floor trying to decide what to do, the stranger took on all four remaining soldiers simultaneously. Del Verde was awkward but powerful, Calvados agile and tricky, Martinez a good if unimaginative swordsman, and Sergeant Lobo had not received his nickname because he was devoid of ability. Watching, Torres could only hope that the sound of battle, the percussive ring of metal on metal, would bring reinforcements running.

As it happened, that hopeful noise died down very quickly—along with half of its proponents.

Sword point held out in front of him like the horn of a charging bull, del Verde broke from his companions to charge the visitant, intending to overwhelm the intruder with sheer brute strength. Instead of trying to parry the thrust, the stranger stepped aside at the last possible instant. Encountering the black-clad interloper's right foot del Verde spilled forward, his eyes going wide as he tripped. His momentum carried him down and over the first stone step, after which there was a series of equally unyielding subsequent steps. These finally terminated in the ground floor, and unconsciousness for the big soldier.

As del Verde descended Calvados, Martinez, and Lobo engaged the visitor with their own rapiers. The ease and skill with which the stranger parried the tripartite assault was something to behold. Looking on, Torres felt his own sword pressing against his hip. Then the intruder performed a twisting maneuver with his rapier that was so fast it seemed physically impossible, and Calvados found himself disarmed. As quickly as he had remembered them, the corporal found it expedient to forget the presence of his weapons.

As the stranger stepped away from the wide-eyed Calvados to engage with a grim-faced Martinez, Lobo whirled and ran. Divining the intruder's intent, the Sergeant was removing the heavy key ring from his belt as he ran toward the large open window at the far end of the corridor. Lightly nicked but with the implication that worse was to come if he persisted, Martinez clutched at himself, turned, and ran. Before the visitor could reach him, Lobo flung the ring and keys as hard and as far as he could. To his considerable satisfaction, they landed high in the oak tree opposite the window. Sword held at the ready, he spun to confront the attacker.

"Whatever happens now, the prisoner will stay where he is!" Leaning back into the window through the thick adobe gap, the Sergeant opened his mouth to shout into the night air. "Hola! Sound the alar…!"

The "alar" was not sounded because as the Sergeant attempted to buy time with a side parry, the stranger had pulled something from his own waist and flung it forward. The bullwhip cracked as it snapped around Lobo's ankles. Wrenching sharply backward on the whip's handle and putting his weight into the effort, the stranger yanked the Sergeant's feet out from under him. No gentle cushion, the hard floor made a sickening sound as Lobo's head connected with the brown tile.

Glancing to his left, Torres observed that the stairway was unoccupied. Leaning into the window, the stranger was busy trying to locate the hurled key ring. If I run, the corporal thought hurriedly, will the assassin follow or will he stay behind to try to free the prisoner?

He rose quietly to his feet. The door to the interior rooms where the American was being held was thick, heavy, and barred with iron. No matter what furniture the interloper swung at it, it was unlikely to yield. By the time the masked killer could make any headway, Torres would be back with plenty of reinforcements. With Lobo and del Verde unconscious and Calvados and Martinez dead, he would be a hero.

Gathering himself, the incipient hero fled.

Glancing back over his shoulder, the intruder saw the corporal disappear down the stairs. He hesitated only an instant. He had not come to decimate the military garrison of the city of Chihuahua. Stepping back, he laid the length of the bullwhip out behind him, gauged the distance carefully, and let fly. Shooting through the rectangular portal of the window, the tip of the whip reached its maximum length and cracked sharply around the iron key ring that was lying precariously atop one branch of the old oak. In almost the same instant, the whip was snapped back—its end wrapped securely around the ring.

Trapped in his quarters, Pike had heard the sounds of fighting outside. Helpless to participate or even to observe, he could only wait for whatever might come. Suffice to say, it was not what he expected.

The black-clad figure that threw aside the heavy door was as unexpected as he was formidable. Reaching for the only weapon at hand Pike picked up a chair, held it out in front of him, and prepared to defend himself.

"Lieutenant Pike, of the American army?" The intruder's English was heavily accented but perfectly intelligible.

"I can hardly deny it." As the lieutenant gripped the chair tightly his eyes never left the point of the intruder's sword. "Have you come to kill me, sir?"

"I've come to save your life, if you'll let me. Soon after sunrise, Comandante General Salcedo intends to have you shot as a spy. As an example both to your men and to your government."

Pike lowered the chair halfway. "He wouldn't dare! The status of my expedition is still a matter of discussion between the government of the United States of America and that of your country."

"Spain is my country, but the government of Spain is not necessarily my government. It taxes unfairly, imprisons unjustly, and kills with impunity and without trial those it deems to be the enemies of a corrupt and fading monarchy." The tip of the sword gestured. "Unless you intend to sit in it, would you please put that chair aside?"

"What? Oh." Pike complied. As he did so, he leaned slightly to his left in an attempt to see around his—what? he wondered. If not executioner, then…?

"It is against my nature to see anyone murdered without a fair trial, especially by the Spanish military. Please come with me. Otherwise I fear there is a corporal with a slow mind who may prove our undoing."

Pike started to follow his liberator toward the door. Catching himself, he returned to a table where he began frantically digging among the impressive pile of paper on top.

At the door, the masked visitor was growing impatient. "What are you doing?"

"My maps! I can't leave them behind. They represent everything my expedition was instructed to accomplish." Hastily rolling the papers into a thick tube, he finally joined the stranger in sprinting for the stairs.

They reached Zorro's waiting horses just before Corporal Torres returned with what seemed like half a battalion in tow. As the soldiers arrived on the other side of the building, no one saw the two riders vanish into the night.

An hour later, both men were ensconced in a simple but clean church well outside the city limits. They relaxed from the hard ride, enjoying food and drink brought to them by the priest's mestizo servant whom the masked man had befriended earlier.

As he ate, Pike gazed across the room at the singular individual who had rescued him—however temporary his freedom might be.

"Who are you, anyway? An agent of the Mexican resistance?"

The man looked at him sharply. "What do you, an American, know of a Mexican resistance?"

From a chalice Pike guzzled cold well water. "I know that my interpreter Juan Pedro Walker has spoken often of local unhappiness with the way the citizens of New Spain are treated by their mother country. You yourself spoke earlier to me of the injustices perpetrated by that government on its American citizens." He smiled encouragingly. "On this new continent we are all Americans. Your people and mine have far more in common with each other than you do with the British monarchy or mine with that of Spain. Perhaps some day our governments, our people, will be as one."

The black-clad fighter considered the lieutenant's words. "While it is true that I personally admire much of what is said in the founding documents of your country, it is difficult for me to envision such a thing coming to pass. Even those among my acquaintances whom I respect are wary of your country's interests. I, for example, am from California, a land I cannot truly imagine voluntarily deciding to join with your English-speaking states."

Pike's attention perked up. "California! I've heard a great deal about it, and hope to see it myself one day."

A black-clad arm swept wide. "It is the finest of all countries, full of fish and fowl, highly suitable for the ranching of sheep and cattle, and blessed with air so pure that the part I call home is known as The City of the Angels." He sat up straighter. "You must be tired, Lt. Pike. Hopefully the opportunity will present itself for us to talk again. I would learn more of your country."

"And I of yours, which after all is the reason my expedition was sent to—visit it." Rising, he extended a hand. The black-gloved grip of his rescuer was strong and assured. "You continue to have the advantage of me, sir."

"Ah. It is better for both of us if my true name remains unknown to you. As a military man, I am sure you understand that. Some call me El Zorro."

"Very well, Fox. I thank you for saving my life." Turning, Pike began carefully unrolling his maps. Gazing at the sheets of intricately inscribed paper, the stranger reached out a hand to stop the lieutenant.

"I assume that if you return your own country you will wish to take

71

these documents with you?"

Pike nodded. "As I said, they represent everything my expedition was sent to achieve."

"Then they must be well hidden, or Salcedo will surely see to it that you do not leave with them in your baggage. Might I make a suggestion?"

"Of course."

"Roll them separately, and much tighter. If you are permitted to depart, your weapons will certainly be returned to you so that you will be able to defend yourselves. Slip one document apiece into the barrels of your rifles. Those are not usually searched for contraband."

A wide grin broke out on Pike's face. "That is a fine notion, sir. One I will most assuredly keep in mind." Then his expression fell afresh. "You say, 'if' we are allowed to depart." He indicated their surroundings. "With your help I am certain I could make my way safely homeward, but I won't leave my men."

The flat-brimmed hat bobbed as the stranger nodded. "I did not think that you would. You will be safe here." He turned to go. "If you need anything, these people will look after you."

"Wait! Where are you going?"

El Zorro paused in the doorway. "Salcedo will not be pleased to learn that the man he proposed to make an example of is no longer in his custody. Troops will be searching for you. Your government must be informed of what is taking place here. I have contacts. I go now to make use of them."

Then he was gone, a wraith swallowed up by the night. An exceptionally well-spoken wraith, Pike thought as he turned back to his maps. Though he was exhausted, he did not immediately retire. Instead, he spent an hour seeing how tightly he could roll the broad sheets of ink-marked paper.

"Outrageous! Simply outrageous!"

"I know, Comandante General. I concur completely."

Salcedo could barely restrain himself. Standing outside the livery as the invaders were mounted up under guard, he wanted to draw his own pistol and blow the smug smile off the face of the American lieutenant. But he dared not. Word had reached Chihuahua that the intruders' property was to be returned to them. They were to be escorted, albeit under official protest, to the border with Louisiana, there to be allowed to cross freely back into their own recently acquired territory.

Not with anything of military value, though. At least Salcedo had been allowed to disabuse them of any such potentially seditious items.

"You wanted to see them," he growled as the horses of prisoners and escort alike formed up. "Do they meet your expectations, Don Diego?"

"My dear Comandante, they exceed them!" The young landowner put a hand over his mouth. "It is all I can do to stand here downwind without falling from a recurrence of my consumption!"

The aristocrat's freely expressed contempt made the General feel a little better. Perhaps Diego de la Vega was not as useless as he appeared—though in a fight Salcedo would rather have had his back guarded by a flamenco dancer armed with nothing more than castanets. As the troop prepared to move out—the Americans holding their returned long rifles, their escort with banners flying from the tips of their lances—something caught the General's eye. He had not noticed it previously, but that was hardly surprising. His interest had been focused on the Americans' intentions, not their kit. It looked recent. Something crudely stitched in gold on the saddlebags of the American commanding officer that surely had not been there before. The letter "Z".

"Now why would the lieutenant have the letter Z newly embroidered on his saddlebags?" he wondered aloud.

Enveloped in a cloud of choking perfume, Don Diego de la Vega advanced delicately to stand alongside the staring General. "Do you not recall, Comandante? The American's first name is 'Zebulon'. A most ridiculous personal designation, is it not?"

"Indeed," agreed Salcedo. "For some reason it reminds me of some odd news recently arrived from the western provinces. Do you...?"

But Don Diego had already left to enter the waiting carriage that had brought him, and as he watched his prisoners ride on northward and out of sight, the fuming General forgot what he had been about to say....

BROTHER AT ARMS

BY JOE GENTILE

Fray Felipe was getting ready to turn in for the night. He longingly looked down upon his cot, wishing he was already in it.

Another back-breaking day where he and the San Gabriel Mission's Indian neophytes tended to the crops, while baking in the heat from sun up to sun down. The vineyards were coming along quite nicely this year, and it made Felipe feel good that he accomplished something of value. He didn't get the chance to make it into town to see to the infirm like he had wanted to, but perhaps tomorrow would bring him more time to do so.

He lay down very gingerly, allowing his muscle groups to relax from the strain of the day. The instant he was comfortable, he could feel the warm beckoning of sleep take over. He welcomed it with open arms.

WHAM!

Felipe woke with a start. Someone was pounding at the back entrance! He knew that meant something was wrong. Very wrong.

WHAM! WHAM!

He leaped out of bed and left his room at a run. He was a strong man and he used that power when the Lord called upon it. Most people did not equate strength or combat skill with a Fray, but they might have forgotten that Felipe used to be a soldier, and a very good one.

He reached the heavy wooden door, and heaved it open.

A large black horse was silhouetted by the moonlight, and was about to make another head-butt to his door when the Fray caught its bridal and led the muscular mount into the entryway. It had to duck to get in.

"Toronado? What is wrong?"

The horse was breathing hard, and Felipe knew that to be very unusual. This horse could run for twenty miles without much rest, so it must have traveled more than a day's ride to get here. Toronado shuddered to the ground in a drawn out huff of exhaustion.

Felipe saw the problem. Zorro was unconscious and lying across the horse's saddle on his stomach, with his head dangling over one side, and his legs dangling over the other.

"*Madre de Dios*" whispered the Fray as he immediately grabbed the sweat-soaked form of Zorro off the saddle. He was shocked by what he saw as he lay Zorro on his back. His clothes were ripped and strewn with blood, and his face was covered with bruises and welts. His sword was still in his scabbard, which was a good sign, but unexpected. The whip was missing, and his hat was gone, but his wraparound bandana mask was still intact. He had really taken a beating, but somehow Toronado had gotten Zorro here.

Felipe checked for a pulse and was thankful to feel one. He gathered up his own cloak from a peg by the door and put it under Zorro's head. He retrieved a pitcher of water from a nearby shelf. He then cradled Zorro's head very gently, giving him a drink.

Zorro's eyes fluttered. At first they were wide-eyed crazy, but then his expression softened as he recognized Felipe.

"Toronado…how is Toronado?"

Felipe looked over at the muscular steed. Every breath the horse took was more steady and calm.

"He is fine. You both made it."

"Give my magnificent friend some water." Zorro said. He then managed to drag his bloody arm over to where Toronado was lying. The horse nuzzled into his master's hand.

"I owe you, my friend," Zorro said. "I promise you delicious apples all week."

He got a neigh and a nod in response. Zorro smiled. Then his eyes closed and rest fell over him like a curtain.

Earlier that same night…

"Gentlemen, please allow me to introduce myself. My name is Zorro. Please try to take this personally, as I give you something to remember me by."

Zorro had dropped from the tavern ceiling right onto the wooden bar. With a flourish of his cape, and a bow at the waist, he grabbed his whip off his belt before any of the men could speak. He swirled the whip over his head once and with just a slight flick of his wrist, he sent it snaking forward with a loud crack. His audience froze, slack-jawed.

With a second snap of Zorro's wrist, a man at the rear of the bar was astounded to discover his cigar no longer in his mouth. The next whip crack had that same man gasping for air as it wrapped around his neck like a leather noose. The man went down with a gurgle.

Zorro had tracked the men to this location and wanted to wait for the right moment to strike, but his emotions were getting the better of him, and he reacted quickly.

They were a bad lot to be sure. Worse, in fact, than greedy *politicos*, for these men had little motive for what they did.

Zorro had caught up with them after they had burned a village to the ground and they took what they wanted from it—mostly the women…and some food…just for fun. They were wild animals, and he felt a painful need to put them down…*hard*.

Now, normally, Zorro would be sharing further witty repartee with these brigands, but not tonight. This was a different Zorro. There was a glaze to his eyes that was unsettling. He seemed reckless.

One of the brigands, a small furtive man, dropped prone and crawled out of the tavern while the going was good.

Zorro's whip lashed out and wrapped around the ankle of another. With one strong yank, Zorro pulled this man hard to the ground where the man's head struck the floor with a thud. Another man leaped over the bar. Zorro kicked him in the teeth, but still kept his whip ready. Someone threw a chair; Zorro caught it with one hand, and then boomeranged it right back into the crowd, knocking men down like bowling pins. But the fun was just starting.

With another crack of his whip, Zorro was able to wind it around one of the ceiling's wooden cross beams. He swung through the angry mob as more than one bullet missed its mark. At the apex of his swing, he dropped to the floor and rolled under a table. It was done so quickly, and out of the line of sight of most of the men, that there was a slight pause in the fight.

Then without warning, the table was launched into the air, and Zorro launched himself after it with the agility of a circus acrobat. The table fell onto two men, who dropped to their knees upon impact. Zorro had timed his leap so perfectly that he was able to land directly on the table with a stomp, and that put an end to their struggle underneath it.

That was it, then. The element of surprise was over.

Zorro surveyed his handiwork. Six jackals down. A dozen more to go. He grinned, liking the odds.

Without a weapon in his hand, he motioned the remaining men to approach. And approach they did.

In such close quarters, there was no more room for firearms, or even swords. Zorro felled two men with quick shot-put like punches, but that was not enough, and he went down almost immediately under a pile of flailing fists and kicking boots. He tried to keep moving, figuring that being a constantly shifting target was his best bet. He managed to roll away from the crowd and leaped to his feet.

Grabbing a glass of ale from a nearby table, he smashed it into the first face he saw.

Eleven to go.

He ducked under a flurry of punches from a large bearded man, and launched his own series of blows to his attacker's oversized midsection. The man bent over with the assault, and then Zorro gave him an over-hand, two fisted strike, and he flopped to the ground like a bag of wet sand.

Ten to go.

Zorro jumped onto one table, and then leap-frogged from table to table, while the men vainly tried to grab at the moving target, toppling each table in turn. He ended up on top of the bar, and when the men reached him, he again did something unexpected: he dove right into them. He took two to the floor with him, banging their heads together, and those two stayed down.

Eight to go.

Someone punched him behind the ear. He zealously returned the favor with a double punch to the man's kidneys and a quick uppercut, then elbowed a second, rail-thin man in the jaw.

Six to go.

Now, the pace of the evening had caught up with Zorro, as the men matched the speed of his movements. Even though he was trying his best to roll with the blows, he took several hits to the face and body. But even though his training told him to wait for an opening or beat a hasty retreat, he continued to dish out punishment as he received it.

He fell to the floor, where the kicking commenced.

Someone smashed a chair over his head and his vision blurred. He struck out with both of his boots, and connected with the nose of someone who was leaning over him.

Five to go.

As Zorro felt himself losing consciousness, he let out a shrill, high pitched whistle. It was so unexpected that the men stopped their punching and kicking for a moment. When nothing happened, they continued their brutal attack.

Seconds later came the crescendo drumming of hooves, and then the front door of the tavern thunderously exploded inward as a mountain of a horse burst through.

Toronado stood atop the broken door like a giant in a doll house, and rearing back with a loud snort, he pawed with his front hooves and bared his teeth.

The five men were so shocked at the sight, they didn't move. Toronado muscled his way forward, knocking aside chairs and tables like children's toys. With a quick turnabout, Toronado kicked out with his massive back legs, and two of the men struck the wall as if they had been shot from a cannon.

The last three men ran like they were on fire. Toronado lowered his head to his master, gently nudging him, trying to get him to stir. Zorro groaned painfully in response. Toronado slowly sank to the floor to make it easier for his master. One bloody inch at a time, Zorro crawled onto his horse.

"Diego, my son, when is this going to end?" said Felipe. "When you are dead? Then who will protect the people?"

"Fray Felipe, I can't stop myself—"

"You must! You cannot survive another night of this behavior."

"I'm not sure it matters." Diego softly said with a far way look in his eyes.

Diego looked at the ground of the small Mission chamber where he sat and shook his head slowly. "I don't know who I am anymore."

"You are hope, my son," Felipe said. "And you are needed."

"Yet how is it that I feel just the opposite?"

"Diego, I know it has been hard since—"

"She was everything! My heart is so empty, Felipe, so empty. I don't know what to do."

"You must draw upon your memory of her, and she will be there for you."

Felipe tried to look into the eyes of his friend, but found their usual sparkle was gone and replaced by an unfocused blackness. He knew he would have to do something drastic to reach inside and find the Zorro that was in there.

"I have heard that kind of thing before as you counseled the grief stricken. It just sounds hollow to me now."

Then Felipe struck with the speed of a mongoose. He grabbed his friend by the shirt, and dragged him off of the bed. Then, using all of his strength, he slammed him against the wall and held him there.

Zorro reacted instinctively and grabbed the front of Felipe's robes. "Felipe," he said in a soft, gritted whisper, "have you lost your senses? Believe me, you do not want to do this."

Felipe ignored the fear rising in his chest, and silently prayed that he was doing the right thing. "Diego," he said, "you have to think!"

He strong-armed Zorro up a couple of inches up the wall with one arm, and pinned his friend's right arm to his side with the other.

Zorro struck out in sudden anger. Felipe's response was to dodge the blow and apply more pressure, holding his forearm under Zorro's chin and effectively cutting off his oxygen supply.

Zorro kicked out, but Felipe was ready for that too, as he was standing at the right distance and angle to minimize such an attack.

"Diego, you are striking blindly…this is not how Zorro fights."

"What are you talking about?" Zorro said. He tried to punch his friend again, but failed to connect.

Felipe was sweating with the strain. He couldn't avoid Zorro's assault forever, nor could he expect him to be able to breathe much longer either. He had to make his play now.

"Diego…think…think about how you trained with your sword."

"What? What does that have to do with why you are attacking me?"

"It's everything. It's everything you have forgotten."

"You are insane!"

"I think not, my friend. Remember the countless hours of practice? Remember the uncounted days and nights where it was just you and your sword, repeating the same moves over and over again until you couldn't think anymore?"

Zorro, who was struggling with the strength of a madman, lashed out and this time punched Felipe right in the jaw. The fray took it, barely moving his head with the attack. That just further infuriated Zorro, so he struck his friend again, and instantly wished he could have taken it back. Felipe spit out blood as his head rocked with the blow. He slowly lost his strong grip on Zorro, and then slid to the floor.

With slumped shoulders Zorro stood over his fallen friend.

"Damn it, Felipe. Why would you attack me so? I didn't want to hurt—"

At that moment, even before Zorro was done speaking, Felipe's leg whipped around and caught Zorro, unaware, right behind the knees. He went down ungraciously on his back, but leaped up and jumped on Felipe who was still prone. He had his fist raised to attack and yelled.

"What is wrong with you?"

"Just trying to prove a point," Felipe said.

Zorro was now leaning over, face to face with his friend. "And what would that be? How to court death?"

"In a way, yes!" Felipe shook his head. "You need to stop reacting with your emotions, or you will soon be dead, and thereby useless to me, your people, and the memory of your wife. I mean, when was the last time Zorro was able to be bested so easily…by a fray no less?"

"Bested?"

"Are you going to get off me now?"

"Are you going to throw me against a wall again?" Zorro said.

"Not if you listen to me this time,"

Both friends sat side by side against the wall, breathing hard.

"Zorro…Diego, I plead with you. You need to change your thinking."

"To what?"

"Remember the sword training. You need to have your mind empty so the trained body can react. Right now, you are dangerous to everyone. You have been very lucky so far…no innocents have been killed. It's only a matter of time, for luck doesn't hold forever. I know you. You do not want an innocent death on your conscience. It would be impossible for you to bear. Take it from me."

"Felipe?"

"Never mind that, just listen. Tell me how you felt when you were with her."

"Why, wonderful, of course. You know how I felt about her."

"Now, when you were not with her, did any of that good feeling remain with you?"

"Of course." Zorro said.

"That is what I am talking about. You have lost that."

"She is dead, so yes, that is gone."

"No it's not gone. You have covered it up." Felipe said.

"What?"

"Diego, reach inside your soul here…close your eyes…drag up that good feeling that even when you were not together, you were happy."

"Felipe–"

"Do it!" Felipe said, making his bicep bulge and pointing to it, "What, you need more of this?"

Zorro took a hard look at Felipe. He knew the fray was serious, but he couldn't help but smile, "No, *senor,* you are indeed mighty."

"Are you mocking me?"

"Never."

"Then, be quiet and close your eyes."

"I will try for you, because only good friends try to kill each other, yes?"

Felipe rolled his eyes upward in silent protest, but was glad to see Zorro complying.

"I can't do it," Zorro said.

"Of course you can! You need to let her into your heart, not keep her from it. You need to do this. Not for you, but for her. Do not lose her, my friend."

"I would do anything…"

Felipe waited as his friend closed his eyes and took a couple of deep breaths. He waited. Time passed. He became aware of the pulsating ache of his jaw, heard the wind whisper outside, and listened to the rustle of leaves skipping along the stone path.

Finally, a slight smile appeared on Zorro's lips.

Felipe knew he had one more thing to do for his friend. Without a moment's hesitation, he back-handed a closed fist strike at Zorro's face.

Without opening his eyes or losing that small smile, Zorro blocked the strike with a raised arm.

"My dear Fray, I did not know you were such a violent man."

He opened his eyes and the two friends smiled at each other.

"Welcome back, Diego," Felipe said.

"It's good to be back, Amigo. And, I am really sorry about hitting you, my friend. Although, I must say, you are full of surprises. I underestimated you."

"Drastic measures in dire circumstances," Felipe said.

"Somehow I think it is more than that. Regardless, I think I may have you accompany me on some of my midnight rides."

"Why?"

"Need you ask? You could be my bodyguard...or, um, Fray-at-Arms."

Felipe stared at Zorro silently for a few seconds. Then he got up off the floor, rubbed his sore jaw, shook his head, and walked out of the room.

"You mock me," he called out. "Here, I risked my very life to help you, and you mock me."

"Hey!" Zorro said to an empty room. "I was serious."

"Felipe?"

YOURS AND MINE

BY JENNIFER FALLON

Don Diego de la Vega was accustomed to fear. He knew how dangerous a racing heart, dry mouth and moist palms were in battle. He knew how soul destroying the agony of terror was. If one couldn't conquer their panic, they were at the mercy of their enemies.

He'd studied long and hard to master his fear so that at a time like this, when it really mattered, he could face his most terrifying foe with a steady hand and a bold heart.

With the sun beating down relentlessly, Don Diego stepped forward, forcing himself to take a deep, calming breath and then smiled as he offered his nemesis his hand so she might alight from her carriage.

"My dear Aunt Eudora! Welcome to California."

Doña Eudora de la Cruz, Diego's great-aunt (several times removed), matriarch of the de la Cruz clan, matchmaker extraordinaire, stepped from the carriage and cast a leery eye over the hacienda. She took in the adobe buildings with their red tiled roofs, the large main house, the humble stables, servant's quarters and storage buildings, the dusty roses and the dry fountain, which had recently faltered under the strain of several weeks without rain, not at all pleased by what she saw.

"This place is a fortress," Eudora said, frowning at the high walls surrounding the central courtyard. "You have problems with the natives?"

"Of course not," Don Alejandro said, stepping forward with a gracious bow. He smiled—mostly at his son's discomfort, Diego suspected—and kissed Eudora's hand. "We are cautious, *Tia* Eudora, not under siege. Welcome."

Eudora sighed dramatically. "I shall have to make do, I suppose."

This was shaping up even worse than Diego feared. She hadn't even said *buenos días*, yet.

Before he could add anything, another gloved and elegantly poised arm protruded from the interior of the carriage. Bernardo hurried forward to assist. A young woman emerged, of middling height and a voluptuous build, followed by two more women, both a little taller and younger. All three wore lace mantillas over their dark hair that shaded their faces.

Eudora turned, indicating her companions. "Don Alejandro, Don Diego de la Vega, allow me to introduce *Señorita* Tierra Castilla-Ramírez, *Señorita* Maria Arroyo y López and *Señorita* Angelina García de la Cruz.

The star-struck one on the left was Maria. The youngest-looking around with a calculating eye—was Tierra.

"Encantada, Don Diego," the short, voluptuous one replied with a coy smile as she raised her mantilla. This was Angelina.

Oh Lord. She's already flirting with me.

"Bernardo, would you see to the luggage?" Don Alejandro suggested. *"Señoritas*, I'm sure you'd like to wash away the trail dust."

Eudora nodded and turned toward the house, the girls in her wake. Diego caught Bernardo's eye. "This was not *my* idea, you know."

Bernardo said nothing. His eyes said it all. *We don't have time for this. Zorro has work to do.*

As usual, Bernardo was right. Zorro's intricate plan to expose Luis Ramon's shady dealings with the Deep Gorge Mine several miles from the Pueblo Los Angeles was at a critical point. He'd been exchanging letters with Ramon (under a pseudonym) for months now, and almost had the *Alcalde* to a point where he was ready to meet his mystery investor. Then Zorro would expose the details of the *Alcalde's* plans, which Diego was convinced were a complicated web of lies and deceit, all bound up in a mine that produced nothing but unsuspecting paupers.

Diego didn't need the distraction of a determined matchmaker like Eudora getting in the way.

He could say nothing to Bernardo now, however. Instead he forced a smile at Eudora and her hopeful charges, wishing there was a quick way to extricate himself from this awkward situation that didn't involve him getting married again.

"When I received your letter, *Doña* Eudora, I was surprised," Alejandro said, as the *Doña* looked around, taking in everything with a glance so shrewd, Diego wondered if she was able to calculate their net worth with a single sweep of the room. "Delighted, naturally," he added.

"But surprised."

"Why surprised, Don Alejandro?" Tierra asked. She too, had been examining the room, but seemed more interested in the swords hanging over the fireplace, than the Indian rugs, which gave the room such a comforting feel. "Is not California teeming with unwed caballeros looking for a pretty virgin from good Spanish stock, on which to spend their millions?"

"Tierra!" Eudora gasped. "Hold your tongue!" She turned to Alejandro. "Have arrangements been made as I requested?"

"They have," Alejandro assured her as Carmen hurried in with a tray of chilled juice. "And now that you have arrived, formal invitations can be sent."

"I will ride into Pueblo de Los Angeles this afternoon and deliver them myself," Diego volunteered, thinking it an excellent excuse to escape the hacienda.

Eudora was hard pressed to find fault with that. Tierra, however, seemed unduly excited by the news, barely even glancing at the drink she was offered.

"Then the sale is on!" she declared, her words giving lie to her cheerful tone. "We shall all be sold off like prize brood mares before the month is out, *primas*." She turned to Diego. "Tell me, Don Diego, will *Alcalde* Ramon be one of the buyers?"

"Tierra!" Eudora scolded again, looking mightily displeased. Diego found it rather unsettling that this feisty young woman seemed uncowed by the indomitable Eudora, while he was quietly terrified of her. "Apologize at once for offending our hosts."

"They are not offended," she said, turning her dazzling smile on Diego. "Don Alejandro and Don Diego understand how these things work. Are you looking to replace your tragically departed wife anytime soon, *señor*, or is *mi tia* Eudora simply indulging in a spot of wishful thinking?"

Don Diego stared at Tierra, unable to think of a coherent response.

"Tierra, you are horrid," Angelina declared. She put her glass down and hurried forward. "I'm so sorry, Don Diego. Our cousin is tired and not conscious of what she's saying. Could we be shown to our rooms?"

"Of course," Maria agreed hastily, stepping up beside Angelina which effectively put Tierra behind them. "With rest, I'm sure our cousin will find her misplaced manners."

Diego nodded wordlessly. Fortunately, he didn't need to explain anything to Carmen, who held her arm out, pointing toward the door.

"If you would follow me, *Señoritas*," the maid said. "I would be happy to see you settled."

Eudora waited until they were alone before apologizing. "I am sorry, Alejandro, that you and Diego had to suffer Tierra's insults. She is somewhat...ambivalent about coming to Alto California."

Diego didn't blame her. It was bad enough being in the sights of a matchmaker. He couldn't imagine how uncomfortable it was being one of her wards.

"She is young," Alejandro said. "I'm sure—under your guidance—Tierra will fall madly in love and be glad of the chance to settle in California."

Diego didn't believe that for a moment. "Does she have a suitor in mind?"

"Why do you ask, Don Diego?"

"She mentioned the *Alcalde*, Luis Ramon."

Eudora shrugged and put down her glass on the long polished table. "Pay no attention. She is a foolish young girl harboring foolish ambitions."

"To marry Luis Ramon?" he asked.

"No, to restore her family's fortune."

"Not by marrying Ramon, surely?" Alejandro asked. Even he seemed alarmed by the notion.

Eudora shook her head, brushing a fleck of dust from her long black skirt. "She blames Ramon for the death of her brother."

"That's tragic."

"All the more tragic because the fool boy died by his own hand," Eudora said, unsympathetically. "Maximilian fancied himself a businessman. Invested the entire family fortune in a gold mine here in Alto California. Of course, it proved worthless. These things always do. But the shame is still raw. I suppose it's easier for Tierra to blame her brother's business associates than her brother." Eudora cocked her head, eyeing Diego curiously. "Does she intrigue you, Don Diego, my feisty little pauper with the pure Spanish blood?"

She certainly did, but not for the reason Eudora thought. Were Tierra's family another victim of the Alcalde's Deep Gorge Mine?

Zorro needed to look into this.

"Alas, I am still in mourning my wife," Diego said, wondering if he could find an excuse to leave that didn't involve him pretending to faint.

"Lolita has been dead for more than a year," Eudora pointed out with the same lack of sympathy she showed Tierra's tragic tale. "It is time to move on, Diego. Time to think of the future."

"Trust me, Tia Eudora, I do." He smiled pleasantly. "And in my immediate future, I see an afternoon dedicated to delivering fiesta invitations. If you will excuse me?"

Diego sought the *Alcalde* out when he arrived in Pueblo de Los Angeles later that afternoon with the invitation to the fiesta Don Alejandro had agreed to host, so Eudora might introduce her charges in a socially acceptable setting. He found the *Alcalde* on the veranda outside his office, dusty from the trail, having just returned himself. Ramon was berating Garcia for some slight that had the sergeant rolling his eyes as the *Alcalde* turned away.

"Ah, de la Vega!" Ramon said, when he caught sight of Diego. "What brings you to town?"

"I have an invitation, *Alcalde*," he said, tying his horse to the post. "My Aunt Eudora has arrived from Spain. We are holding a fiesta in her honor."

"In *her* honor?" Ramon asked with a raised brow, a leer on his handsome face that made Diego wish it was Zorro delivering the invitation on the point of his sword, not the mild-mannered Diego de la Vega. "Or in honor of her wards?"

"Either way," Diego said, ignoring the leer, "my father and I would be honored if you would join us."

"I wouldn't miss it," Ramon assured him, flicking the blond hair from his eyes before attempting to brush the dust from his trousers. "Have you met the *señoritas*?"

"Naturally," Diego replied, feigning puzzlement. "Why do you ask?"

"Are they pretty?"

"I suppose. I didn't really notice."

"Then you'll no doubt be a widower for some time yet," Ramon laughed, turning for his office. "I wonder how you got married the first time, de la Vega, I really do."

Diego watched Ramon disappear inside the cool darkness of his office, scowling.

"Pay no attention to him, Don Diego," Garcia advised, leading Ramon's dusty, lathered horse toward the stables. "The *Alcalde* can be... insensitive."

"He's a busy man," Diego conceded, more interested in what Ramon was up to, than his attempts at humor. "What takes him out of the *pueblo* at this time of day?" Diego was worried the *Alcalde* had found some new way to torment Bernardo's people. If he had, then Zorro would have to do something about it.

"Sorry, Don Diego, I am sworn to secrecy."

That was never a good thing. Diego smiled, falling into step with the sergeant. "Then I would not dream of trying to extract the secret from you, Sergeant. Besides, if the *Alcalde* is up to something, I'm sure Zorro will ensure he is reprimanded."

Garcia shook his head. "Oh, this is nothing to concern Zorro, Don Diego. It is just a business venture."

The Deep Gorge Mine? Or another scheme to enrich himself at the expense of the people of California, Diego thought. *Perhaps Zorro will have to ride again.*

Preferably for the entire length of Eudora de la Cruz's visit.

He clapped the sergeant on the shoulder with a smile. "I never thought of the *Alcalde* as a shopkeeper."

Garcia laughed. "This is not a shop, Don Diego. It's a... actually, I must not say." The sergeant's face fell as he realized he'd almost given the game away.

Diego pretended not to notice. "Then I shall leave you to your secrets, Garcia. And to that poor horse. He needs to be cooled down for some time yet."

The sergeant let out a long-suffering sigh. "*Adios*, Don Diego. Think of me while you're delivering invitations. In cool places like the *taberna*."

Diego slapped him on the back. "I shall have a drink in your honor, Garcia."

"*Gracias*," Garcia said wistfully.

"Tierra's family makes it nine investors Ramon has cheated that we know about," Diego informed Bernardo, as his friend helped him unsaddle Toronado. Zorro had been abroad this night, not to fight, but to put the final touches on his plan to expose the *Alcalde's* scheme to defraud unwitting and often naïve investors like Tierra's brother, of their wealth. Maximilian's fortune must have been quite a bonus for Ramon. The other eight families he'd fleeced could ill afford the loss of their hard-earned savings. Diego had tossed aside Zorro's hat and mask, but was still wearing the black. "She may be trouble."

Bernardo cocked his head curiously.

"Tierra is seeking revenge," Diego explained. "And she doesn't strike me as the type to be satisfied by anything less than bloodshed. I fear our fiesta may prove a little more exciting than my father anticipates."

Bernardo gave him a pointed look.

"You're right," Diego said, nodding as he hefted Toronado's saddle onto the rail of the stall. "She needs to be convinced Zorro has the matter in hand."

Diego turned back to find Bernardo holding his mask and hat out to him, his warm dark eyes conveying amusement in the lamplight.

Diego sighed and took the mask. He wasn't done this night.

Zorro had one more job to do.

Carmen had put all three girls in one room. Maria and Angelina had taken possession of the bed. Zorro stepped silently over the balcony and slipped through the door. They were sleeping soundly, their faces serene and untroubled in the moonlight.

There was no sign, however, of Tierra.

With his sword sheathed, Zorro crept forward.

He stepped cautiously...until he was halted by the unmistakable pressure of cold steel against the side of his neck.

"One more step, *Señor* Zorro," Tierra said softly, "and you will be bleeding all over Don Alejandro's exquisite Indian rug. It would be a shame for such a legend to die such an ignominious death."

Zorro froze. "You've heard of me?"

"Everyone has heard of Zorro."

"I have not come to harm you, *señorita*."

"Which is why you came through the window, I suppose?"

Carefully, he turned to face Tierra. Although dressed in her nightgown, she seemed in control but he could feel the blade trembling against his neck. "I came to speak with *you*, *señorita*. About your brother."

"My brother?" Tierra jerked the sword in surprise, nicking him in the neck.

"Ouch!" he hissed in a loud whisper, fearful of waking her companions. He slapped the blade away, pulling his own sword out and disarming her in a blur of steel she had no hope of countering. Within seconds the tables were turned. Now it was Tierra with a sword at her throat.

Tierra paled, not nearly so brave now she was unarmed. "I'll scream!"

"And who will rescue you, *señorita*? That fop, Diego de la Vega?"

"Don Diego is a *gentleman*," Tierra shot back. "Which is more than I can say for you."

Zorro forced himself to keep a straight face and sheathed the sword. "My manners may not be those of your host, but you would do well to heed my words, *señorita,* however rudely and unconventionally they are delivered."

"What have you to say that I care to listen to? And what do you know of my brother?"

"He is not the only man to lose a fortune investing with Luis Ramon's mine."

"How do you know?"

"Because I've spent months preparing a trap for the *Alcalde*. If you spring it too early *señorita*, then not only you, but no one tricked by him will ever see their money again."

Tierra was stunned. "You can recover our money?"

"I believe so."

"But you cannot bring back my brother."

He could hear the pain in her words and wished he could answer differently. "No."

She was silent for a moment. Then Tierra squared her shoulders and asked, "What do you want me to do?"

The night of the fiesta, Diego came down with a terrible stomach fever, brought on—he informed his father with convincing pathos—by eating the rather suspect *jamón serrano* from the *taberna*. He was in no state to entertain company and was devastated to miss the fiesta. Diego then retired to his room, waiting until everyone was in the courtyard. When the music started up, he sneaked back through the house to the fireplace and the secret entrance to Zorro's hidden lair.

Zorro watched the fiesta from the roof, in the shadow of the chimney, relieved he'd found an excuse to forgo the party. He could see Eudora targeting likely suitors with one or other of her wards in tow. In the background, he could just make out the chimes of the clock marking the hour. Right on schedule, Zorro spied Tierra making her way toward Ramon. She introduced herself and then leaned forward to whisper something in his ear.

The *Alcalde* stiffened in surprise, turned to excuse himself, and with a cautious glance to see who was watching, followed Tierra.

Zorro allowed himself a small smile.

It was time to teach Luis Ramon that he could not trifle with the lives—or the livelihoods—of those under Zorro's protection.

"I was not expecting such a lovely emissary," Ramon said, as he stepped into the darkened study, shutting the music of the fiesta off with the door. Zorro once again waited in the shadows, this time with his sword drawn. "But I was hoping to meet *Señor* Milan in person."

"*Señor* Milan is a recluse, *Alcalde*," Tierra said with admirable calm. "I have the papers." She indicated the writing table where the contracts Zorro had so carefully prepared were laid out. "Once they are signed, title of Deep Gorge Mine will be transferred to *Señor* Milan, and your payment will be arranged from *Señor* Milan's bank in Barcelona."

Zorro held his breath, waiting for Ramon to refuse, but greed overruled prudence.

The *Alcalde* glanced around the room and then turned to Tierra. "Could we have a little more light?"

"*Señor* Milan was adamant this deal remain confidential, *Alcalde*. More light will attract attention. If you could sign here?"

Even in the gloom of the poorly lit study, Ramon seemed annoyed, but he strode to the table, dipped the quill in the ink and after a slight hesitation, signed the papers where Tierra indicated. Once they were done, she folded his copies of the documents and handed them to him. "I must ask that you not mention my part in this, *Alcalde*. My aunt thinks I'm here to find a husband."

"I am sure one as lovely as you won't have to look too hard," Ramon said, slipping the papers into his coat. "Shall I leave first? To protect your reputation?"

"That would be very chivalrous of you, *señor*."

Ramon nodded, closing the door behind him as Zorro stepped out from the shadows, sheathing his sword.

"How did I do?" Tierra asked, unable to hide her grin.

"Exceedingly well, *señorita,*" he said. "If Eudora fails to find you a husband, I am sure you'll do well as a professional confidence trickster."

Tierra beamed at him, thrilled by her part in Zorro's charade. And no doubt the imminent restoration of her family's fortune. "What will you do now?"

"Ride through the night to San Francisco," he told her. "These papers need to be lodged at the bank there before Ramon has a chance to read his copies and renege on the deal."

"Shall I ever see you again?"

Zorro raised her hand to his lips. "Not if justice prevails, *señorita.* There will be no need."

The morning after the fiesta, in the privacy of his quarters, Ramon opened the folded contracts, smiling. The sale of Deep Gorge Mine to a recluse in faraway Spain was a stroke of genius. Now he could buy enough genuine gold ingots to reassure those pesky investors who had grown suspicious. He may even get more investors, once they saw real metal.

Ramon glanced down at the contract, his smile soon changing to a frown as he read. Each page revealed a horror more awful than the one before.

This was not the bill of sale he thought he'd signed.

Each page was a transfer authorization from his secret account in San Francisco to the investors he'd swindled. For the full amount plus interest, on their original investment!

If these papers were lodged with the bank before he could contact them, he was ruined.

Furiously Ramon scanned the pages, thinking it a sick prank, until he came to the end page. His heart sank as he realized this time, he was the victim.

The last page had only one mark on it.

A large, bold "Z".

EL LAGARTO

BY STEVE RASNIC TEM

El Lagarto lay stretched out along the edge of the rise beneath the falling sun much like his lizard namesake, so aware of his skin against the sand and the heat of the dying day. He peered down the rifle barrel that poked through a hole in the curtain of fine mesquite. He'd rested the gun within a fork in the shrub to steady his aim. He had no idea whether such a technique was wise or not, but he did not worry himself. He was learning his own way of shooting, and if he made a mistake it would be his, and no other's. That was the best way to acquire an original talent, perhaps a reputation, and to avoid the oft-repeated mistakes of others. In this way he might become the greatest fox hunter in all California.

He tried to remain focused, but called for the boy. "Josue, are you looking for the fox? Tell me you haven't fallen asleep!"

The young boy stirred behind him, his muffled yawn escaping. "Of course not, Senor Salazar! I am like the halcón with one eye, who therefore has no where else to look!"

"I have told you that when I am hunting you are to refer to me as El Lagarto. And please do not attempt metaphor—it makes you sound like a fool. Hawk, indeed."

"Of course, Senor Sal—of course El Lagarto, Senor, my apologies. But one thing I do not understand—"

"One thing?"

"Si, one thing, Lagarto, Senor. Why do you trust me to watch out for the fox, when you are the great cazador?"

"I am not yet the great hunter, Josue. That will come later. Now I am simply developing my talent. I require someone with nothing better to do to keep an eye out for the fox, while I prepare to take the unhurried shot."

"And that would be me, El . . . Lagarto?"

"That would be you, Senor Halcón, with one eye."

"I am so honored!"

"Then honor me with your silence, until some unwary fox appears. Meanwhile I will practice my aim on this shallow valley before us."

El Lagarto resumed his meditation on all things hunting. This was his opportunity to participate in that primeval predatory relationship among all members of the animal kingdom—the fox taking its prey as its rightful communion, and he, the lizard Lagarto, taking the fox in turn as his rightful meal as a superior being.

This was simply the way of the world. The fox had his place, as did the lizard. They all had their roles to play. Just as the peasants of this remote pueblo had their place: to labor, to fall ill, to purchase their cures and other supplies from the good vendedor ambulante Senor Salazar. He had traveled to many such backward communities these past few years, but never before had he found a population so needy, so friendly, so unmoored by the relatively recent demise of their beloved padre, who as yet had not been replaced. El Lagarto was plainly needed here, for his stories, his remedies, his sage advice. For what was prey without its predator?

All he asked was to play the part of the noble lizard out in the world a few afternoons each week, watching the desert, playing the camaleon, shedding its tail to escape its enemies, then disappearing into the landscape, both a sprinter and a climber.

The sun had now largely descended into its nighttime burrow, only its glowing breath remaining to illuminate the desert a few more minutes. This was the best time for finding that degenerate creature, which always seemed to overestimate its cleverness. Somewhere beyond the limits of El Lagarto's vision the parasitic fox scavenged, a desert rat eating garbage, small animals, whatever might stumble into its grasp. The fox had only to stray into the small territory El Lagarto had claimed as his own and he would dispose of its salt-and-pepper body without hesitation.

El Lagarto had had a lifelong aversion to the fox. Certainly there were denizens of both the spiritual and earthly planes far more revolting than the skinny fox, although he could not think of any at the moment. His mother believed he might have once been frightened by a fox when he was a child. Perhaps the fox had carried off a favorite rabbit? His family raised rabbits when he was growing up, and they were always disappearing. But no matter. Whatever the reason, their places along the wheel of life were irrevocably fixed.

"Senor Lagarto! I think it is him. The fox!"

El Lagarto raised his hand to silence the boy and leaned forward against his rifle. He snapped shut one lizard eye and raised the lid off the other, then went down into his lizard brain seeking the vision that would permit him to place a hole in the rat's gray hide.

There was definite movement in the brush. Something parted the tall dry grass. The blossoms on a Summersweet bush suddenly fell into pieces. El Lagarto hissed in anticipation, feeling the rise in his shoulder muscles as his finger tensed around the trigger. A nasty triangular head rose from the ground, bright eyes shining within a mask of shadowed fur. The fox looked proud as a hunting dog, the limp rabbit in its mouth. Lagarto sighed his displeasure and jerked the trigger.

The ground exploded and the fox's image paled into suspended dust which the breeze tore apart and spread into oblivion. El Lagarto sprang up, the rifle raised high in triumph. "Josue! The lantern!"

The pair ran down the shallow slope and out into the desert, El Lagarto using the rifle as an extension of his arm to point the way. "There, Josue! Put the light there!" Both circled the spot. There was no fox, dead or otherwise. No dropped rabbit, not even a set of tracks. "Imposible!" El Lagarto cried. "The fox was there! I saw him. He had a rabbit in his mouth!"

"Perhaps something else ate them both!" Josue offered.

"And what might that be, Bobo? La Cucaracha gigante?"

"No. El murciélago gigante!"

Salazar heard the massive flapping, the sound drifting from one ear to the other. And he saw the startled flow of Josue's eyes, following the creature's progress through the dark desert behind him. Salazar twisted around and saw a gigantic bat wrapping itself in its glossy black wings, falling deeper into the desert night, and disappearing.

Senor Salazar settled himself onto the ancient chair of crackling, dried wood in the abandoned tienda and waited to see if it would hold him. One day he would have a fine chair and beautiful furnishings when he turned this store into something far grander than the builder's original vision, but for now this bit of kindling would have to do. The disadvantage of dealing with the poor peasants of the pueblo was, unfortunately, that they were poor peasants. A few vegetables, some scattered chickens, and what passed for the family silver was not going to obtain the golden visions of El Lagarto. Obviously some widows needed to be swindled, some foolish believers gulled into investing in El Lagarto's great enterprises.

As Josue worked outside gathering his customers into an orderly line, Salazar meditated on his aborted hunting trip of the evening before. Obviously he had not seen what he had thought he had seen. Bats of such size did not exist here in California or anywhere else in the everyday world. Perhaps he had simply been overly excited due to the anticipation of the kill, the dim lighting, and Josue's poor assistance. Perhaps it had been a woman's lost shawl, blown by the wind onto a sapling, then blown away again far out into the desert. He certainly believed in a world of spirits and monsters, but they would be on his side.

If such a monstrous bat did exist perhaps El Lagarto had stumbled into its feeding grounds last night. Perhaps the giant bat also sought the destruction of the devious fox, to satisfy its own hunger. Salazar could surely respect that, but supernatural creature or not, Senor Bat had best stay clear of El Lagarto in his quest to destroy the fox. His mission was a personal one, and he would not be dissuaded.

The first client in to his la tienda de maravilla was to be the Widow Mendez. Inquiring around the pueblo, he'd determined that the lady had recently lost her husband after a long and painful illness, and that the guilt she'd felt over her inability to assuage her husband's suffering had driven her to her bed for many weeks. Salazar had sent Josue out to the widow's alqueria with tales of the maravilla he had performed for others by means of his special medicines. He had complete confidence in Josue for such a mission, as the bobo actually seemed to believe in his employer's powers.

A beautiful woman entered. He stumbled to his feet, the chair collapsing beneath him. "Viuda de Mendez!" he said, a bit too loudly. "I am honored you have come. Allow me to get you a chair!"

"Thank you, Senor, but I have been lying in my bed, or sitting in my chair, for days now. Perhaps I will stand."

He made himself smile. "As you wish." He strolled over to a table holding a small canvas bag. "I have been apprised of your situation. I am sure I can help you."

"I am not sure what they have told you." She looked away. "My situation, as you call it, is over now. I am done."

"I was referring to your husband's pain." Salazar frowned.

She jerked her head angrily. "What would you know of that? He is gone. His pain is over!"

"My sincere apologies, senora. How may I help you? I will do anything within my power."

"I have so many headaches," she replied, and her hand went to her forehead and hestitantly rubbed at the skin. "I thought they would stop after my tears dried up, but they have not. I lose sleep because of them, and I cannot do my chores. The boy said you had cures for such things?"

"But of course. Tell me, are they worse at noonday, or after the sun has gone down?"

"Why, they are worse in the heat of the sun, I suppose."

"Then you are in luck—I have just the thing!" He rummaged in a bag and brought out a small bit of powder wrapped in cloth. "Sprinkle this in your tea. You will be much better in a few days."

She took the cloth package and tucked it into her sleeve. She brought out a coin, and when he failed to smile she brought out another, and then a third before he raised his hand to stop her. She nodded, and turned to leave.

He called after her. "Are you quite sure, madam, that his pain is over? Are you quite sure the dead feel no pain?"

She paused, and her shoulders lowered. She turned. "No, Senor, I am not sure, I am not sure at all."

"You have dreamed that your husband is still in pain."

"How could you know such a thing?"

"I sometimes sense such things. The ability has been with me since childhood. Mind you, I am not always correct."

"This time . . . you are very correct. But it is simply my fear, is it not?"

"I wish I could tell you that, Senora. It seems so unfair that a life should end but that the pain goes on. But there are stories I could tell you—"

"Please! No!"

"Do not despair, my dear," he whispered, intoxicated by her smell. "This evening I will come to your farm and we will end your poor husband's torment."

Z

The rest of the day was taken up by the usual assortment of ailments, injuries, disappointments, and dreams. An aging resident of the pueblo brought in his small pig. "He is so small. Surely this cannot be right."

"Some breeds are . . ." Salazar began.

"Can you do something for mi cerdo, Senor?"

Salazar examined the pathetic puerco, considering how it might look on a spit, slow-roasting in the fireplace at the back of the store. Not much bigger than a rat, actually, but meat had been hard to come by here, especially since his hunting trips had been largely unsuccessful."I think I can do something, my friend. But he will require extensive, night and day care. I will keep him by my own bed, feeding him the medicines that will make him grow big and strong."

The old man's eyes filled with tears. "That would be wonderful. But surely such special treatment is expensive?"

Salazar looked the man up and down. "Perhaps we can work out a trade. You are a good worker?"

The old man looked down at his feet. "When I am able."

"Good enough. Come here late this afternoon and I will have a job for you."

During that afternoon Salazar treated a man for his rash with a mixture of sand and water, gave another man a jar full of a similar mixture for bathing his broken hand, prepared a pungent poultice of grease and chicken droppings for a woman seeking a new husband, provided another woman with a few lies scribbled on a scrap of rotted cloth intended to assuage her broken heart. For these treatments he received a few poor parcels of food, some silverware, a rare coin or two, scattered information concerning the pueblo's residents, and the secret fantasies of at least one of the women. All in all a good day, but he would need much more if he were to ever meet his lofty goals.

"Senor Salazar," Josue called from the door. "You have one more, waiting."

"Send them away, Josue. I have done enough for today. A man can labor for the good of others only so long before he must replenish himself with food and rest. I can perform no more miracles today."

"But Senor, this one has money. A great deal of money."

"Someone from the pueblo? Impossible. I would have known."

"No, Senor. A stranger passing through. One Diego de la Vega."

"I have heard of such a man. Send him in."

An elegant, dark-haired young man entered. He appeared to be in some discomfort, and had a silk handkerchief wrapped around his forearm, his stylish sleeve rolled up around it, but creased as neatly as if it were intentionally tailored that way.

"Senor, you have been injured!"

"A bite, I fear. Probably nothing, but one worries about infection in such an environment."

Agitated that he was so poorly prepared to deal with a mark of such obvious means, Salazar frantically scanned the room. In one corner was an old chest. He struggled to drag it into the center of the room. "Josue, quick! Help me with this!" Both men shoved the heavy box out onto the floor. His new customer grinned as Salazar exploded into a coughing fit. Well, Senor, smile while you can, before I take all your money and leave you mired in the tar pits.

"Please, sit," he told the clueless gentleman. "I apologize for these primitive conditions, but when doing charitable work one rarely has access to a palace."

"It is fine, Senor," Diego said, sitting on the chest. "I am honored to be under the care of such a humanitarian."

Salazar slowly began unwrapping the makeshift bandage. He used great care—the rich could be quite particular and easily offended when one was in close proximity to their person. "You are traveling through our beautiful countryside, Don Diego?"

"Yes, I am. I make trips through the countryside on a regular basis, taking notes, making sketches, relaxing in the evening by reading and writing poetry. Such activities reinvigorate me."

The wrapping was overly complicated, consisting of several layers. Salazar wondered if the bite was deep, perhaps infected. This bobo might need genuine medical care, which of course Salazar was unprepared to give. Not that it mattered to him, except that the demise of such a gentleman might invite serious, and unwanted attention. "You said you take notes, Senor?"

"Si. The local flora and fauna. I am a nature enthusiast, Senor—. Pardon me—I just realized I don't know your name."

"I am . . . Salazar." The last few wrappings were coming off. A large quantity of silk and fine cotton bandage material lay scattered across the trunk, spilling over onto the floor. "So many bandages, Senor! This must have been quite the bite!"

"My own fault, really. I had perched myself on a rock to sketch the creature. I had been watching him much of the day to see what mischief he would get himself into. He really is such a devious, underhanded beast. No charity in this one at all. I was simply curious, and wanted to observe his attempts to get out of trouble. But then I dropped my guard, and the coward lurched in and bit me!"

"Cobarde, indeed, senor. What kind of creature was this?"

"El Lagarto, a pitiful, devious thing."

"Con permiso! Excuse me?"

"A lizard, the lowest of the low. He crawls the desert on his belly and steals the food from the people's mouths."

"I see." Salazar jerked the last of the bandages from Diego's wound. And saw nothing but unblemished skin. "The lizard bit you here, you say?"

"Yes, yes. It was a very subtle bite. It was a lizard with very fine teeth, you see. But very painful, I assure you. In fact, I am feeling increasing discomfort now that the wound is exposed. Surely you can see I need treatment?"

Salazar leaned close enough to smell the soap on the rich man's skin, but could find no traces of injury. Obviously this young naturalist was delusional, which would make Salazar's work even easier than usual.

"Oh, yes. I have seen such a bite before. Very, very subtle. And very difficult to treat as a result, I'm afraid."

"Oh, surely you can do something, senor. I can pay you well for your healing talents."

"Oh, senor, I assure you I would treat you without charge if I could, but the ingredients for such a cure are quite expensive. I will treat you at the cost of those ingredients only, but it will be substantial."

"Of course. I assume this will suffice." Diego slipped his free hand into his pocket and drew out a pouch of coins.

The delicious sounds of their tiny metallic collisions drew Salazar's eyes. "Pay me in a few days," he said, somewhat reluctantly. "After I have finished the treatment and effected a cure. I trust you, of course." Sometimes delaying a demand for payment meant a grateful bonus, if properly played. Diego's insults against the noble El Lagarto would cost him dearly. He went through his bag until he'd found a small jar of worthless salve. He handed it to Diego. "Apply this to the area tonight, and again in the morning. Come see me again tomorrow afternoon and I will have a different salve for the second stage of treatment. Four days, four different salves—that will produce the cure."

"You are most kind, Senor Salazar. I am forever in your debt."

"Not at all," Salazar carelessly rewrapped the wound as there was no injury, except in this bobo's mind, to protect. "I shall see you tomorrow afternoon. You may go rest now and, well whatever you like, read some poetry, I suppose."

After Diego left Josue brought in the old man Salazar had hired for the night's job. "Senor!" Salazar shouted effusively, beginning to embrace him, but then reconsidering, held himself an arm's-length away. "I have a humanitarian mission planned for this evening. We have a grieving widow who would so love to see her dear, departed husband once again."

Salazar sent Josue out to hire a wagon and in the meantime had the old peasant help him gather a huge quantity of candles and powders from his collection of chemical effects. Tonight would be a costly endeavor, completely depleting many of his supplies, but after satisfying the widow, and tomorrow providing Don Diego with his second treatment, he was sure to have funding for any future projects, if future projects would even be necessary.

Salazar gave Josue and the peasant a few basic instructions on the way out to the widow's farm. To the peasant he explained that they would be giving the widow the gift of her dead husband, whom she needed to see one more time "if she is ever to have peace of mind." To Josue he gave a few more indications as to what his true intentions were, but not so many that the boy's ineptness might cause problems. Sometimes, the full range of one's plans and ambitions is best cherished alone.

Perhaps it was because of his very good luck of the day, or the anticipation of a larger than average payday to come, but the closer they came to the widow's farm Salazar experienced a gradual transformation taking place. He felt himself grow more confident, stronger, more cunning. He could sense the change in his legs, his belly, his chest, his throat. He was becoming El Lagarto, the lizard, the driving force of all such reptilian creatures trapped in an inhospitable desert. Oh, his companions might not see any physical evidence of his change, but those foxes out in their burrows, surely they must sense his stealthy approach and must now be quaking in fear. In fact, he was sure he could smell those quick and elusive foxes with his heightened sense of smell.

They dropped off the old man a short distance from the farmhouse and told him where to wait until Josue fetched him. The widow took her time coming to the door.

"Viuda de Mendez, I have come, as promised," El Lagarto said, bowing deeply.

She appeared none too pleased by his presence. "I have been reconsidering. This seems quite disrespectful. My husband was . . . conservative."

"Oh, but we mean no disrespect, Senora. Our concern here is strictly spiritual. I know your husband cared, still cares, about your happiness."

"We are good Catholics here."

"As am I," the lizard exclaimed. "I do God's work, whenever possible. We intend only to pray with you, good lady."

"Very well," she said, though her posture showed her reluctance.

Once they were inside the widow's modest home he had Josue retrieved the numerous candles from the two large canvas bags and arranged them around the room. He asked the widow's permission to rearrange the chairs for their prayer session and she agreed, but not without some fuss concerning the necessity of it all. Josue then lit all the candles. "Increíble!" she exclaimed. "It is like the daylight!"

"It is the light of true knowledge! Only liars, thieves, and foxes hide in the shadows!" He closed his eyes and bathed in the light and heat.

"What are you planning here, Senor Salazar?"

"I plan to pray with you, Viuda de Mendez. Pray to end your dead husband's suffering! And to end your suffering as well. You are a good woman, you treated your husband well. I am sure also that you gave everything you could to the church. So surely you deserve some peace of mind!" He looked down at her, and imagined he could smell her sadness and grief. "You were a good wife, were you not? And generous to your church?"

She looked up at him, crying. "I was not always patient. My husband could be . . . a difficult man. And I am poor—sometimes I am not able to give to the church as much as I would like."

El Lagarto met Josue's eyes over the hunched form of the weeping widow. One of the first things he had taught the boy was that good and generous people seldom if ever think they are good enough, or generous enough. "I am sending my assistant out to the wagon for some medicine to make you feel better, dear lady." Josue left the room. "There, there."

He bent over her. "Sit up proudly, madam. I can tell you are a good woman. I have never been fooled in that way." He handed her the last of his clean handkerchiefs.

She sat up. Her eyes glistened in the brilliant candlelight. "God bless you, Senor."

He pulled a smaller bag out of one of the others. "I have here a kind of incense. I will be using a great deal of it, madam, for this is a very great prayer we are making for your husband who suffered greatly. I fear it will make things smoky for a time, and you may find that breathing will make you light-headed, so hold the handkerchief over your mouth. I am sorry, but this is necessary, I assure you."

Josue came inside and nodded, handing El Lagarto a small bottle which he passed to the widow. It contained only a strong licor and some herbs. "Drink this and you will feel better, madam. Drink the entire bottle. It will fortify you for our prayers."

El Lagarto then went from candle to candle sprinkling variously-colored powders into the flames. Smoke spontaneously erupted, the plumes entwining and filling that end of the room with a pastel curtain of cloud. As he fed the candles he shouted, "We pray for the tormented soul of the departed Senor Mendez. We pray for his loyal young wife who misses him so dearly. We pray for the poor people of the pueblo who will benefit so greatly from the unprecedented generosity of the Viuda de Mendez. In the name of the holiest of holies please give us a sign!"

All during this loud prayer the widow's sobs ballooned louder, culminating in a sorrowful scream as the old man materialized out of the curtain of smoke, his face painted luminous green except for the bright red circles drawn around his eyes. "Mi esposa!" he shouted. "My wife!"

"Mi Dios! Mi Dios!" she cried, falling to her knees.

El Lagarto grinned magnificently, so pleased with himself he threw back his head and stuck out his tongue as if to taste the air. And stopped, sure he had smelled and tasted fox. "The fox?" he croaked.

Two giant black wings came out of the dense smoke on either side of the old man, beating the smoke away. A long silver tongue sliced through the air and beheaded many of the candles. Then above the terrified old man the great dark shadow of a fox's head appeared, eyes burning brightly in the hollows of the blackened triangular shape.

El Lagarto devolved quickly into Salazar again and ran screaming from the room.

Josue called desperately after his master, not knowing what to do. He turned to escape when a black-gloved hand grabbed his arm and spun him around. Josue cowered, looking down at a set of black leather boots which grew legs and then a torso as the tall man slowly tipped Josue's head upwards by means of a rapier wedged beneath his chin. Finally Josue was staring into the man's eyes peering from holes in a coal-black mask.

"No more hunting foxes, with lizards, eh Josue?" the man said in near whisper. "I know you are better than that."

"Si, El Zorro. Si."

Josue was sweeping out the abandoned tienda when Don Diego strolled in, presenting a bare forearm and carrying his little sack of coins in the other hand. "I think it is muy better," he announced, "but I am ready for Senor Salazar's second treatment just in case. After all, what harm can he do?" He looked around the room. "Where is my good and generous médico?"

"He has crawled away into the desert like the lizard. He is not good, or generous, or a medico. Don Diego, you really should be more careful with your money. If I were a rich man, which I never will be . . . my apologies, Don Diego, for introducing you to him. El Lagarto, Senor Salazar, he was a very bad man."

"But Josue, I am shocked! Were you not his assistant?"

"Mi madre, she has been ill, and there has been little to eat. I thought I could help her, but I have only brought her dishonor."

"The truth is like the wind during a violent storm, muchacho. At least it clears the air, however difficult the experience." He tossed the bag of coins to the startled young man. "For your mother, and a new start." He turned to leave.

"Wait! Don Diego!" Diego turned and the boy continued. "So, I do not want to be like the lizard anymore. Should I be like el zorro, the fox, wise and swift on his feet?"

"Oh, muchacho, too much metaphor will give you such a headache! I could tell you no, be like the bird, and spread your own wings, but even then some hunter might shoot you out of the sky! Leave the zoológico behind, live among people for a change."

And then he was gone.

BY MOONLIGHT:
A TALE OF ZORRO

BY JOE R. LANSDALE

It was hard to know the nature of the road, the dust was so thick and high and white you could not see the sun, but somehow, the driver, thick of body, and hard of soul, as if by instinct, was constantly on it. The horses snorted and shook their heads against the dry powder their hooves knocked up and caused to settle across their noses, heads and manes like snow.

Duarte and his fresh bride, Juanita, rode in the back of the wagon and all their earthly goods bounced about them. Already, some of their beautiful dishes, touched with colors unique and fine, had broken. The overhead canvas of the wagon held the heat and made the air inside the wagon not only dusty but heavy, made them feel they were wrapped in woolen blankets.

Duarte said, "Driver. There is a lady here. Can you not drive more gently?"

"The dust does not care for ladies or gentlemen," the driver said, tugging at his sand-colored hat. "It does not care for drivers like me. The dust does as the dust does and is not at my command. Let me eat the dust in peace, Senor."

"You can slow it down," said Duarte.

"And then you will complain about how slow we go."

Duarte knew this was correct, for he had done just that an hour ago, so he said nothing more for the time being. He sat and thought about how just a year before, they would have been riding in style, with servants, but, his fortunes, though still good, were not what they had once been.

They rode on through the hot day and breathed the sandy air, and finally they stopped beneath a growth of cottonwood trees beside a spring where someone had dug it out and laid rocks around it for a pool. The pool flooded over on one end and fled down into the trees and fed a creek that gurgled through them.

They dipped rags in the pool and wiped their faces and the backs of their necks, drank, filled their water bags and canteens and let the horses sip.

Duarte took two chairs from the back of the wagon and put them under the shade of the cottonwoods, side by side. He held Juanita's hand and guided her toward one of them. She sat, and though exhausted she was lovely in the dying light of the sun and the dropping of the dust; her hair was raven black and her eyes were even darker, and the bones in her face were sharp like the aristocratic bones of her ancestors, her lips full. Duarte looked at her and his heart hurt. He sat down beside her and watched the driver take care of the horses.

"Are you all right Juanita?"

"I am."

"Still sick?"

"Some."

"Is there anything I can do?"

"In nine months you can hold your son."

Duarte turned and looked at Juanita. She was smiling at him.

"A child?"

"Yes. I know why I'm sick now. I should have known before. My sisters have all had the sickness, and then the baby."

"You are sure?"

She nodded. "I am sure."

"Wonderful," Duarte said. "Driver," Duarte said standing from his chair, "did you hear that?"

"A baby," said the driver. "I have had five. Trust me, the idea loses charm in time."

"I'm to be a father," Duarte said paying no attention to the driver's reply. "Did you hear?"

"Said so," and then the driver softened. "Congratulations. Now, I suggest we rest awhile. It will be a full moon tonight. We rest for a couple of hours and push on. The road is rockier a mile or so from here. Less dust and at night it will be cooler."

"Will it be bumpy?" Juanita asked.

"Very much so," the driver said.

"Then we must go slow," Juanita said. "Because of the baby.

"Yes," Duarte said. "You must drive slow, like my wife is made of glass."

Juanita said, "Glass? So far we have broken a lot of glass."

"Slower then," Duarte said, holding her hands in his, smiling. "Slow and careful as if you are the butter on a butterfly's wings."

In the night, the young man and his wife, lying on canvas that was topped by soft blankets, wearing only the night air and their fine clothes for covering, they slept, and then, suddenly, Duarte awoke. He sat up and looked across the countryside and saw a rise where the earth had coughed up itself, and above that, he saw the moon, big and shiny like the back of a new pocket watch. Bats were flying across the face of the moon. He watched as they flapped and glided their way across the sky; it caused a chill to climb up his back. He thought: Bats. Rats with wings. Is this an omen? He laid back down, his ear to the ground. He heard horses.

He sat upright, and up the rise, backed by the moon, came four horses and four riders. They paused there and sat and looked down at where Duarte and his new bride lay. Duarte looked for the driver. But he was nowhere to be seen. He was gone from his place.

And then he felt the tip of something sharp against the back of his neck. He turned to see the driver holding a long, sharp dagger.

"I am sorry about your bride, about the child, but a man, he must make a living. And driving you and your goods is not as fine as having your goods. You should have hired someone more honest. Me, I'm not so honest...Should I shoot your wife now? Those men up there. They will want her."

Juanita had come awake, and she saw all this and heard all this, and if she had any words, they froze in her mouth. All she could do was slowly stand as her husband stood, and watch as the riders came down from the hill.

So down the riders came, and it seemed as if it took forever, and Duarte hoped it would be forever, but they came, arrived and dismounted.

Among the riders was a big man and the big man appeared to be their leader. He gave the reins of his horse to one of the men behind him, stood and looked at the pair and pulled his sword and let it hang loose in his hand. The others stood behind him, holding their horses.

The driver, without being asked, went away then, and came back with a lantern. He held the lantern up so that it lit up Duarte and Juanita's face. The big man said, "She is as lovely as I remember."

And then Duarte knew he had seen the man before, the others too. The town from which they left, the men had been there. Two of them had been among the hired help who had loaded their wagon. The others had watched from under the overhang of the Mercado. It had all been planned from the very start.

"Do what you wish with me, and the goods in the wagon," Duarte said, "but give my wife a horse and let her go."

"We do not have a spare horse," said the big man. He turned to the others. "Do we have spare horses?"

"No," said a dumpling of man. "We just have the ones we ride."

"Let her go," Duarte said. "Leave her be. She is with child."

"Ah, ripe with child," said the big man. "The thing that would have been best for my mother was that I was never born. Perhaps it is the same with your child, huh? We kill you both and the child is never born to grow up to worry his mother. What do you say?"

Duarte said nothing. Juanita took his arm and held it.

"That does move me," said the big man. "It always moves me to see true love. But...I must not leave you to talk. We are robbers. It's our job. And, unfortunately for you, we are murderers too. It does not always pay well, but sometimes, like tonight, it pays well enough."

"I am sorry," said the driver, lowering the lantern. "I have nothing against you."

"Shut up," said Duarte, "you are a coward like all the others."

"This is true," said the driver. "I am a coward. And a coward knows his place."

"Give me a sword, and I will kill you one at a time," Duarte said.

"Now," said the big man, "why would we do that? We do not want to die. We want you to die. Come, let us go away from here, on out from beneath the cotton woods, away from the wagon. We will stay here tonight, and we do not want the stink of your deaths to be where we sleep. And perhaps, before the woman dies, we can give her a moment of pleasure. We are not so young and handsome, but we are men."

"You are animals," Duarte said.

"Perhaps," said the big man. "Come. Come now."

As Duarte and his wife were marched before the desperadoes, there feet moving as if pulling weights, Duarte thought of many things, but mostly he thought of his wife and his child who would never be born, and he decided he would fight to the death before he would merely stand and die. Then out of the corner of his eye, he thought he saw a horse and rider move on the hill from which the robbers came. But when he turned his head to look, there was nothing. It had only been hope that had put the horse and rider in his eye, not real rescue, and he felt his bravado drain out of him.

At the edge of the cottonwoods they stopped walking and stood under the moon light, and the big man said, "Turn around and look at us."

Duarte and Juanita turned. Duarte looked at the grouping of men before him and blinked. Before there had been the four from the hill and the driver, and now there was one more, one who stood slightly back from the others, just at the edge of the cottonwoods, not out in the open.

Six, thought Duarte? Had he miscounted from the start?

The big man moved across in front of the others, and Duarte followed him as he moved. The big man smiled and the moon gathered up in his teeth and made them gleam.

"Do you know what it's like to be poor, and for you to be rich?" said the big man. "It disappoints."

"You may have all we own. Just let my wife go."

"We already have all you own," said the big man. "I was born poor. I've never grown used to it. Fat dogs like you, you should give up things that the rest of us need. Am I right, my friends?"

The crowd agreed almost in unison, and when Duarte turned his attention from the big man and looked at the others, he saw that now they were one less.

But the man standing by the cottonwoods, still stood.

"I am first in everything," said the big man. "So, young woman, come to me. You might as well."

"But," said a voice, "she does not want to come to you. She is not a dog."

The robbers turned to look. The big man said, "Which of you said that?"

"I must confess," said the man nearest the cottonwoods, "that would be me."

The man at the rear of the group had stepped back and was deeper among the trees than before. He could barely be seen.

"Who are you?" asked the big man, and then he hesitated, noted one of his group was missing. "And where is Manuel?"

"Ah," said the voice in the shadows, "he is sleeping, and when he awakes, he will have quite the headache. I tapped him not so gently with the butt of my sword."

"Come out of there," said the big man. "Come out and show yourself."

The shadow shape in the trees moved, stepped to a spot where the cottonwoods split and the moon light shined through. The man was dressed in black, wearing a black hat, and a black mask. The moonlight caught a cold wink of silver—a drawn sword.

"Zorro," said one of the robbers."

"Good of you to recognize me," said Zorro, moving forward. "I am flattered."

Silence ruled for a moment, and then Zorro whipped his sword through the air and the moon tracked along it; it looked as if he were whipping a silver ribbon in the air.

"Do any of you care for a taste?" said Zorro. "Which coward is first?"

"Take him, Rafael," the big man said. "Give him a taste of your sword."

"Not me," said Rafael, and he moved back a couple of steps.

"Then we will all take him," the big man said. "He is only one man."

There was a long silence. Then, somewhere in the cottonwoods a night bird called, and a horse snorted.

"That snort," said Zorro, "that would be my horse, Toronado. He is disgusted with your cowardice."

The driver held up his hands, said, "I have admitted I am a coward. I am nothing more."

The driver took off running.

"Come back here," yelled the big man, but his words had no effect. The driver ran in the direction of the wagon.

"He will find I have borrowed his horses, hidden them away," Zorro said. "Now, enough! One at a time or all at once. Do your worst."

One of the men drew his sword and broke forward with a yell. Zorro's sword poked like a hat pin through dark velvet, and then the point of it found the man's knee and he fell. Another would have attacked, but Zorro danced forward and his sword licked out and tasted flesh as the man drew his own weapon. Zorro jerked the butt of his sword to the man's chin, and he went down. That left two; the big man and a skinny fellow who reached for his sword. With the precision of a seamstress, Zorro wove his sword in such a way he plucked the weapon from the brigand's belt, flipped it back behind him.

The big man charged forward with a yell, his sword waving above his head.

Duarte sprang forward, grabbed the big man by the shoulder, turned him and hit him with his fist. Hit him so hard the big man nearly turned completely around before he fell on his face.

The last man, unwilling to draw his sword, dropped to his knees and clasped his hands in front of him and begged.

Zorro commanded him on his stomach. He looked at Duarte, who had now pulled Juanita close to him, and smiled.

"What say you return to the wagon and bring back some rope if you have it, and a knife?" Zorro said. "If you see the driver, knock him down, though my guess is, without horses, he is on the run."

Duarte got the rope from the wagon. The driver was nowhere to be seen. He went back and they tied the robbers up and left them there. Duarte said, "What will happen to them?"

"I will come back for them," Zorro said. "Do not let it worry you."

Zorro brought the horses out from the trees where he had hid them, and he whistled up Toronado. Duarte hitched up the horses and drove the wagon with Juanita by his side. Zorro rode along with them on Toronado.

They found the driver beside the road, having collapsed from exhaustion.

Zorro rode where the driver lay on the ground, breathing hard. He leaned out from his horse. "All that effort for nothing."

"Please, Zorro. Do not kill me. I am not a bad man."

"Oh, yes you are. You certainly are. Young gentleman, have you any more of that rope?"

Z

They tied the driver and left him, continued on. Zorro said, "Where is your destination?"

Duarte told him. Zorro said, "You are but a short time from there. The driver duped you. He took you a back way to tire you out and to have you away from others. You are lucky I was returning from...We will call it a business trip...and saw your situation."

"Lucky in more ways than one," Juanita said. How can we repay you?"

"Remember the less fortunate. That is payment enough. Now, there is a better road just ahead, and we will take it."

Z

They had come to the lights of a town now, the town where Duarte and Juanita were traveling to, and Zorro halted and Duarte tugged the horses to a stop.

"There is where you want to go," Zorro said, pointing.

"We're starting our married lives there," Juanita said.

"You will do well, "Zorro said. "I know it." He smiled. "I have to leave you now. I must go back to our friends," Zorro said. "I am going to deliver them to someone who will make sure they get their just desserts. And so, farewell."

Zorro wheeled his black stallion and galloped off into the night. Duarte climbed down from the wagon and watched him go. He watched him race down the road and come to a hill and top it. Saw him pinned there by the moonlight. Then Zorro stopped and turned in the saddle and took off his hat and waved it. Duarte lifted his hand to wave in return. Then Zorro rode behind the hill and out of sight.

ZORRO AND THE FILIBUSTER

BY KAGE BAKER

In other countries, winter was a time of hellish ice and snow. The *pobladores* of Pueblo de Los Angeles knew it rather as a season of delights. In winter, abundant rains made the hills green, lush with golden poppies and blue lupine, and water actually flowed in the river bed!

No, the hellish season in Alta California came at the end of summer, when long months without rain had made the hills dry and brown. Then cattle roamed the dusty plains, searching without success for something upon which to graze. When the rancheros saw their herds in danger of becoming lean, they knew the time for the *matanza* had arrived.

Whooping like devils, the vaqueros would circle the herds, striking with braided *riatas* and expertly cutting out the fattest of the steers. The panicked animals would be driven to the place of slaughter and felled. Their hides were taken for leather, their fat rendered down into tallow for candles, but the rest was left to rot on the open plains. The well-to-do *pobladores* ate beef so often they had no need of thrift, and so circling vultures and a towering stink of decay completed the picture of Hell.

By night the vultures flew away to roost, to be replaced by scavenging coyotes. But on one hot September evening in the year of our Lord 1820, the coyotes found themselves driven back by a single fox…

"Patience, muchachos." Don Diego de la Vega peered through the darkness at the darker shapes circling the carcass. "We won't be much longer. Will we?"

Bernardo, stolidly hacking away with a machete, shook his head. The steer had been slaughtered only hours ago, just before sunset, and so the meat was still fresh. Bernardo tossed a chunk of prime beef onto the tarpaulin he had spread. One coyote, bolder than the others, started forward, drooling at the scent of fresh steak. The business end of a whip cracked scant inches from his nose. He yipped and somersaulted backward.

"A little less noise, my friend. We don't want to wake our hosts the Verdugos, do we?" Diego coiled his whip. He glanced at the distant lights of the Verdugo hacienda. In his heart he would have welcomed an uproar and a chase, but he conceded to himself that such excitement was unlikely tonight.

Bernardo chopped out a couple of good marrowbones and added them to the heap on the tarpaulin. Stepping back from the carcass, he gathered up the tarpaulin's corners into a bundle and tied them tightly. He carried it to his mule and paused only to wash his hands and the machete, with Diego helpfully holding up the bota of water they had brought. Behind them, the coyotes fell to on the carcass at last.

"Well, give my regards to Manuel and his wife," said Diego. "Tell them the meat will last longer if they smoke some of it."

Bernardo gave him a wry smile. Manuel Cota and his wife were poor *mestizos* with eight children and Manuel had been unable to work for six weeks, after he had broken his leg in a fall. The meat was unlikely to go uneaten long enough to make preserving any necessary. Bernardo climbed into the saddle and Diego handed him the tarpaulin bundle, and stood watching as his foster brother rode away on the errand of mercy. With a sigh, Diego swung into his own saddle.

"Let's go home, Toronado," he told his black mount. "It's a dull night in Hell, after all."

He found his way to the bank of the dry river and rode along its bed a while before cutting across a low range of hills. As he was descending to the plain beyond he heard the clatter of hooves on hard dry earth, and the crack of a pistol shot. Looking down, he saw a drama being played out: four horsemen were in hot pursuit of a fifth, a man whose mount was heavily burdened with a pair of big saddlebags. The hunted man rode well, but clearly it was only a matter of time before he was overtaken.

"Toronado, I think I spoke too soon," said Diego, with a grin. Reaching into an inner pocket he drew out a black kerchief and bound it on his head, adjusting it so as to be able to see through the holes he had cut for his eyes. "Four against one? What unfair odds!"

Even as he spoke, the fleeing mount stumbled and went down. Its rider was on his feet in an instant, drawing steel that glinted in the starlight.

"Oh, bravo, señor!" Diego urged Toronado down the hillside. Though he had not worn Zorro's full costume that night, his clothing was dark, and his swift approach through the dry grass went largely unnoticed by the four attackers. As they circled the solitary man, one of them drew a pistol and aimed it, meaning to do murder. Before he could fire, the thief felt a pain like a branding-iron in his wrist, and the pistol went flying. Inexplicably something yanked him by the same wrist from his saddle. He fell heavily and found himself staring up at a dark rider on a coal-black stallion.

"El Zorro!" he gasped.

"Time to think about a change of career, my friend," said Diego. His whip uncoiled like a live thing and snaked out again to crack beside the ear of another thief's mount. The startled animal bolted, carrying its rider away. The third rider, more cowardly than his companions, turned his horse's head and rode away for dear life. Only the fourth dismounted and drew a cutlass, swinging it like a meat cleaver as he strode toward his intended victim.

"*En garde,*" said the other, and struck at him with the lunge of an accomplished swordsman. The thief beat the blow back with difficulty.

"Ruiz, find your gun and shoot him!" he bawled.

"I wouldn't do it, Ruiz," said Diego mildly. He recognized the man on the ground as one of the stevedores who worked at San Pedro, when he worked an honest day at all. The man with the cutlass sounded English, and the one they had been pursuing was clearly a Frenchman, from his style with a saber. *What a cosmopolitan place Alta California is becoming,* thought Diego, as he slid from the saddle and grabbed up the pistol. "Really, Ruiz, take well-intentioned advice when it's given. Ride away while you can."

Both he and Ruiz looked over, startled by a hoarse scream. The thief with the cutlass staggered and fell. His opponent turned menacingly, sword ·point raised once more. Ruiz needed no further warning. He scrambled to his feet and was in the saddle in one bound, galloping off.

"Had they been chasing you all the way from San Pedro?" inquired Diego, catching the bridle of the Englishman's mount.

"They had, monsieur. *Merci mille fois.*"

"You defended yourself well, señor." Diego led the horse to where the Englishman lay, and prodded him with his boot. "You! Let's see your—oh. He's dead." He saw now the black spreading stain on the thief's shirt, from a clean saber stab through the heart.

"One less scoundrel and murderer in the world," said the Frenchman. "I will shed no tears." Wiping the blade of his weapon on a handful of dead grass, he looked curiously at Diego. Diego returned the favor. He beheld a man of about his own age, of a stiffly upright bearing. He was handsome, with prominent green eyes, and a set of neatly-trimmed whiskers that gave him a military air.

"Why are you masked, monsieur, if you will pardon the question?"

"To conceal my face, señor, why else?" Diego grinned at him. "But I am no thief, if that was your next question."

"*Bien*." The Frenchman sheathed his saber and went to inspect his horse, which had gotten to its feet and was shivering, head downcast. "Poor creature! She may have been injured. Monsieur, if I might impose on your kindness further—will you assist me in removing the saddle-bags? I will take the ruffian's horse."

Diego assisted him in transferring the saddlebags to the other horse. They were large and tremendously heavy. "Whoof! What have you got in these, señor, books?"

"Some books, oui. In the one I have my trunk, containing my personal effects," said the Frenchman, buckling the saddlebags in place. "In the other is a gift I bring to all of California."

"How generous, señor."

The Frenchman climbed into the saddle and, urging it forward, took the reins of his previous mount. He looked down at Diego thoughtfully.

"*El Zorro,* the brigand called you. I will remember it."

He rode away into the night.

Z

When the warehouses at San Pedro were full of stacked hides and tallow, the rancheros would hold a fandango to celebrate their prosperity. This year the gala was held at the splendid hacienda of the Lopez family. It was customary to bring some sort of house gift, nominally to defray expenses for the host, but it was also customary to vie with other guests to bring the most expensive and extravagant contribution.

"French champagne," said Diego with satisfaction, lifting a bottle from its packing case. "Or so the smugglers swear on the honor of their sainted mothers. What do you think, Bernardo, shall we give them a dozen bottles?"

Bernardo rolled his eyes, but took the bottle and carefully loaded it, with the others, into a pair of wicker panniers strapped in the back of his mule. Diego dusted his hands and glanced down to be certain no straw clung to his knee breeches or silk stockings. "There! Still a flawless peacock. It's been months since I had a chance to do any serious competitive flirting."

Bernardo did not smile. Diego knit his brows. "Is something troubling you, brother?"

Bernardo nodded. Signing, he explained: *My wife's family tells me a foreign white man has been seeking them out, asking what they know of a man called Zorro.*

"Ah!" Diego remembered his strange encounter of the previous week. "What did they tell him?"

Only that Zorro is a spirit of justice who walks at night. But there is more, brother. This man asked them many questions about themselves, about how they live and how they are treated by the rancheros. He told them he is their friend and will help them.

"Very good! Undoubtedly a Frenchman who has been reading about Rousseau's noble savages. And he wants to help them? Good for him." Diego patted his pockets to be certain he had his dancing slippers. As he swung himself into the saddle, he wondered briefly about the weight of the mysterious saddlebags. Had they contained gold? Perhaps the Frenchman intended to start a charity for the Indians.

The first chill of autumn made the sight of the Lopez rancho especially appealing, with the greasewood torches lining the long drive to the house and the lights blazing in its windows. The wide courtyard was already crowded with carriages and tethered horses when Diego and Bernardo arrived, but Don Alfonso Lopez still stood by his open door, welcoming in guests.

"Don Diego! Fashionably late, are you?"

"Am I not always?" Smiling, Diego dismounted. He could hear the musicians tuning up in the ballroom, and the excited cries of young ladies. "My father sends his regrets, but I'm happy to say his cold is much improved. And where may my servant put these?" He opened one of the panniers and drew forth a bottle for Don Alfonso's inspection. The older man took it and peered at it, holding it out at arm's length to read the label.

"Champagne! You are too generous, my boy. It's curious, you know; we have a gentleman visiting from France, inside."

"Have you?" Diego raised his eyebrows. "Perhaps he can tell us about the latest fashions!"

Don Alfonso made a wry face. "He is no dandy. A little sour, if you ask me. He's a friend of the schoolmaster's, as I understand it. But come, come in! Have your man take the wine around to the kitchen. There is still a little ice from the cellar."

Having entrusted his boots to a solemn Indian servant and put on his dancing slippers, Diego joined the party. The musicians struck up a *seguidilla*, and in short order Diego found himself paired with the youngest of the Lopez girls, Incarnacion. He assumed his most sparkling and frivolous air, but Incarnacion's attention was elsewhere.

Following her darting gazes, he spotted the Frenchman he had rescued the previous week, standing close against the wall. His arms were folded, and he watched the dancers with a faint ironical smile. Beside him stood the schoolmaster, Señor Balendin, who did not appear to be enjoying himself. As Diego watched, he drew out a handkerchief to mop his sweating face, and threw a nervous glance at the Frenchman.

"Señorita Lopez, I am crushed! I wore my most magnificent swallowtail coat to this occasion, and you haven't given me so much as one look of astonished admiration! How can you be so cruel?" Diego murmured to his partner, as he turned in the dance.

Incarnacion Lopez looked demure, yet a dimple was visible at the corner of her mouth. "Don Diego, you are quite the silliest man in Alta California. But—haven't you traveled?" She looked up at him in sudden interest. "You *have*, I remember, Mama said you were educated in Spain. Did you meet any Frenchmen? Do you know anything about them?"

"Yes," said Diego, without missing a step.

"Does he seem well-born to you, that man standing by Señor Balendin? Can you tell if he is a man of quality? He is so handsome, and yet his whiskers are so fierce!"

"Alas, Señorita Lopez, I can tell you nothing more than that he has the bearing of a soldier," said Diego, truthfully. "I thought he was your guest. Do you mean to tell me your sisters have not learned all his secrets yet?"

"No." Incarnacion, pouting, stole another glance at the stranger. "Papi sent an invitation to Señor Balendin and he replied that he was unable to attend our fandango, because he was entertaining a friend from France. Papi wrote back and told him his friend was invited too. So he's here. His name is Guillaume de Payan and that's all I know. Such distinguished features! And you don't know anything about him at all?"

"You're asking his hated rival?" Diego flung up his arm and turned gracefully. "Well, then, his real name is Señor Satan and he's milk-brother to Napoleon Bonaparte, and he's as poor as a tailor."

Incarnacion struck him with her fan. "Don't be so mean! He looks much younger than Señor Balendin, don't you think? Funny that they should be friends. The schoolmaster isn't dashing at all. Oooh! Estrellita Covarrubias did tell me her father told her Señor Balendin was mixed up with the French, what were they called? Jacobites? Something like that. When he was a young man. But he never teaches sedition at the school. My brothers would say something if he did."

"I don't doubt it for a second," replied Diego. As the dance ended and he took Incarnacion's arm to escort her to a chair, he thought: *The schoolteacher a former Jacobin? Interesting!*

There were many men who had fled to the New World to escape a dangerous or shameful past. Diego wondered whether the schoolmaster was one of them.

The *sarabande* was danced, the minuet, the waltz, and yet Guillaume de Payan remained in his place by the wall, with something of well-bred contempt in his general attitude. So irresistible were those whiskers, however, that when the musicians took a break the Lopez girls headed for him in a breathless line. Consuelo, the oldest, got there first.

"Señor schoolmaster, why will your handsome friend not dance?"

Señor Balendin gave a forced smile. "He is—that is to say, he doesn't—"

"I am only here to bear witness, mademoiselle," said de Payan, with a sardonic bow.

"Witness to what, Señor?" inquired Diego, who was ladling up a cup of sangria from the punchbowl. "If you'll pardon my inquiry."

"The spectacle of the landed gentry disporting themselves," said de Payan.

"And what a spectacle it is," Diego agreed cheerfully. "Have you ever seen so many people with two left feet in your life? We haven't the undoubted polish of the French court, señor, but no one can say we aren't enthusiastic dancers."

"I wouldn't know how the *Ancien Regime* amuses itself," said de Payan. "Since I have not visited the country of my birth in some years."

"Ah! A Republican, are you? One of those fire-eaters in favor of old Roman virtues? A revolutionary?"

"No, no, Don Diego, he is only fond of spouting nonsense," said Señor Balendin, with a ghastly attempt at a hearty laugh.

"You cannot deny, monsieur, that the Roman Republic was an admirable thing," said de Payan.

"I suppose it was. I have never bothered my head with history books. This is California, señor!" Diego raised his punch in salute and drank. "Why should we concern ourselves with the old world and all its wretchedness?"

"You will find California a hospitable place, I assure you, señor," said Consuelo, but without much warmth, for she could see that the handsome stranger was disinclined to court anyone.

"Hospitality is an ancient and sacred custom," said de Payan. "Otherwise I would speak freely."

"Guillaume—" the schoolmaster went pale.

"No, no, señor, speak your mind, please!" Diego bowed after Consuelo, who had wandered away in annoyance. "We provincials are always eager for enlightenment."

"Then I will be frank, monsieur. I see in this room all the worst vices of the old world: its tyrannical nobility indulging themselves in wine and feasting, while worthier men are relegated to the outer darkness. They labor in your fields, your vineyards, your gold mines, they stand in your yards with brute patience and hold the reins of your horses. The noble savage is oppressed here as foully as the peasants of old Europe!"

"Guillaume, keep your voice down, please!"

Diego had a sip of punch. "Actually, señor, we have no gold mines up here in Alta California. You're thinking of that *El Dorado* story, yes? Nothing but cows up here, I'm afraid. Cows and a lot of bad dancers."

"If you were a less frivolous man, I would call you to account for your tone," said de Payan, leaning close to stare into his eyes. Diego smiled and shrugged.

"Unfortunately you are looking at the worst swordsman in all of Alta California, señor. Nor am I any use with a pistol. You wouldn't kill me over a few jokes, would you?"

"No," said de Payan, leaning back and folding his arms again. "But others may claim that duty, one day. And it may not be so far off! I have heard certain stories of a leader among the Indians, a certain Zorro, who rides the night righting injustice wherever he finds it."

"Oh, him." Diego waved his hand. "He's just some lunatic in a mask."

"Laugh all you like, monsieur," said de Payan, with a sneer. "This Zorro may bring about a day of reckoning sooner than you think."

Some days later, Diego woke to the familiar sound of Bernardo bringing in a pail of hot water. He roused himself and pulled on his trousers while Bernardo filled the washbasin and laid out the razor and shaving mug.

"Well, brother, what's the news?" Diego inquired, as he daubed his chin with shaving soap.

Bernardo faced him in the mirror and signed, *The stranger from over the sea has been riding among the villages again, asking where he might find Zorro.*

"Persistent fellow."

More. He brought them printed papers to read. He was angry when it was explained to him that most of the villagers cannot read French or Spanish. He called everyone together and talked for a long time.

"Talked. About what?"

He told them much about his own people and how they suffered for many years under cruel masters, until they turned the earth upside down and became their own masters instead. He said he wanted to help the villagers do the same. He said his own people had done it with fire and the sword.

"Hmmm!"

And he said that once the villagers had done this, they too would be their own masters. And each man should have his own rancho and farm like the white men.

"What did the Indians think of this?"

Bernardo smiled with his eyes. *Most of them thought it was only another white man telling them they must be more like white men. The stranger became angry again. He asked Zorro to step forth, so he could speak with him. It was explained to him that Zorro is a spirit. He would not believe this. He told them all to send word to Zorro that he must meet with him.*

"You know, our friend M. de Payan seems well-intentioned, but he is going about this the wrong way. I think we must indeed arrange a meeting between Zorro and this man." Diego took up the razor and carefully set about sculpting the perfect lines of his mustache.

Z

Some miles northwest of Pueblo de Los Angeles was the village of La Nopalera, in the Cahuenga Valley. At the rear of this valley it was possible to follow a switchback trail up a steep canyon. The rider doing so emerged at last onto a peculiarly flat-topped hill with a breathtaking vista of the plains before him on three sides, even to the sea and a distant island.

The few *mestizos* living at La Nopalera shunned the high hill, for there were stories that it was haunted. Indeed, Don Diego de la Vega himself claimed to have once seen a ghostly *baile* in progress there, with skeletal dancers and musicians. Not even the bravest of the local men would venture up there after that.

This suited Diego perfectly, for the hilltop provided an excellent view and was well suited as a meeting place for any occasional business Zorro wished to contract with others. He waited now, immobile on Toronado's back. He spotted M. de Payan's approach, from far out on the plain, long before the wind carried the sound of hoofbeats.

In due course the Frenchman came riding up the trail. Diego rode to the hilltop's edge. De Payan looked up and saw him silhouetted against the stars, just as a gust of wind spread his black cloak behind him.

"Zorro welcomes you, señor."

De Payan urged his horse up the last few meters of the trail, staring hard at Diego. "When last we met, I took you for an Indian, monsieur. Now I find you dressed as a *chevalier*."

"A man must wear many disguises, in my line of business," Diego replied. "You have asked to meet with Zorro; here he is. How may I be of service, caballero?"

"Rather, I hope to be of service to you," said de Payan eagerly. "I have learned that you and I are brothers-at-arms in the struggle to bring justice and liberty to the noble Indians."

"Are we? I am delighted to hear it."

"I will introduce myself. I am Guillaume Robespierre de Payan, formerly a child of France, now a son only of the glorious Revolution. My family was obliged to go into exile following the infamous events of the Ninth Thermidor."

"Unfortunate. Bear with an ignorant man, my friend: what was the Ninth Thermidor?"

"The day on which traitors to the Revolution denounced my noble godfather, Maximilien Robespierre," said de Payan. "His ungrateful nation consented to his execution, and see what happened! The vile Corsican Bonaparte rose to power, and made it possible for the *Ancien Regime* to creep back in turn. It broke my father's heart. For my part, I saw that France did not deserve her liberty. I have dedicated my life to bringing the struggle for liberty to other nations."

"I believe I have heard of men such as yourself," said Diego. "They are called *filibusters,* are they not?"

"Exactly! I have wandered the world spreading Rousseau's philosophy. In Lima and Cartagena the old aristocracy was too entrenched to be overthrown, but here I feel it might be possible. Imagine my joy in discovering that a fellow campaigner is already here and hard at work!"

"You are too generous with your praise, señor," said Diego. "I am merely a simple man following one creed: To seek justice, nourish the hungry, clothe the naked, protect widows and orphans, give shelter to the stranger, and never spill innocent blood."

"Profoundly admirable." De Payan bowed in the saddle. "And how it must enrage your heart that you have been unable to bring about any real change for the better."

"I wouldn't say that, señor! I chip away patiently and, gram by gram, down goes what used to be a mountain of injustice. The Indians and the *pobladores* have learned to live in peace, for one thing."

"But that is exactly what they should *not* do!" De Payan urged his horse closer. "My dear sir, do you not see that as long as the fat landowners possess such vast estates, the Indians will remain poor and downtrodden? There is only one way to restore the natural order, and that is by violent change! My friend, for the sake of your fellow Indians, let us bring the Revolution to California."

"I should confess something, señor." Diego chose his words carefully. "I received an excellent education at the Mission San Gabriel. What I learned there of the French Revolution was that in the end it betrayed the very people it had been intended to serve, because of something called the Terror."

"Pfft! You were taught by a priest; of course he would say that. The Terror was in fact entirely necessary, and an excellent thing. My godfather used to say that we needed both virtuous intent and the Terror, for without the Terror mere virtue is impotent. Terror is essential. Terror is swift, severe, indomitable justice!"

M. de Payan waved his arm at the plain below. "Look down there, monsieur. Imagine that great plain once again the property of its noble and rightful owners, no longer hunting buffalo and living in tipis, but properly educated revolutionary citizens farming their own land!"

Diego looked down at the village lights, the little communities here and there. He imagined yet another European system forced upon the Indians, "for their own good." He imagined the plain below all one vast *matanza*—not of cattle, but of human beings.

"Actually we didn't live in tipis here, señor," he found himself saying distractedly. "Or hunt buffaloes. You're thinking of the tribes out on the prairies. But I'm quite sure that many innocents were killed in the Terror, señor, and I have sworn never to spill innocent blood."

"Ha! Then that is why you have made no progress here, my friend. A rotting limb must be amputated," insisted de Payan. "And, see! I have brought the surgeon's knife."

He threw back the flap of the saddlebag his horse bore, and with some difficulty wrestled out a heavy oblong package wrapped in thick cowhide. Unfastening it, he displayed something that caught the light of the stars overhead.

"The blade of *La Guillotine*," said de Payan, with reverence. "A holy relic of better times. We need only a carpenter to build the frame."

Diego stared at it a long moment, before smiling his widest smile. "A gift for princes. You have convinced me. But, señor think! The rancheros have powder and ball. Should we not arm the poor? I know where to obtain weapons."

A week later, Diego had made all the necessary arrangements. He waited at San Pedro in the shadows beside an abandoned fishermen's hut. The tide was in, sparkling across the mud flats, and wind sighed in the reeds of the slough. As arranged, de Payan rode out of the shadows at midnight, looking this way and that. With a soft whistle, Zorro beckoned him over.

"Did you bring the money, señor?"

"I did," replied de Payan. "Balendin is a coward; I threatened to reveal his past unless he provided us with ready cash."

"Bravo, señor! Now, just down this trail you will see a whaleboat drawn in among the reeds. It is loaded with rifles and ammunition. The Yankee sea captain will happily unload them for you, once he sees the color of your gold. Hurry!"

"Will you not go too?"

"Alas, señor, while they have admirable ideas about liberty, the Yankees do not trust poor Indians. He told me he would only turn the weapons over to a white man."

De Payan nodded and rode down the trail. Diego peered out at the dark horizon, where he could just make out the schooner *Lelia Byrd*. He knew, in his heart, that the days of the gracious haciendas were numbered; but it would not be the Terror that ended them, if he could help it.

There was a sudden scuffle from below, de Payan's voice heard in a short cry of outrage before breaking off in a muffled snort. A moment later the whaleboat moved out across the shallows. At the oars were a pair of sturdy Sandwich Islanders, in the sternsheets sat Captain Johnson, and between them in the bilges lay the bound, gagged and furiously struggling M. de Payan. The captain, spotting Zorro, tipped his hat.

Diego grinned and waved. "Adios, Señor de Payan," he said quietly. "Enjoy your journey to Shanghai."

HORSE TRADING

BY CAROLE NELSON DOUGLAS

The day of Don Gilberto Ortiz's funeral the air was crisp and clear. The people of Pueblo de Los Angeles would mark the Don's passing on a beautiful spring morning, with the magnificence of the funeral mass in the Mission Church of San Gabriel Arcangel, and a post-interment feast at the Don's hacienda.

Not every day did the Los Angelinos bid farewell to a major landowner. Don Gilberto had been a responsible and decent man. From fellow rancheros to the humblest peon, people all around mourned his passing, and none so much as the widower's only daughter, Calandria.

Don Javier, the dead man's brother, had arrived from Spain two months before, alerted by Don Gilberto's failing health. A man of autocratic manner and immaculately trimmed silver goatee, he stood in the hacienda's courtyard, receiving the many mourners, who filled the cool inside rooms and overflowed into the sunshine. Flowering vines framed the hacienda, draping it in heady scent, fountains played pizzicatos on earthenware, and the mood, if regretful, celebrated what Don Gilberto had achieved in his life among his neighbors, friends and dependents.

"A great landowner," Fray Felipe declared to Don Javier. "Everything that flowed from Don Gilberto's fields, or winery, or good works was a blessing shared with the Church and every worker, from overseer to peon."

"Indeed," Don Javier agreed, "my brother's success in this unsettled and uncivilized land has been a tribute to our homeland heritage in Spain."

"We are not so uncivilized. Our wines deliver good vintages and our horses spring from the finest Spanish bloodlines of the Conquistadors' steeds," said a dignified man nearby, Don Alejandro de la Vega.

"Not pure, however." Don Javier frowned. "The prime bloodlines remained in Spain. Conquistador mounts may have been worshipped by ignorant savages when they first saw them, but, alas, once on this untamed continent they slipped their masters and interbred with the lesser, wild breeds."

"Still," said Don Alejandro, "we have imported stallions from Spain for our personal use and breeding, and the tough Spanish mustang is outworked by no breed, pure or cross, on our thousands of ranchland acres."

Don Javier shrugged. "I believe you New Spain settlers try your best to mimic the motherland, Don Alejandro. However, I have no passion for ranching, or horses. I prefer wine, books, and art."

A soft clap of hands caught the two men's attention. A third had joined them.

"My congratulations," Don Diego de la Vega said with a bow to his father and the visiting Spanish caballero. He'd been watching the two men as the conversation had developed. "I admire your taste in pursuits, Don Gilberto, but perhaps that is because they mirror my own. The first families of our humble pueblo have striven to cultivate the finer things here, but it takes time. May I assume that Pueblo of Los Angeles is likely to lose you back to the city of Seville in Spain?"

"Ah, Don Diego," Don Javier responded with a rare smile. "You certainly are one of the more civilized products of New Spain."

He eyed the young man's silken ruffled shirt and suit of finest wool broadcloth and his exquisitely barbered hair and mustache. "Don Alejandro, you have reared the flower of Andalusian fine breeding. All that is missing, in fact, is a well-bred wife to extend your line."

"True, Don Javier," Don Alejandro agreed with a laugh. "So I tell the lad, but he enjoys the refinements of courting, the flowery speeches and love poems, far too much to wed. I assumed when you asked to meet with the local landowners after the funeral feast that you plan to sell your late brother's magnificent hacienda and ranch, but I didn't anticipate that you would be eager to act as matchmaker."

Don Javier impatiently eyed the colorful throng. "Of course, I must settle my niece, Calandria, on a husband, since she refuses to return to Spain as my ward. She is pretty enough to attract a noble suitor, but this New Spain upbringing has made her unsuitable for that. Where is she? I told her I wanted her here immediately after the funeral. Why does she always fail to honor her father, and me?"

He glanced at the other men. "Perhaps such manners are acceptable in this new land? It will be difficult to find a husband here without the dowry of the ranch, and her willful ways are no help."

Father and Son exchanged a shocked glance.

"Don Gilberto did not provide a dowry for his daughter?" Don Alejandro asked, as only a grandee of Don Javier's equal in New Spain could inquire so bluntly.

The man finished his glass of wine and held it out for a passing servant girl to take.

"He doubted his illness was fatal and waited too long to make his wishes known, so I must settle it all. I will do what I can, but I have little time for such . . . subtle arrangements as marriage. The *Isabella* sails from San Pedro harbor for New Spain in nine days. I intend to be on it with the proceeds of the hacienda's sale. The journey around the Horn is arduous and long. My affairs in Spain have suffered too much already... but what is this?"

Don Gilberto's question and narrowed eyes attracted the de la Vega men's attention to the archway of the enclosed yard where carriages and their horses were prepared.

Don Diego audibly caught his breath.

A magnificent black steed's hooves danced a flamenco on the flagstones, a steed mounted by a figure swathed in a cloak of black from stirrup to shoulder.

He felt his father's hand tighten on his forearm.

"She has gone riding after her father's funeral mass?" Don Javier burst out. "I cannot believe it. What barbarous behavior is this?" He took one long booted stride forward. "Calandria, come here, you disobedient child."

Don Diego had by now realized that a woman's long black riding habit, tumbling over a sidesaddle, would resemble a man's cloak.

"For a moment," Don Diego said with a laugh, "I thought that our local legend, the outlaw cut-throat Zorro, had come to mourn our neighbor."

"Zorro?" Don Javier was too annoyed to pay attention to some local jest. "What have foxes to do with this? No, that appalling vision is only my wayward niece. Come here, Calandria."

"You do not want a horse in the courtyard, my uncle," she answered.

"Dismount first, you hoyden."

Calandria obeyed, but she didn't drop the reins. Instead, she led the horse behind her, its hooves ringing out to attract the guests' attention as conversation slowed.

"Not the horse!" Don Javier ordered.

Calandria seemed disinclined to release the reins held tight in her small, black-gloved fist. Don Diego would wager that her knuckles were white as bone within them.

"Oh, let us see the horse, by all means," he said quickly. "What a magnificent animal," he added, watching horse and dismounted rider part the murmuring guests. "What name does it bear?"

By then Calandria had stopped before the three men. "Fortuna, Don Diego," she told him.

"A mare, of course. I admit I am not a great expert in horse flesh, only in beauty. I imagine it cost the fortune it is named after."

"Fortuna is beyond price to me," Calandria returned.

"And why are you dressed like this?" Don Javier demanded of his niece. "The habit is appropriately black but you smell of hay and the stable. Have you no respect for your dead father?"

Calandria had the same slender neck as her mount, a mane of shiny black hair gathered into a large snood at her neck, and eyes of liquid brown.

"Fortuna and I followed the inspection route of the hacienda lands we did with my father every week while he lived. It seemed a proper way to bid him goodbye."

"Well, you can bid that damned horse goodbye. I'm selling the hacienda, livestock and all. And since you refuse to travel docilely to Spain with me, I'll send *you* to a convent."

The young woman gasped at this abrupt disposition of herself and her horse, causing the sensitive animal to dance away from the man's harsh words, and lift its forelegs off the stones in a minor buck.

Don Javier stepped forward to snatch the purely decorative riding crop from his niece's hand and raised it high to strike the animal across the head and eye.

Calandria leaped between man and horse, arms raised to take the blow.

Don Javier would have struck despite her, but Don Diego pushed so hard against his side and shoulder that he spun half away from his target.

"Oh, my deepest apologies," Don Diego said, "I thought Calandria would slip and my gallant attempt to prevent her ended in my own clumsy misstep."

"I was not about to slip," Calandria said, turning from her uncle to Don Diego. "And you are a clumsy oaf, for all of being the flower of Californian manhood. My uncle is right that I would not marry you or any man in this pueblo merely to place a roof over my head."

"Perhaps you'd rather live on the wild hills with your precious horse," her uncle suggested angrily.

"Perhaps. I certainly will not submit myself to a convent, nor my horse to whoever buys the hacienda. My father bought Fortuna for me. She is mine."

"You may be mistress of your horse, but you are not mistress of yourself, Señorita Sauciness. I am your uncle and guardian and if I wish this horse whipped to tame its unruly manners, it will be so. And what punishment the good nuns find for your unmannerly ways will earn no objections from me. The Convent of Santa Rosa is within a couple hours' ride."

"You would threaten what my father loved best in his life after his death? You came here only from greed. I can't believe he would have left me unprotected."

Don Javier lifted the crop again.

"Peace," Don Diego urged as his father moved to stop Don Javier and Fray Felipe's brown-robed form emerged from the crowd. "You would waste an opportunity to fetch a small fortune for such a fine horse, for this well-named Fortuna. Don Gilberto spent generously on his daughter and the animal's quality is obvious, even to a man of letters like me. A public auction in the pueblo's central plaza would attract heavy bidding."

Don Javier was nodding agreement. "You are wise, young de la Vega. Too wise to offer for this she-cat in marriage, I suppose."

"I doubt she would have me," Don Diego said with a smile. "She prefers a wilder temperament in both horseflesh and husbands, I fear."

"You are right," Calandria said. "Have you always lusted after my horse, Don Diego? Now that you've arranged a public auction for Fortuna, I suppose you'll take her in the bidding."

"And it will not just be an auction for the horse," Don Javier added with a sly smile. He raised his voice. "Don Gilberto's lands will go to the highest bidder, but there will be a tempting extra inducement. My brother's daughter has no dowry, but she is a pretty piece. What man here is eager to tame both horse and rider? If you bid on Fortuna, you will get her mistress too."

"Uncle! That is outrageous." Calandria was aghast.

"Perhaps, but well within my rights. I am your guardian now. The auction will be held in the public plaza a week hence, I think, so ca-

balleros far and wide may hear of the opportunities and festivities, gather
their gold, and come to compete for the prize. Horse and rider belong to
whoever pays the most for the ranchero, a rich bride and bridal price. I
will take only gold on the spot."

He nodded at the de la Vegas.

"That could be you, Don Diego. You seem to admire the horse, at
least."

Calandria turned on her possible suitor like a rattlesnake. "It is thanks
to this . . .this meddling dandy of an idle, so-called scholar and gentleman that Fortuna and I are to be sold like slaves. This cannot happen.
Don Alejandro, you were my father's dearest friend." Her desperate
glance caught the friar's eye in the crowd. "Fray Felipe!"

"I fear your uncle is correct and within his rights, my child. Resign
yourself."

Calandria's eyes sparkled with furious tears, but her uncle ordered
her duena forward to escort her into the hacienda and called a groom to
lead off Fortuna.

"Both prizes will be kept under guard and lock and key for the next
week," Don Javier announced to the crowd. "At noon Thursday next the
auction will take place. Tell any likely men of means who'd like to add
to their land, their livestock, and household. They may take my niece for
a servant rather than a wife. I care not."

Distressed murmurs arose among the guests, but some of the older,
widowed landowners pressed forward with interested eyes.

Z

"What have you done, my son?" Don Alejandro asked when they
were once more in the welcome shade of their own hacienda rooms an
hour later.

"I only saved Señorita Sauciness's beloved horse from being beaten
and sold."

"But now she is as much for sale as any horse," Don Alejandro ob-
jected, taking an agitated turn around the room.

Bernardo, Don Diego's—and Zorro's—milk brother and personal
servant to the larger world, poured a glass of wine for Don Alejandro
and his master.

Don Diego sipped while his father fretted.

"I cannot believe," Don Alejandro said, "that Don Javier left no will. He treasured his daughter and would never want her driven from the land and hacienda of her birth in this fiendish manner—*Dios mio*. Every greedy wifeless landowner for miles around will offer fortunes for such an indecent prize. I see no hope for it . . . save that you attend the auction and outbid any offer. Even our coffers could be severely tried, yet to witness her falling into the hands of any brute who bids for her . . . ."

Bernardo clapped both hands to his head and shook it in woe. While Bernardo did not speak, his observant eyes translated words and gestures faster than some hearing people could gather the import of a conversation.

Don Diego idly paged through a book lying on a heavy wooden table, then put down his wine glass. "*Padre mio*, you are right. There is no help for it."

"Just what I have been bemoaning," Don Alejandro lamented.

"Are you saying that I should risk all our holdings to win the auction for the land, the lady and her horse, no matter the cost?"

Don Alejandro groaned. "She would not welcome that outcome. She is a pretty and spirited woman, and all I could hope for in a daughter-in-law, but she hates you now for making the suggestion that Don Javier escalated into this travesty."

Don Diego's twinkling dark eyes lifted to the ceiling, contemplatively. "Changing such a spirited lady's opinion might be an intriguing challenge for so mild and civil fellow as I."

He turned to clap his father encouragingly on the shoulder.

"Worry not, my father. I am sure that heaven will provide for such an ill-fortuned lady."

"Heaven! You leave far too much to heaven, my son, and too little to your own actions."

By now Bernardo was beaming a knowing smile.

Days later, Bernardo's hands fluttered over the clothing he'd set out the morning of the auction. Already strains of guitar music thrummed from the square as bees buzzed among the bougainvillea blossoms climbing the de la Vega hacienda walls.

In the shuttered bedroom, Don Diego was preparing to look particularly splendid in a ruffled saffron shirt and suit coat of gold serge festooned with sky-blue braided soutache designs along the lapels and cuffs and down the sides of the black pants.

Zorro's silken black shirt was beneath the lighter clothing. The soutache work along the pants' side seams was only basted on here and there, ready to be ripped off in an instant.

"Toronado is primed for a daytime ride and accoutered with all the Zorro accessories and weapons? You will ride into the pueblo early and hide him in the tack room niche near the town stables?" Don Diego asked, his hands etching a stroke of the horse's neck and a round gesture like the sun.

Bernardo nodded, pantomiming that the spirited black stallion was at first balky about taking the bit and bridle at such an unaccustomed early hour. Toronado usually made midnight excursions with Zorro.

Diego grinned. "It will do the rascal good to make a more public appearance. Don Diego will excuse himself from the burning sun of the outdoor auction to step into the *taberna*, slip through the back to the stable area, stripping and hiding Don Diego's plaza clothing in the feed trough.

"Once Toronado leaves the plaza, you will wait for us on your own horse beyond the pueblo to execute the rest of the plan. The timing will be crucial, but I count on our brave stallion showing off in front of the mare, which is in season. Ah, spring as it flowers into the lush, full bloom of summer. A time indeed made for love and larceny."

Bernardo looked alarmed and pantomimed furiously.

"Toronado and Fortuna are the least of my problems," Don Diego said. "As usual, the most dangerous stumbling blocks are human. Fray Felipe says the clever and desperate Calandria has been leaving messages for Zorro in the folds of his robe sleeves when he goes to her uncle's hacienda to give her daily communion."

Bernardo displayed his shock at this new ritual.

"Don Javier had not noticed before that she is so devoted to daily mass, but couldn't deny her since she'd managed to get a message from her duena to Fray Felipe that she wished to receive the host. The greedy and brusque Don Javier takes it for a ploy to show docility and get him to change his mind. What a battle of wills between niece and uncle!"

"No, Bernardo," Don Diego added, reacting to the worry in the man's eyes and rapid hand gestures. "Señorita Calandria doesn't suspect that Fray Felipe is a friend of Zorro. She tells him to put her folded paper money—with her name and plea for rescue and the letter *Z* scrawled into the intricate scrolling—into the church collection plate as if she were actually present. She's hoping a clever fox like Zorro has spies among the people. Had I not a double life to lead, I might be tempted to wed this clever girl.

"Stop grinning, Bernardo, like a duena who has trapped a suitor for her adored charge! Meanwhile, we have to prepare everything for this noon's show. We must be fleet and surprising, all of us, two-footed and four. The angels of the pueblo truly must be on our side."

Don Javier's auction produced a throng of curious people and at least a dozen landowners from miles around the pueblo de Los Angeles. Lace mantillas and flat-crowned men's hats topped the church-going garb on the first families of the area, and mingled with the colorful woven wear of the local Indian people and peóns.

Don Javier had provided music, food and wine for his guests and bidders. For the rest, there was the square fountain and vendors of corn and bean tortillas.

When the sun was directly overhead, making every eye squint slightly and glinting off the plentiful gold braid of Capitán Monastario and his soldiers at the side of the area, Don Javier stepped onto the scaffolding that had been set above a long wooden table. A velvet-and-brocade upholstered armchair from the Ortiz hacienda provided an elevated throne-cum-auctioneer's podium.

"People of Los Angeles," he hailed the assembled populace. "Here is the prize I promised. A deed to the lands of the late Don Gilberto, and the additional prize of his daughter's hand in marriage, or in whatever state you wish it, and her fine steed, Fortuna."

A groom led out the prancing black horse. Calandria, mounted sidesaddle, wore a spectacular gown of ivory lace ruffles from bare shoulders to the ends of the trailing skirts, which spread over Fortuna's hindquarters in a peacock-tail-wide swath. An intricately carved ivory comb in her piled dark hair held a blond-lace mantilla that fell in lavish folds as far as the horse's back.

The crowd's gasp was as vocal as the wind that heralds a coming storm. From among them men in richly decorated riding suits pressed forward to the table, clutching laden saddlebags. They began shouting out sums as they each staked out a place for their gold coins, adding bags to their piles as the bidding increased.

All the while Calandria surveyed them, her uncle, and the crowd with bitter disgust. Fortuna's reins were in a groom's grasp. Her hands were bound by silken cords and a short lead to the pommel of her sidesaddle, concealed by her skirted knee hooked around it.

Don Diego and his father stood at the crowd's rear, both sober figures despite the glint of metallic and silk embroideries on their suits

"You do not bid, Don Diego," Calandria called out during a lull. "It was your cruel notion to auction off Fortuna that led to this public travesty."

"I agree, señorita," he called back. "I apologize deeply. What I meant to preserve your horse has become the excuse for an inexcusable and distasteful auction. I can no longer watch."

With that he strolled away into the shade of the taberna's overhang, leaving his father fuming behind him.

Calandria lowered her gaze to the unappetizing and greedy men clustered around the gold-heaped table. Her last hope of a civilized intervention had departed with Diego's withdrawal and his father's silence.

"Coward," she muttered, unheard over the contending bidders. "Turncoat to your neighbor. Traitor to my father."

She clenched her teeth and fisted her hands and touched her heel lightly to Fortuna's skirt-hidden side. The mare responded with a forward lunge, but the groom's tight hold on the reins jerked Fortuna's head roughly around, causing the metal bit to twist cruelly in her tender mouth that Calandria had never abused.

"Beast!" Calandria berated the groom, her face paling rather than coloring with anger. She knew she was truly caught in this vile charade for now. Any real escape opportunity would only come after the ranch lands and house were lost to her, and she had become a permanent prisoner subjected to more than public indignity.

Her voice gentled Fortuna to submit to the groom's control, for the horse's sake. They were truly lost. For the first time, the proud high-held heads of both rider and mount drooped in helpless fury and fear.

The farthest fringes of the crowd had begun murmuring unhappily to see Calandria's gallant escape attempt foiled, but those were only peóns and *Indios* who were as bound to the hidalgos' will as Calandria now was.

"My father would curse you all," she shouted to the milling men below her. "You let his own brother turn you into a frenzy of vultures."

"Your disobedience has brought you here, my girl," one man foreign to the pueblo looked up to say, "but your spirit will be broken, as will your horse's. It is the way of men and the world, and you must learn that to our benefit and pleasure." He turned away to up his bid with another double-fist-sized bag of gold.

"Don Javier," Calandria called. "You will have your money from my father's holdings, and a good price too. Let me and Fortuna go."

"Alas, niece," he said with a small shrug and smile. "I do think you have learned your lesson, but an Ortiz of Seville cannot go back on his word. And I suspect the good price is the result of the 'extras' put into the bargain, both products of the finest breeding Spain can provide in these godforsaken colonies."

"*You* are godforsaken!" she retorted.

He spread his hands with the Valencia lace cascading from his gold-braided cuffs. "Are my hands bound? Do I sit a horse whose reins are held by a common groom? Am I the object of auction lust? I fear not, niece. You must say your prayers and accept your fate."

The murmurs of the farther crowd reached a new pitch as they turned at some commotion behind them, the urgent oncoming clatter of some late-arriving bidder, no doubt.

But, no.

Instead, a riderless black horse wearing a magnificently tooled black saddle, bridle and martingale, came clattering and jingling and cantering through the crowd, whinnying and snorting with a stallion's power to claim the right of way.

Fortuna's silver-studded black bridle rang in counterpoint as she lifted her head and flared her soft nostrils.

Calandria stared, silenced by the dramatic arrival of this self-driven horse out of a tale of El Cid.

The crowd's murmur became a buzz, a bee-like buzz taken up by throat after throat, until it reached the front row of puzzled bidders and assumed a meaning.

Zzzzzzz . . . zzzzz . . . . zzzzz

"Zorro!" Calandria cried triumphantly. "I knew he would come."

"Who is 'Zorro?' This demon horse that accepts no rider?" Don Javier asked, dumbfounded yet shaken. He was too new to Pueblo de Los Angeles to know its history and legends, but now was about to meet one.

145

From the red tile roof behind and above him, a black shadow of storm-cloud surmounted the peak and came flowing down to the rim, landing with a booted thump beside his lavish chair as a pen-tip sharp point of inflexible Toledo steel pricked the skin sheltering the heart's-blood artery of his neck.

"*Dios!*" Don Javier whispered between his teeth, not daring to enunciate more or look to see who his standing captor might be, and still watching the hellish black horse charging toward him.

"First he calls on demons, now God," a black-caped, masked and hatted Zorro announced to the crowd. "Don Javier is somewhat confused. Certainly not sharp-witted enough"—the sword point dropped a centimeter and prodded again— "to handle such a fortune as weighs down this table before us."

The horse had stopped before the table, scattering the bidders as it pranced and lifted to show its hooves.

"Groom!" Zorro tossed a set of black leather saddlebags down to the man beside Fortuna. "Drop those reins and fill these bags with the purses of gold until I say stop. Or Don Javier's noble blood will rain down on every bag and truly make it blood money."

"Now, Zorro, you show your true colors as a thief," Capitán Monastario shouted from his post fifty feet away.

"My true color is black, black as Don Javier's greedy, merciless heart," Zorro riposted, waving his sword for an instant before it settled on Don Javier's quivering throat again. "Do you wish officers of Spain to come calling on you, asking how such a nobleman died in your jurisdiction?"

Zorro's hat dipped as his masked eyes surveyed the table. "A heavy leavening. Don Javier has the golden touch. Now, groom. Sling the saddlebags over the stallion's back. Attempt to run and his hooves will smite you down."

Zorro whistled and the black horse reared, screaming a challenge, his forelegs and sharp hooves two-man heights above the ground, high enough to make Don Javier, on his makeshift auction throne, feel the wind of their churning pass him.

"*Dios,*" he muttered again as the horse heavily stomped back to ground, raising a cloud of dust that made all the bidders sneeze and Fortuna dance sideways, flaring her nostrils.

The once-empty saddlebags bulged so heavily the groom staggered to lift one side onto the saddle, then pushed that over until the burden drew the other side up and his body played counterweight.

"Lash them to the cinch and buckle them down," Zorro ordered.

Don Javier finally found a voice that didn't call on the Deity or tremble. "You can't just ride away with all that gold unscathed. The soldiers will shoot you and that hell-horse the minute you turn your backs on them."

"Of course," Zorro said in mock regret. "How could I have forgotten that once I remove the sword from your neck we are helpless? I suppose I should settle my affairs before I perish." He wrenched a leather bag from his belt and threw it to the now-empty bidding table before them.

"Here's payment for your brother's land. Thirty pieces of gold."

He laughed and eyed the restless horse, shouting, "Away now, to your brother the wind!"

The stallion dug in his muscled hindquarters, spun and vaulted into the scattering crowd as if winged. Toronado galloped past all the cowering gawkers, swiftly disappearing from the pueblo view behind a cloud of his own dust.

"You have trapped yourself," Don Javier croaked as the sword point at his throat eased. "You are a dead man."

"With a very rich horse? I think not. You have provided me with more than gold, unwilling *amigo*, but a fine and fine-blooded means of escape."

With that, Zorro sheathed his sword, then took a running leap off the platform onto Fortuna's back behind Calandria, drawing his sword again and nudging his heel against the mare's startled side.

"Away, Fortuna!"

The mare needed no second invitation, having chaffed at the groom's rough control. Besides, all her instincts had been urging her to follow Toronado on the run. He was having all the fun.

As if she felt no burden and inhaled the wind, Fortuna whinnied her freedom and spun onto the open path the great stallion had forged. Calandria's bound hands twisted in Fortuna's mane as she leaned to the side of the horse's neck to aid her speed.

Zorro's flowing black cape and Calandria's streaming white skirt train formed a parti-colored flag too conjoined to risk shooting at as they disappeared into their own veil of dust and distance.

Oh, how the crowd milled in confusion. How Monastario and his men cursed as they mounted and tried to goad their sleepy, sun-lulled steeds into a spirited pursuit. It was already the beginning of the end to another wondrous tale of Zorro.

Don Javier sank back into his chair, dabbing his red-dotted neck with a handkerchief more lace border than useful linen. Bereft bidders buzzed around him like angry hornets, bewailing their lost gold, each claiming he'd won the land and that the land was his no matter what.

And, to add a last, comical touch, Don Diego finally came limping back into the fringe of the crowd, the soutache filigree along his pant seams mostly torn off, and his splendid jacket dusty and disarranged.

"What happened to you, my son?" Fray Felipe asked, rushing to the young man's aid.

"I was attacked by a dust devil . . . *two* of them in quick succession just outside the plaza, both as black as Satan himself." People gathered to hear his tale. "Barely had one grasped me in the wind of its appearance and turned me around like a top, then another soon followed, this one a stream of black and white flames that spun together into a blinding eddy."

A woman in the crowd laughed. "Those were no dust devils, Don Diego, but that brigand Zorro and his black horse. He has taken all the gold and Don Gilberto's beautiful daughter, and her prized mare as well."

"Zorro!" Don Diego cried. "Would that I had been wearing my dress sword to the auction instead of my purse."

Which drew another laugh from the crowd. They had lost nothing that day but viewing more of a shameful spectacle, and most of them were decent enough to be pleased about that. The idea of Don Diego as a swordsman up against Zorro was amusing beyond words.

That evening, Don Diego, now dressed as Zorro, visited the hidden cavern below the de la Vega hacienda to bring Toronado an apple for his impressive solo performance that noon.

After greeting Bernardo with a "Well done!" he explained how matters had gone after he'd returned to the plaza as Don Diego and then asked how Bernardo had fared.

"You, er, wore your own disguise and deposited our charge and her steed at the convent of Santa Rosa with gold enough for her keep for a night or two until her uncle's ship sails?"

Bernardo made a long series of gestures that Zorro interrupted from time to time to confirm their meaning.

"Yes, I am sure she was very angry. Oh, she was *most* angry that *you* were her escort to the convent. She demanded to know why Zorro had deserted her? And she took your adamant silence for cruel indifference." Zorro laughed. "I am sure she is not used to cruel indifference from most men. I'm sorry you had to be the object of her disappointment. It was necessary for Don Diego to show himself in the square.

"A splendid gallop you made alone, *amigo*," he turned to tell the impatiently waiting horse. "You seem subdued. My two truest companions are both annoyed with me? A shame. Did you miss having me on your back, Toronado? Or...do you miss the dainty Fortuna? She made a champion run herself, with two of us aboard."

Bernardo sketched a gesture.

"Yes, my brother. Señorita Calandria is indeed very beautiful and brave. And proud."

Zorro patted Toronado's neck. "Now you will get the long ride you crave."

He and Bernardo hoisted the laden saddlebags to the horse's back.

"Bernardo, you kept perfect count of which landowner bid which bags of gold for the Ortiz holdings?" Zorro asked. Bernardo nodded with a wink.

"That mathematical memory of yours is a gift." Zorro eyed the written list Bernardo offered. "I'll make the rounds of their haciendas and toss the money bags at each front door, a return of their fruitless investment, excepting a twenty percent donation to the Church for the poor, of course."

Toronado danced sideways in anticipation after Zorro mounted. "Yes, a good, long ride, my friend. We won't be back until dawn. For once we will return money to the rich."

And that would write finis to one more successful escapade in the career of Zorro, except that Don Diego took Bernardo aside two Sundays later.

He unfolded a piece of paper money and pointed to the Z written into the scrolled border.

"There is other writing," Zorro said, whisking it away from

Bernardo's gaze. "Toronado and I have an appointment in the hills tonight."

Bernardo's expressive eyebrows performed acrobatics.

"All my apologies, brother. This one mission is between only Toronado and me.'"

Z

Spring was becoming fragrant summer and the almost full moon painted the hilltops silver.

Along the ridge a silhouetted horse and rider were cantering toward another, waiting horse and rider.

More than the night made the horses and riders appear black.

Calandria Ortiz reined Fortuna to a stop as she came abreast of Zorro.

"A fine steed," she said, "a peerless stallion, and as brilliantly trained as the tides the moon rules. He must be amazingly in tune with his rider."

"Indeed, my humble thanks," said Zorro. "Fortuna is a marvel of strength and beauty herself. She never faltered on that perilous run through the plaza and past Monastario's rifles."

"Thank you in turn. I am afraid I am not so humble."

Zorro laughed. "I never thought so."

"I knew you would come," Calandria said.

"Tonight, or that day in the plaza?"

"Yes."

There was a silence before she spoke again, softly, so he had to lean over Toronado's shoulder to hear.

"As my uncle charged, I am an ungrateful girl, I fear."

He waited.

"I am here to ask another favor."

"And that is, señorita . . . ?"

"It is most bold of me."

"I would expect no less."

"I would like Fortuna to run free, with your stallion."

"His name is Toronado. And why this boon?"

"I want a foal to found a line of the finest horses in California on my father's *rancho*, now that you have preserved it for Don Javier's true family. I should be coveting a future stallion for breeding purposes, but I'm hoping for a filly as fast as the wind I can call Zorrina."

"Perhaps Fortuna will live up to her name and produce more than one foal."

"You mean twins?"

Zorro smiled, the whites of his eyes and teeth luminous in the moonlight. "Or another assignation."

"I'm sure I can speak for Fortuna's agreement."

There was a silence before Zorro spoke again. "May I help you down?" In a moment, the black of her riding habit spilled into the black spiral of his cape.

Zorro stripped Toronado of his bridle and martingale and saddle and blanket, as she did the same with her Fortuna, but first she detached a basket.

While they worked, the horses nickered, anticipating a rare freedom, and nosed each other. Fortuna was the first to wheel away along the ridge, her long tail streaming like a banner. Toronado head-butted his thanks to Zorro's chest before he capered and cantered in playful pursuit.

"This may take some time," Zorro observed. "All night, perhaps."

"That's why I brought refreshments." Calandria hoisted her basket. "Bread, cheese, grapes, glasses and linens. A bottle, or two, of wine."

"And a corkscrew?"

"Oh. Oh! There is always your sword, I suppose."

Zorro laughed and swirled off his cloak to let it settle on the ground, his hand assisting Calandria down.

In the distance against the moon-rinsed clouds two black horses danced where earth and sky met.

ZORRO'S RIVAL

By Win Scott Eckert

1820, El Pueblo de Los Angeles

The darkly cloaked figure arrived at the shore, dismounted, and knelt at the edge of the cliff, overlooking the sea. A half moon hung over the horizon, lending a silver cast to the lapping water of the Pacific.

A ship lay anchored across the bay. As the dark form watched, three longboats rowed to shore and the group gathered on the beach. A smaller shape—that of a child—darted from the others and ran away. A bearded man carrying a pistol and cutlass followed, and a whip lashed out with a solid "crack." The child cried out and fell to his knees in the sand. The man grabbed the boy by the arms and viciously dragged him back to the others.

Now other cries reached to the cliff-top, the voices of children surrounded by the few large men. The longboats were clearly coming to collect them.

Slavers.

Like a living shadow, the watcher deftly scampered down the cliff face, using branches and outcrops of rock for hand- and footholds, landed behind a large stone, and took stock of the situation. Three men guarding ten children. Two more men in each of the approaching boats.

One of the slavers stood slightly apart from the others. Not smart. A whip unfurled, the end snaring the slaver's neck with an almost inaudible snap. The cloaked prowler dragged the choking and disoriented guard through the sand, then dispatched him with a punch to the face.

Shaking a gloved fist slightly, the dark figure noted the zig-zagging pathway up the cliff face. It was toward this the young boy had run.

The longboats drew near.

The shadowy form clambered up the large stone and leapt into the midst of the group, flipping in the air to land feet-first, blade drawn. The stalker's cloak whipped like obsidian wings in the moonlight.

"Run! Up the path to the left!"

The children darted and scattered, while the two remaining slavers growled in surprise. Then the one who had whipped the boy—massive, bald, and heavily bearded—laughed and aimed his flintlock pistol at the interloper. A slender blade darted out and ran straight through the colossal man. He fell to his knees and writhed in the sand, then collapsed, blood dribbling from his dead lips.

The other slaver gaped and ran, following in the direction of the children. Ignoring the cries of alarm from the longboats, the cloaked intruder fell into hot pursuit, catching the slaver by the ankle halfway up the cliffface. A solid yank sent the hapless man through the air, screaming. The scream ended abruptly as the man met the rocky ground below with a solid thud.

The dark intruder continued to scurry back up the path, ignoring the distant musket shots from the longboats. The prowler heaved over the cliff ledge and scanned for the children.

There they were.

Huddled behind a masked man and his magnificent ebony stallion.

Zorro collected the escaped niños pobres, the poor children, behind Toronado and took stock of the figure who had just come up over the cliff. The newcomer was dressed in a cloak and hood, similar to that of the Franciscan monks. Both were of a crimson so deep it was almost black. A sword hung from a scabbard on one hip, a coiled whip on the other. Not unlike Zorro's own armaments.

Zorro and the other silently assessed each other.

"Your name?" Zorro inquired, after a long silence.

"El Halcón." The Falcon. The voice was a scratchy whisper.

"Ah, the infamous Halcón. Your reputation precedes you, Señor."

"As does yours."

"Bouchard's men approach, Halcón." Zorro gestured below to the men pulling the longboats up on the beach. "Shall we fight, or fly?"

"Bouchard?"

"Hipolito Bouchard. Pirate captain. Slaver."

"Ordinarily I'd say fight," El Halcón replied. "However, in this instance I believe discretion dictates flight. El Commandante's soldiers draw near."

Zorro turned slightly and observed the approaching men, never letting El Halcón out of his field of vision. "You are correct, Señor Halcón. Does El Commandante seek your head?"

Cloaked shoulders moved slightly. It might have been a shrug.

Zorro smiled tightly, a hint of white teeth bared under the thin moustache. "While it might be amusing to play with El Commandante's toy soldiers, these children come first. Let's exit the field of play and let the soldiers and Bouchard's men clash."

"I will take the children now, Señor Zorro," El Halcón said.

"Perdón?"

"The children. I will take them into the pueblo, and see they are reunited with their parents."

"With all due respect, Señor Halcón, I will undertake that task. These children are frightened, but they know me. You are...an unknown quantity."

"Unacceptable," El Halcón countered, sword drawn. "The reward is to be mine!"

"Reward?" Zorro laughed, but his own blade met Halcón's in a flash, metal clanging on metal. "You are fresh off the boat, aren't you, Halcón? There are no rewards in the Pueblo de Los Angeles for rescuing niños pobres. Instead, deeds such as these are regarded by those in charge as the acts of an outlaw."

The two regarded each other in silence, their swords pressed against the other, sliding down to the hilts.

"What will it be, Halcón? Bouchard's cutthroats and the soldiers approach," Zorro said.

El Halcón's face was shadowed beneath the hood, and Zorro could see no expression. However, the pressure of Halcón's rapier gradually lightened. A moment later, the blade withdrew.

"My horse is that way," El Halcón said. The interloper turned and began walking away, then looked back. "I will meet you again," Halcón added, then disappeared into the night.

"Come children," Zorro addressed the wide-eyed and shivering pobres, "there's no time to waste. Let's make for the cover of that hillock." He pointed and led the way, going slow because they were on foot.

At the top of the small hill, Zorro and the children turned and watched as the soldiers met Bouchard's slavers. Then he kept them moving. With a group of children on foot to protect and see safely to their homes, he didn't have the luxury of waiting to watch the battle's outcome—or involving himself in it, much as he might want.

Z

Why are there no "Wanted" posters for El Halcón? Diego de la Vega thought to himself.

The noonday sun beat into his skin. He pulled his flat-brimmed hat closer down over his brow and turned the corner. As he made his way to la taberna, he looked around the central plaza of the Pueblo de Los Angeles and took in the many sheets, old and new, offering rewards for the capture of El Zorro. Everywhere one looked—from the fortifications of the Presidio at the north end of the plaza, to the shops in the marketplace, to adobe walls of Victoria Escalante's tavern—crude depictions of Zorro's masked visage were evident.

The Alcalde, Ignacio de Soto, was obsessed with snaring the Fox.

So why not El Halcón as well?

Diego shook his head and stepped into the relative darkness of the tavern. He tossed a wave and a smile to Señorita Escalante, and pulled up a chair at a small wooden table which was made even smaller by the portly frame of the person occupying the other seat—Diego's boyhood friend (and unwitting informant) Sergeant Garcia. Diego signaled to Victoria for wine, a cup for himself and a third to complement the sergeant's two empties.

"Buenos tardes, Sergeant Garcia," Diego greeted his friend. "Keeping our pueblo safe from the depredations of El Zorro this fine afternoon, are we?"

"Greetings, Señor! But I fear you are teasing me, mi amigo. You know that Zorro mainly comes out at night."

"Ah, well, all this talk of Zorro is tiresome, is it not? He's old news. Tell me Sergeant, what do you hear at the Presidio of this new masked man? What's his name again?"

"El Halcón?"

"Yes, that was it. El Halcón. Surely this new masked madman is giving de Soto as many fits as Zorro." Diego shook his head mournfully. "Imagine, twice the trouble! Not one, but two vigilantes causing problems in our quiet pueblo."

"Indeed not, Diego!" Garcia replied. "In fact, El Halcón is a friend of the people—"

"And Zorro, that wastrel, is not of course."

"Of course, Señor. You yourself were there for the Aldcalde's speech a few days ago."

Indeed I was, Diego thought, reflecting back on de Soto's performance. The Alcalde had called the townspeople for a rally, a short speech which was blatantly self-serving.

"Aha! Many thanks, Garcia! It was such a fine presentation, I had almost forgotten it."

Garcia looked confused and sipped his wine, while Diego recalled the scene in question: los peónes, soldiers from the garrison, and caballeros all gathered in the plaza, while Ignacio de Soto, dressed in the finest clothes befitting his office, addressed the crowd from the balcony of his villa. El Commandante and some of the other higher ranking army officers stood behind de Soto.

"My friends," de Soto had intoned, "the people's hero, El Halcón, captured a group of outlaws led by the notorious highwayman Vargas last evening, and in the process saved the latest gold shipment, destined for storage at our fine pueblo, for the benefit of all citizens. I was present as Vargas and his men were turned over to the Commandante and imprisoned in the Presidio's cárcel, awaiting transfer to El Diablo Prison."

Diego had closely scrutinized the crowd during the performance. He sometimes gathered valuable information by observing others' reaction to the propaganda the Alcalde spewed. In this case he found it interesting that a newcomer to the pueblo, Felix Calderón, had gathered up his easel and painting supplies and left in the middle of de Soto's speech.

De Soto continued. "In a display of swordsmanship rivaling that of our finest soldiers, the brute Vargas was soundly defeated by El Halcón. Vargas has troubled us before, and was arrested by the esteemed Capitán Monastario. He escaped only two weeks ago, no doubt with the help of his fellow bandit Zorro.

"Of course, Zorro put in an appearance, but he was conveniently too late to help capture Vargas—because he and Vargas are in it together! El Halcón ran him off, and the Fox scurried away with his tail between his legs."

Diego had burned at this bit of fiction—he had not even been present—but controlled his reaction in keeping with his pose as a bored dilettante.

"The fine people of el Pueblo de Los Angeles can rest easy in the knowledge that Vargas will not bother us again. And El Zorro is next!" de Soto had concluded.

Now, in the dim coolness of la taberna, Diego sipped his wine and thought back to his own run-in with El Halcón, the week before. El Halcón had not seemed eager to encounter the soldiers, but hadn't seemed particularly worried either. Halcón also showed little fear of Bouchard's pirates.

Who could El Halcón be? A longtime resident of el Pueblo de Los Angeles, who decided to join Zorro in his quest to right wrongs and help others? It seemed unlikely, given Halcón's interest in a reward. Halcón hadn't been here long enough to discern that such actions were not valued or rewarded by those in power.

On the other hand, de Soto's speech cast Halcón's desire for reward in a new light. Were the two in league, somehow? Perhaps El Halcón had had legitimate reason to expect remuneration.

Was El Halcón a newcomer to the pueblo? There were a few candidates. A French merchant, M. Durand, had arrived two months before on the last supply ship, along with his daughter Violette. Alcalde de Soto had taken an obvious liking to Mlle. Durand, and was actively courting her.

Diego couldn't blame de Soto, for the girl was quite lovely, with lustrous dark hair bracketing a heart-shaped face.

As for M. Durand himself, he appeared to be his early '40s—his dark hair grayed at the temples—and appeared fit. He could easily be El Halcón, although Diego had noted no trace of a French accent—or any accent at all—during his encounter with the cloaked vigilante. He'd have to remember to pay more attention if he met El Halcón again.

Two others from the last ship had also stayed on in the pueblo, the brothers Calderón. Jorge Calderón was Durand's associate, assisting the Frenchman in navigating the intricacies of Spanish business requirements and laws. Felix Calderón, who had slipped away in the middle of the Alcalde's fine words, was an artist who had accompanied his brother. He kept to himself, exploring the hills and bluffs, and painting scenic vistas.

Of the three men, Diego felt Felix Calderón was the most likely candidate for El Halcón. The loner would have the greatest opportunity to familiarize himself with the surrounding locale, and to slip away at appropriate moments.

None of which explained Alcalde de Soto's beneficent attitude toward the new interloper.

The noonday sun blazed in as the tavern's door opened. Diego watched as several newcomers—M. Durand, Mlle. Durand, and Señor Jorge Calderón—entered the cool sanctuary and took seats at a table in the corner.

Speak of the Devil, thought Diego. He excused himself from Garcia and went to greet the newcomers.

"Buenos tardes, Monsieur, Mademoiselle, Señor. May I join you?" Diego gave a courtly bow. Mlle. Durand extended her hand, which Diego took in his own and made a brief gesture of a kiss. The girl pursed red lips, and Diego's heart skipped a beat.

Then he sat and the group spoke of the weather, and El Halcón's daring capture of the bandit Vargas. M. Durand's favorite topic, however, was the wine trade and the quality of the local vineyards, or rather the lack thereof.

"Indeed, Monsieur. Then, may I ask, what exactly keeps you here in our humble little pueblo, if the wine business here has not proven fruitful?"

Diego pretended to laugh at his own pun, but Durand sighed. "To be sure, Don Diego, I have wasted much time here. I would have moved north weeks ago if your Alcalde de Soto had not been so persuasive."

"Ah, yes, our esteemed Alcalde can certainly be most...persuasive," Diego said pointedly, staring at Mlle. Durand, who had the good grace to blush. "And you, Mademoiselle, how do you find our pueblo? Could you make it your permanent home?"

"Surely," Mlle. Durand replied, "Alcalde de Soto will not be assigned here forever. He will move up to bigger and better postings."

"I could pretend insult at the aspersions you cast on our humble pueblo, but I understand. I too yearn for the museums, and the culture of Barcelona, where I spent much of my youth."

"Then why don't you return there, de la Vega, and bother the señorita no more," a new voice interjected.

Diego turned to see Ignacio de Soto standing over their table. Longish ash-blond hair and a goatee framed an expression that was grim, at best.

"Oh, Ignacio, don't be such a beast. Diego meant no harm. And he certainly was not bothering me. In fact, I find him quite diverting. " Mlle. Durand touched the Alcalde's arm, but his expression hardened even further and he continued to glare at Diego.

"Indeed, Alcalde, shouldn't you be out hunting masked swordsmen? I hear we have a second one to contend with now."

"El Halcón poses no threat to our pueblo or our way of life, de la Vega."

"Well, that's a relief!" Diego paused, then went in for the kill. "Tell me, Alcalde, how do you come by this unwavering opinion?"

"He caught Vargas and saved the gold shipment, didn't he?" de Soto said.

"Yes, thank God El Halcón saved the gold. Certainly los pobres and los indios are also thanking God for the bounties this precious gold will undoubtedly bring to them."

"Careful, de la Vega. Your words skirt with treason."

Diego laughed. "Come now, Alcalde, you know I don't have a political bone in my body. It's just that you make an excellent sparring partner!"

"Perhaps you'll unsheathe your sword and we'll spar with blades, then."

"Ah, now, Señor de Soto, you know that I carry no sword!" Diego grinned equably.

"I will escort you to your hacienda, to retrieve it."

"Ignacio, really!" Mlle. Durand exclaimed, while her father and other tavern patrons gasped.

Jorge Calderón, on the other hand, smirked in anticipation of a duel, his hand going to his own sword. "I'll second you, Alcalde. This dog needs a lesson in humility."

"Now, now, Alcalde," Diego said, ignoring Calderón, "you know I have no taste for such things as swords and duels. Very messy. M. Durand, I think the Alcalde needs some wine to calm the nervous tension from which he seems to be suffering. Perhaps you'll help him select a nice, soothing vintage?"

Over at the bar, Victoria Escalante quickly stifled a small laugh.

Diego gathered his hat and politely offered his chair to de Soto. The Alcalde sat, gritting his teeth, but at a pointed look from Violette Durand he maintained a grim silence.

Jorge Calderón shook his head in disappointment, but sat as well.

Diego made his way confidently to the door, then paused and turned. "Oh, Alcalde, one last thing. Thank goodness El Halcón captured that ruffian Vargas, but how did Vargas escape in the first place? Surely you can't mean to say that Zorro can come and go at will from the impenetrable Diablo Prison?

Then he made a quick exit, to the sounds of the patrons' roaring laughter and smashing glass.

Several days later, Diego rode the bluffs and trails above the de la Vega property, his horse easily navigating the trail. He was returning from el pueblo, after learning that his quarry had set out for the vicinity of his own hacienda.

There he was, sitting in the shade of a tree with a sketchpad in his lap, capturing the broad vistas below.

Felix Calderón.

"Hola, Señor," Diego called. "May I join you?" He dismounted and sat next to Calderón before the other man could respond.

The younger Calderón brother shrugged and kept sketching. He had dark eyes, an aquiline nose, and strong jaw line. Despite his silent artists' temperament, and slight build, there was an aura of quiet strength about him.

They sat in silence for a while, Diego watching the younger man as he skillfully depicted the panorama. Then he gently broke the quiet.

"I return from el pueblo, Señor. No one speaks of anything except the news about the lovely Mlle. Durand, and the Alcalde."

Calderón grimaced at the mention of Violette Durand. He said nothing for a long moment, but stopped sketching and looked hard at Diego.

"Sí, your Alcalde de Soto holds her prisoner in her own rooms. Soldiers are posted at her door. She is being held to...encourage her to make up her mind about marrying him."

"Not *my* Alacalde," Diego replied. He paused a moment. Then: "You are in love with the mademoiselle?"

"From the moment we boarded the ship in Europe."

"And yet?"

"I am a simple artist, beneath her notice. My brother courted her most strenuously, and she ignored him as well. We had thought her incapable of such affections, until she responded to the Alcalde's attentions."

"But now he holds her prisoner," Diego said.

"I heard from my brother of what happened in la taberna. She was displeased with his performance toward you. He was...displeased with her displeasure, and jealous that she defended you. Now, what he cannot accomplish with his dubious charms, he seeks to achieve with force."

"Her father has raised no objections?"

"He cares only for his business, and the Alcalde will pay him well for the privilege of her hand," Felix said.

"And, is there nothing you wish to do about this unfortunate situation?" Diego asked cautiously.

"What am I to do?" Calderón asked. "I am not a swordsman."

"Well, I am not much of a swordsman either," Diego confessed. "Perhaps El Halcón will intervene. The townspeople say he's made a public vow to free her before the criminal Zorro does."

"Sí, I have heard that, and pray that it will be so," Felix said. The young man was so earnest; Diego had trouble believing there was any guile behind his words.

Z

Diego sat at a large wooden table in the caverns below the de la Vega hacienda. Candles cast flickering orange light across his unmasked face. In the stable, Toronado was saddled and ready to ride.

Bernardo sat across from Diego, questions etched on his dark features.

"I know, mi hermano," Diego said. "El Halcón could be what de Soto claims, a 'friend of the people,' which really means a friend of the Alcalde, his cronies, and the military oppressors. In which case they've orchestrated all this and are working together. Or...all is as it appears, and El Halcón is truly working for justice. In that case, de Soto could have learned from his mistakes with me. Rather than making an enemy of El Halcón, the Alcalde may be manipulating events to make it appear that he and El Halcón are allies."

Bernardo shook his head. He wasn't following Diego's line of thinking. He made hand gestures, communicating with Diego as he had since boyhood.

"There are no reward posters seeking the capture or death of El Halcón," Diego answered. "Thus, de Soto is either in cahoots with El Halcón or de Soto wishes it to appear that El Halcón's activities are sanctioned and condoned by those in charge at the Presidio. Likewise, no one escapes from El Diablo. You know that. De Soto must have freed Vargas so that El Halcón could 'recapture' him. El Halcón was either in on the scheme or, if not, is being used by de Soto. El Halcón captures the evil Vargas, and de Soto trumpets the news at his staged rally, once again making it seem that El Halcón operates with the consent of the powers-that-be. In other words, El Halcón may be legitimate, but de Soto could be trying to drive a wedge between us and set us against each other by creating the appearance that El Halcón works with the corrupt authorities.

"At least," Diego concluded with a wistful note, "I hope that is the case..."

Bernardo's hands gestured again, this time with a strong note of skepticism.

"Ah, I know, mi hermano. El Halcón's vow to free Mlle. Durand.... Is it the braggadocio of a true rival? Or a lure? I will not be careless, I promise."

Diego grabbed the black mask and pulled it over his eyes. He secured the flat-brimmed hat on his head. His brown eyes gleamed in anticipation in the candlelight as he approached Toronado's stable.

He mounted the Andalusian in a blink of an eye, and tossed a salute off to Bernardo.

"Tonight, Zorro rides!" Diego called with joie de vivre, as the black stallion took off toward the hidden entrance to the caves.

Leaving Toronado in the shadows of the street below, Zorro skillfully clambered up the ivy-covered walls and vaulted the iron railing of the balcony to Violette Durand's suite of rooms, adjoining her father's. The chambers were dark, but Zorro's night vision was excellent, and he navigated her rooms with ease.

There were three strikes against Felix Calderón's tale.

First, Violette Durand was not present.

Second, soldiers clumsily scrambled down ropes from the roof and onto Mlle. Durand's balcony, behind Zorro. Another cadre of soldiers rushed up the stairs and burst in the door. Both groups of soldiers completely surrounded and covered Zorro with their rifles, while staying out of each other's line of fire. He was effectively boxed in.

Third, El Halcón rolled from beneath Violette Durand's mahogany four-poster bed, sword drawn and at the ready. Draped in the trademark dark crimson hood and cloak, El Halcón put the sword point against Zorro's chest.

"A trap," Zorro said. "How disappointing."

"Disappointing for you, Zorro," Ignacio de Soto said, entering Mlle. Durand's chambers, but making certain to remain behind the soldiers. "Yet, so satisfying for me. Except...what have you done with Mlle. Durand?"

"What have I—?"

"Don't pretend with me, Zorro!" the Alcalde cried. "Enough of your perfidy! I demand to know where she is!"

"Ah, I see," Zorro said, a light going on in his head. "A duel, then."

De Soto looked at Zorro quizzically. "A duel?"

"Of course, a duel. Me against your new champion." Zorro gestured at El Halcón.

De Soto laughed. "Why would I allow that? You're caught, Zorro." He signaled the soldiers to prepare to fire. "Tell me where Violette is and I'll make your death quick and painless."

"I've escaped from worse before, Alcalde. And I'm about to, right now. Or, El Halcón and I can duel. Are you saying you're afraid your champion might...lose? How much do you really know about this newcomer, anyway?" Zorro taunted.

"I—"

"Do you hear that, men?" Zorro continued, addressing the soldiers. "The Alcalde is not convinced El Halcón can take me. He publicly praises his new hero's exploits, and yet deep down he is unsure. When was the last time your Alcalde publicly praised the fine soldiers of el Pueblo de Los Angeles, my friends? When was that? Your Alcalde has partnered with a masked hero and doesn't even know who it is! Do you, Señor de Soto?"

The men were grumbling, and Zorro pressed his case, over de de Soto's rising protests. "Let us duel, I say! If El Halcón wins, then the Alcalde has made a wise choice! If not....Either way, I will reveal the whereabouts of Mlle. Durand—but only if we duel first."

"Very well!" the Alcalde yelled. "Very well." He signaled the men to lower their weapons, but keep them at the ready. He nodded to El Halcón as everyone stepped back.

Zorro knew, however, that if he defeated El Halcón, de Soto would still order the soldiers to kill him. Or at least to try. Even if Zorro won, he'd need to create another distraction to escape.

Fortunately, he had something in mind.

Then El Halcón was on him, and Zorro had no time for planning future distractions. He drew his Spanish rapier, "Justine," and was fighting for his life.

The two figures whirled, parrying and thrusting in a deadly dance. Their swords rang out as metal met metal. El Halcón was smaller in stature, a fact that the voluminous crimson cloak hid at a distance. The Falcon also didn't quite have Zorro's physical strength, but made up for these deficits with extraordinary agility and skilled swordsmanship.

Their swords locked at the hilts, and the two opponents pushed back and forth in an effort to release their weapons and gain the upper hand.

"Why did you help those children," Zorro gritted out, as he fought to release Justine.

"Why not?" El Halcón's scratchy voice replied. "I was there anyway, hoping you'd show yourself. And if I helped, it would keep you guessing about me."

The two broke apart, each tumbling and regaining their feet at opposite corners of the room.

"Then you gave no thought to justice, to doing it because it was right?"

In answer, El Halcón attacked and Zorro deftly leaped above his adversary's slashing blade.

"It's unfortunate you were not what you appeared," Zorro said, counterattacking with a series of rapid cuts, faster than the eye could follow.

The lower part of El Halcón's long cloak fell to the floor in shreds, exposing legs with breeches tucked into black leather boots. El Halcón spun and kicked out, a boot connecting with Zorro's sword arm. Zorro, however, retained his grip and renewed the attack.

"What were you going to get out of it," Zorro continued, "once you helped the Alcalde trap and dispose of me?"

"A quarter of the latest gold shipment, of course, and I still will!" El

Halcón slashed through Zorro's defenses, and Zorro felt hot blood pumping from his upper arm.

Not his sword arm, fortunately. Nonetheless, de Soto and the soldiers cheered.

"A point to you," Zorro conceded. "He'll never let you get away."

"Not if he can't find me once I collect my payment."

"Aha!" Zorro cried. He called out even louder, his words aimed at the Alcalde and the surrounding men watching the duel: "I was right, you really don't know who El Halcón is, do you de Soto?"

Zorro leaped atop a table, flung his whip around a hanging iron candelabrum, and swung in an arc behind El Halcón. His sword expertly sliced through the upper sleeve of his enemy's cloak, without breaking the skin beneath.

Skin that was revealed as alabaster white, lacking the dark hair that a more masculine forearm would have.

A collective hush came over the gathering as Zorro landed behind El Halcón, grabbed the cloth of his rival's hood, and with a swift cut deftly separated the hood from the cloak.

"Violette!" de Soto shouted in fury, then clamped his mouth shut.

"Why, look everyone, it is Mlle. Durand, whom the Alcalde has been wooing," Zorro taunted.

Violette's blade fell to the floor, the fight gone out of her.

"Really, de Soto, sending out the love of your life to duel in your place. And consorting with masked vigilantes! You should choose your female companions more carefully in the future."

In the ensuing shock and confusion, Zorro bounded toward an open window and leaped up, crouching on the sill.

He turned back and briefly locked eyes with the Alcalde.

"What will Governor Montero think, de Soto, when he hears of this?" Zorro asked. Then he vanished under the shroud of darkness.

Diego sat in the caves below the de la Vega hacienda. Bernardo bandaged the cut on his upper arm, while Diego rubbed salve into the calluses on his right hand.

He finished recounting the night's adventure to his friend. "Mlle. Durand must have concocted the plot once she and her father arrived in el Pueblo de Los Angeles, and learned of the Alcalde's rewards for my head. De Soto never would have believed a woman capable of defeating me, so she made up 'El Halcón' and approached him that way."

Bernardo nodded.

"I wonder who she really is? I mean, what sort of life and upbringing she's had? Her father must have been in on it. There was no other reason for him to remain here, given his dim view of the quality of our vineyards.

"What skill with the sword," Diego mused, admiration evident in his voice. "And skill with people. She played de Soto, like a violin. Felix Calderón, too, manipulating him into spreading the rumor that El Halcón would beat Zorro to her rescue."

Bernardo shrugged.

"Such a dainty creature, Violette Durand. At least, she appeared so," Diego amended. "She never should have let me kiss her hand."

Bernardo looked at his hermano de leche, the question in his eyes.

"Her sword hand, Bernardo," Diego said, smiling and holding up his own. "Calluses."

Bernardo smiled back, then signed with his hands. His contacts among los peónes in el pueblo had passed on the news: the Alcalde had decreed that Mlle. Durand and her father were to be executed at dawn.

Diego sighed. Violette and her father weren't shining examples of humanity, but they didn't deserve death just because de Soto was humiliated.

He pulled his mask and hat back on.

When justice called, there was no rest for El Zorro.

A WORLD WITHOUT ZORRO

BY CRAIG SHAW GARDNER

"I do not believe it," Juanita said in that tone her husband knew all too well. "Does he think he can take everything?"

Sergeant Demetrio Lopez Garcia stood behind his wife, silently watching the procession march down the street. A dozen men on horseback approached, their brightly colored uniforms covered with dust. They were led by the garrison's new comandante, Capitán Morato. Garcia took a step back into the shadows of his kitchen as the Capitán passed. Morato was known as the Blade, and it was well known that his gaze might cut you in two.

The Capitán's personal guard were close behind. They sat straight and stiff as steel lances riding on by; their faces not bothering to look down upon the peónes so far beneath them. Behind them—a good hundred paces to the rear—came the men driving carts laden with the spoils of the Blade's most recent trip. These were men with simpler uniforms than those before them, plain dark jackets without epaulets or ribbons, men with tired faces that did not hide their misery. These were Garcia's men, the real soldiers of the garrison. They kept their eyes straight ahead as well, but they did so because they were ashamed.

"Look at my men!" Garcia spoke in a harsh whisper. He had never seen them so downhearted. And rightfully so. They were little more than pack animals to the whims of the Blade. "I have deserted my troops! I should be out there with them."

His Juanita looked back at him with a frown. "And share your sickness with all of them? You left the barracks for a reason, my little soldier."

He sighed. She was right again. Garcia's mood softened a bit with the use of his pet name. Her little soldier. Juanita had called him that from the day they first met. She would always call him that, even though no one ever thought of him as little.

169

Garcia coughed into his fist. It was nowhere near the cough he had had only three days before. He and his middle child, little Esmeralda, had been quite ill with the fever. He had lost the better part of the week to the sickness—a week in which the Blade and his men had been very busy.

Still, his family had been spared the worst of it. Three of the elderly and one infant had died elsewhere in town, and there were rumors of more deaths on the outlying farms and among the Indians. But Garcia and his family had survived. Esmeralda was already out playing with the chickens behind the house. And the sergeant himself was feeling fit enough to return to duty. He pulled his uniform trousers over his ample belly. If only his wife's cooking wasn't so good!

As Garcia adjusted his suspenders, he thought of the day, two weeks ago, when everything changed. The Blade and his men marched into town with official orders. Garcia had seen the envelope himself. The wax seal on the letter was very impressive. But those orders were nothing compared to what followed. The sickness had descended on the town that very day, carried in with the hot Santa Ana winds. The Capitán's Plague, the people had called it. But never in front of the Blade.

The last of seven heavily laden carts passed their door. Capitán Morato had brought another kind of illness with him, the illness of greed.

"What will he take next?" Juanita whispered. "Our lives?"

"All for the glory of Spain." Garcia shook his head. That was the only explanation the Blade gave for all his actions. "What can a man do?"

"And where is Zorro?" his wife whispered.

Zorro?

It was Garcia's business to uphold the law. Zorro was an outlaw, a mysterious man with a price on his head.

Still, Zorro was not the worst of men. On occasion the sergeant had even agreed with the masked man's aims, if not his methods. When someone like the Blade was turning the whole town upside down, even Garcia might wish for Zorro's return.

"Sergeant Garcia!" He looked up as someone called his name. "You are needed at once." He saw Corporal Aragones, a tall stick-figure of a fellow, rapidly striding toward his front door. The Corporal saluted as he approached.

"I trust you are feeling better Sergeant," the corporal said brusquely.

Garcia shrugged. "As well as one can feel under the circumstances."

His underling studied him with a frown. "We need you, sergeant. The soldiers are grumbling. Many can't take much more of this." He waited a moment before adding. "And Capitán Morato has called for you. Immediately."

"Is that so?" Garcia felt ice in the pit of his belly.

"He is in an agitated mood, but when is he not? You need to talk to him. For all of us."

Garcia sighed. He was not one to shirk his duty.

"Then I will go."

Aragones nodded, as if he would expect no less. Garcia felt his wife's hand on his shoulder.

"Be strong, my little soldier," she whispered in his ear.

Garcia nodded back to the both of them. He would do the best he could.

Z

Garcia tried not to stare. This was the first time he had stepped into his superior's office since Capitán Morato had taken control. In the past, this modest room had been simply furnished with a desk, three chairs and a plain wardrobe for the comandante's belongings. Nothing on walls, sills or shelves. It was always the office of a soldier.

And what did this make the Blade? Garcia could not see an empty space anywhere in the office. The corners of the room were piled high with silver candlesticks, the window sills piled with golden jewelry. A great tapestry hung from one wall, a portrait of a conquistador in full armor. Garcia knew that this had all been taken from the haciendas and from the surrounding ranchos. Everything of value for fifty miles now sat in this, the Capitán's headquarters.

Morato strode into the room and looked Garcia up and down. Garcia did his best not to stare. The Capitán was a tall, imposing man, and might even be called handsome if not for the livid red scar that ran down the left side of his face from cheek to chin. The scar twisted as he smiled.

"Sergeant. Good to see you back where you belong."

His words were complimentary, but his tone was not. Everything the Capitán said sounded like criticism.

Garcia reminded himself once more that the Capitán had signed orders from Spain. He was their leader, and it was the sergeant's sworn duty to obey.

The Blade continued to watch Garcia closely. The sergeant shifted from foot to foot. Had he forgotten to shave?

"Your men sometimes seem sluggish about following orders," the Capitán said at last. "Perhaps if we shot a man or two."

He paused, glancing past Garcia as if he was looking for someone far more important. "No," he added at last, "that is unduly harsh. I am sure a good whipping would do."

"Mi Capitàn!" Garcia said quickly. "That will certainly not be necessary. Now that I have returned to my duties, they will fall into line."

"I am happy to hear that. If not, my men know how to handle the whip." Morato waved his right hand at the contents of the room. "None of you recognize the serious nature of the situation, no matter what I say! Everything we've gathered here is but a fraction of what we need. What is a little sacrifice when it is for the glory of Spain?"

The sergeant attempted to look attentive. How far away was Spain? Garcia had never seen it. His boyhood friends, Don Diego and his servant Bernardo, had gone there, long ago, to further Diego's education, but neither of them spoke much of it. The sergeant, in the meantime, had joined the army, and the three of them had gone on different paths. That was all he knew about Spain. The sergeant did not pay attention to anything beyond their little Pueblo of Los Angeles and the surrounding hills. Keeping the peace here was enough work for any man.

The Capitán was pacing back and forth before his riches. "The English, the French, the Flemish, all would like to destroy Spain's power in the world, and leave our beloved homeland a ruin. We must do everything we can to insure that never happens." The Blade looked at a small gold pin on Garcia's uniform.

"Some of these medals are made of gold and silver, are they not?" He plucked the pin from Garcia's coat and tossed it on top of the pile of gold. "We must all make sacrifices."

The Blade's scar seemed to glow in the dim light. "And that is what we shall do, now that the men are firmly under your command—and you are under mine. We shall revisit the ranchos and the Indian settlement. We will return to the church; and turn over every bench in the barracks. No one will hold anything back, for Spain must remain triumphant!"

This was horrible. The sergeant felt that he must object, but he did not know where to begin. And would this man listen? He seemed to be on a quest beyond reason!

"Why do you look so worried Garcia? The peasants can always grow more food."

What would this military man know of the soil?

"But Capitán! The rainy season—"

"Enough!" the other man shouted. "You are beginning to sound like the farmers. Tomorrow, I expect you to lead your men to finally fill our coffers!" The Capitán threw back his head and laughed.

Garcia did not think he had had the time to sound like anyone. But he also realized that talk was useless. Capitán Morato would speak of nothing but the glory of Spain, and Garcia feared that very special glory lived only in the Capitán's head. Morato would do what he liked, and there was no one to stop him.

Once again, Garcia thought, where is Zorro?

The Capitán dismissed him, and told Garcia to be ready in an hour. The sergeant hung his head as he walked back towards the barracks and his men.

He jumped when he felt a hand on his shoulder.

It was the young priest, Padre Miguel. Garcia had met him briefly the week before, when he had arrived to give their own Fray Felipe a hand.

"You have spoken to the Capitán, sergeant," the young man whispered. He did not look that much older than Garcia's fourteen year old son, as if he were play-acting by wearing the somber garments of the holy church. "Is he satisfied at last?"

Garcia looked around the plaza. The Capitán and his men were nowhere to be seen, no doubt busily counting all those treasures forcibly taken from the Angelinos.

The sergeant shook his head. "He will not be satisfied until he strips the very walls from our homes."

Padre Miguel did not seem surprised. "I feared as much. This will never do. Beyond Mexico, the world is changing. People have basic rights. It is the talk of Europe."

The young priest sighed. "This is a beautiful place. The life is simple, and people seem to be happy. A priest could have a far worse parish that this. But men like our Capitán seem bent on destroying our way of life for their own ends."

"But what can we do? He is too powerful. And he brought a letter from Spain!"

Padre Miguel paused a minute before he replied.

"Maybe we cannot stop him. But maybe we can find a way to distract him."

"What do you mean?" Garcia asked.

"I have never seen this man called Zorro," Padre Miguel replied. "And yet he is well thought of by the townspeople."

Garcia had seen Zorro more times than he might count. He had even tried, once or twice, to collect the reward on the bandit's head. But this time they really needed him.

"Zorro always arrives in time of need, they tell me," the priest continued. "Zorro protects us all. But where is this Zorro?"

Garcia nodded slowly. These were desperate times, and they required a desperate solution. "Maybe Zorro can be found. I have many friends. I will talk to them and see what I may discover."

"Very well," the young priest agreed. "If you can find Zorro, please do so. We must act quickly." He paused to study the sergeant a moment before he added, "I think we must have Zorro save us, whether we can find him or not."

Garcia was not sure of the priest's exact meaning. But he knew what he must do.

His only truly powerful friends were at the de la Vega Hacienda. If they could not find Zorro, perhaps they could think of other ways to handle the Blade. He must speak to them, and he could not delay.

Garcia thanked the priest and hurried down the street. He called to his corporal to saddle his mule, saying only that he had an important mission. As soon as he told Juanita he would not be home for supper, he was on his way. He would get no rest today. But perhaps he could find a way to keep the Blade from taking everything.

The sergeant urged his steed into a steady trot. His mule, Conchita, might not be the swiftest of beasts, but she was dependable, and would get Garcia where he needed to go without complaint. He wished he could count on everything in his life as much as his Conchita.

He soon left the pueblo behind, and found himself looking up into the surrounding hills.

The day before the Blade arrived, Garcia thought he had seen Zorro, watching from his horse at the top of the Mission Hill. But El Capitán had become ever more bold, and no one had stepped forward to do more than weakly protest.

Where had Zorro gone? Why did he not return? Had the Blade found some way to snatch Zorro away as well?

He must be away on important business, Garcia decided. Everyone knew Zorro protected all of California! But why didn't Zorro realize he was needed here?

Sergeant Garcia knew now that the Blade would not stop until he had taken everything from the pueblo and the surrounding countryside. This should not happen! But who would stop it?

He spurred his mule onward, despite her complaints. Zorro must be found.

And if no one else could do it, he, Sergeant Demetrio Lopez Garcia, would have to bring Zorro back personally. If only he knew how to do so.

Garcia could not believe what he was thinking. He was planning to consort with a known bandit, plotting against the authorities, even against the might of Spain. He could be court-martialed, even shot.

But El Capitán had gone too far.

It was over an hour to the de la Vega estate. It was quiet on the road, and gave Garcia a sense of peace he could no longer find in the pueblo. Perhaps they would have news of Zorro farther from town. He was glad to put distance between himself and El Capitán. He sang softly to himself as he rode, letting his voice wash away some of his cares.

The cook, Rosalita, met him at the gate. Garcia was always sure to compliment her on the excellence of her cooking.

She smiled as soon as she saw him. "Sergeant! What a surprise!"

"And how is my most excellent cook today?" he answered as he dismounted.

"I am well." She blushed. "The sickness has passed by our hacienda." She waved toward the house. "Perhaps I can find you something from the kitchen?"

"Always an excellent idea," he replied with a touch of regret. "But it must wait. I have important business with Don Diego."

Rosalita frowned. "He is not here. He is off to buy horses. He should be back soon—we expected him two days ago—but now I am not certain."

The cook waved him forward, smiling once again. "Come. I am sure Señorita Isabel will be happy to see you." Rosalita led the sergeant across the courtyard before the main house. She glanced dismissively at a pair of brightly uniformed soldiers sitting at a table outside the main house. It was a pair of the Capitán's own personal guard, their colorful jackets slung over the chairs behind them. Why would Morato's men be here? Did The Blade fear the dons that much?

But the guards took little more notice of the cook than she had of them. Seeing Garcia's uniform, they quickly returned to their card playing. The sergeant was glad they did not suspect his intentions. He looked away from them so they might not see the guilt upon his face.

"This is not the best of times for your visit," Rosalita murmured once they were past the soldiers. "Try not to speak too much of politics."

With the guard here, Garcia wondered if he could speak at all. He turned to see the Señorita Isabel de Romeu descending the stairs at the side of the house. The sergeant was always impressed by this fine woman. If, perhaps, she was not the most beautiful lady in the pueblo, she was by far the most elegant and aristocratic.

"Ah, my dear sergeant!" she called as she approached. "It has been far too long. Come. Walk with me." And with that, she turned away from the guards and strode toward the far side of the house. Both Garcia and the cook rushed to follow.

She did not speak until they were out of sight of the card players. "These are dark times for our house," she said softly, "as I am sure they are dark in town. This Capitán acts as though he owns us all."

"He takes from everyone," Garcia agreed. "You have lost valuables as well?"

"We almost lost far more than that." Isabel waved to a figure emerging from the stables at the rear of the house. Garcia realized it was Diego's manservant Bernardo, but he had changed. His right leg was bound by rope and sticks, and he leaned upon a crutch as he approached.

"They broke Bernardo's leg," she explained. "He became angry when they took our silver."

"It was only through the Señorita's intervention," Rosalita added, "that they did not shoot him on the spot."

The situation seemed to grow worse with every passing moment. Garcia realized he could not delay. He leaned close to Isabel, his voice little more than a whisper.

"What do you know of Zorro?"

She looked at him strangely. "Why would you ask such a thing?"

Garcia hastened to explain. "You are a lady of refinement. A lady of the world. You must know much that is beyond a simple man like me."

Isabel smiled sadly at that. "I admit, I have often found Zorro more interesting than I should. He is a bandit, after all." She sighed. "I wish Don Diego were here. He has a way of talking to people that gets them to see reason."

Garcia laughed bitterly at the thought. "Even Don Diego could not persuade the Blade to change his greedy ways."

Isabel smiled ever so slightly. "You might be surprised Sergeant."

She looked out past the stables, where the sun was slipping down toward the horizon. "It is good you have come in the evening. I am restricted to my rooms all but one hour of the day. I am afraid I spoke out against the Blade. But Bernardo has fared far worse."

Bernardo hobbled toward them, his right leg supported by the crutch.

Isabel shook her head. "It will heal. A woman came from his people to properly set the bones and say the suitable prayers."

"Bernardo, my friend," Garcia exclaimed as the servant stopped before them. He gestured as he spoke so Bernardo would understand. Bernardo nodded.

"And do you know what has happened to Don Alejandro?" Rosalita asked.

The sergeant shook his head. He had not seen the elderly gentlemen in the better part of a week.

"He suspected something was wrong with the Capitán Morato's papers," Isabel explained. "Especially after your last comandante was called away so suddenly. Don Alejandro left for Monterey the very next day."

"What did he find?" Garcia asked.

"We should have heard from him three days ago. We fear he never reached his destination." Señorita Isabel looked again to the horizon. "I fear you are correct, sergeant, we do need Zorro."

Garcia was afraid; if Don Alejandro could disappear on his way to Monterey, what might have happened to Don Diego? He only thought these things. He did not wish to worry such fine people overmuch. "The Capitán must be watched," he said instead. "I will do what I can."

Isabel smiled at that. "We know you are a man of honor, sergeant. I will tell Diego that you called. May God be with you."

It was late at night when Garcia returned to the town. He was surprised to see Padre Miguel sitting in the dirt before the Mission, his face in his hands.

The priest looked up as Garcia dismounted. "Capitán Morato has taken everything. We will have none of the sacred vessels used to perform the sacraments!"

"What?" Garcia was astonished. Even Morato could not go that far.

"How will we serve our flock?" The priest said, more to himself than to Garcia. "They took every piece of silver, everything brought here from Spain." He studied the ground at his feet. "I suppose I could bless some earthen bowls—" He paused to take a ragged breath, looking at the sergeant at last. He waved his arm toward a cart hitched to a team of horses that was parked beside the barracks. It was watched by a single, dozing guard.

The priest groaned. "Worse, they sit not fifty feet away! Have they no shame?"

Garcia nodded. "If only Zorro were here!"

The priest looked up at Garcia, that same odd expression on his face. "Maybe Zorro can be here after all." He stood and moved close to the sergeant.

"They have left that cart with but a single guard. Perhaps the man might be called away—or distracted. It would be a shame if something frightened the horses. Who knows what might happen to the cart then?"

Was the priest suggesting they steal back the holy vessels? But then, Garcia realized, how could they steal what already belonged to the church?

"Do not worry, sergeant," Padre Miguel continued. "We will say the horses were frightened, but I will take the cart and drive it somewhere that the vessels will remain hidden and safe. It is my duty as a priest. It will be up to you to raise the alarm once the deed is done."

The sergeant could certainly do that.

"Very well," he said after but another moment's hesitation.

"Good! We should do it now, while everyone sleeps." The priest grabbed a torch from where it burned on a stand before the church. "If you might distract the guard?"

Now? Thought Garcia, but Padre Miguel was already walking toward the horses. Garcia moved quickly in front of the guard.

"What is the meaning of this?" he demanded loudly.

The guard opened his eyes halfway. "What?"

"Sleeping on the job! What were you thinking? You have failed in your duty! I must report you to your Capitán!"

The guard blinked, forcing himself awake. "But sir, I only just dozed. There is no one here save you and me."

"Insubordination! I will accept no excuses! Come, we will see Capitán Morato together!"

Garcia grabbed the guard by the lapel of his uniform and led him towards the comandante's office.

The sergeant was surprised by how easily the words came to him. Still, he had often heard the same scoldings on those occasions when he had dozed.

"Please sergeant!" The guard seemed to become more panic-stricken with each step. "The Capitán knows no mercy!"

"Really?" Garcia looked back toward the church. The cart was now out of sight. He waited until he heard the sound of galloping hooves.

He paused to examine the guard for a long enough moment that the priest might drive away. "Well then." He released the man with a smile. "I'm always willing to give someone a second chance."

He turned and walked back the way he had come. The guard stared after him, open-mouthed. As soon as he turned the corner, Garcia ran back to the wall near the recently vacated wagon. He had one more job to do.

Garcia realized he had better start to shout as well.

"Guards! We are under attack."

A half dozen soldiers stumbled from the barracks. Morato ran swiftly from his rooms, still pulling on his jacket. "What does this mean?"

"What does it mean?" Garcia replied. "I will show you." He waved to his right. A large Z was on the wall by the stable.

Morato studied the letter before turning back to Garcia. "So, this Zorro returns? And he would steal from Spain? What kind of coward is he that he will not show himself?"

"Zorro often uses the dark," was all the sergeant could think to say.

"Well, he cannot have gotten far. Everyone! Search for him! Don't let him get away!"

Both the Blade's personal guard and Garcia's men scrambled for their horses. Sergeant Garcia took a step to follow, but found the Capitán's hand upon his sleeve.

"Oh, not you sergeant. You've been here far longer than I. I may need your help in questioning this Zorro."

But you will not find this Zorro, Garcia thought. He did his best to hide his emotions, an odd mix of happiness at bringing Zorro back, if only for a moment, and fear because of the very same thing.

Garcia prayed the priest had had the time to drive the wagon into hiding. But it was only a matter of moments before a pair of the Blade's guard appeared, dragging the priest between them.

"Have you found my cart?" Morato demanded.

"We found him instead," one of guards replied. "He was thrown from the wagon while attempting to escape."

Padre Miguel smiled weakly at the sergeant. "I was never good with horses."

The other guard added "We found the cart a moment later." As if waiting for that introduction, the wagon, still laden with the spoils from the church, was driven into view. "The cart was only a little way down the road." He kicked the priest sharply in the ribs. "He has confessed to everything. He did not work alone."

The Capitán did not even wait for further explanation. "I suspected you were a weak man, Garcia. Do not deny it. The two of you were plotting, and it will cost you your lives. You shall be shot at dawn. That sounds appropriate. And you do not have long to wait." He waved at the eastern horizon, where Garcia could see the slightest tinge of pink.

"Guards!" Morato called. "Seize these traitors. Tie them up! And place them over there." He waved at the wall on which Garcia had scrawled the Z.

The sergeant and the priest soon stood side by side, waiting for the last sunrise they would ever see.

"If we should die," Padre Miguel said softly, "at least it will be in a holy cause. We shall be martyrs."

But Garcia did not want to be a martyr. He did not want to leave his family. What would they do without him?

As if he had conjured her with his thoughts, his Juanita stood before him. "My little soldier," she said sadly. "I heard that they had made you a prisoner."

Garcia nodded his head sadly. The ropes kept him from any other movement.

"And to save the holy vessels!" Juanita added, stroking his chin with the back of her hand. "How brave you are. I will make sure the children never forget you."

Garcia did his best to smile. He did not want to break down in front of his wife and neighbors. How had this happened? The sun was rising so quickly. How had he become an outlaw?

Four of the Blade's personal guard marched before them. Each carried a rifle. It would be over soon.

Morato strode haughtily after his troops. His scar twisted again as he smiled.

"Do either of you have any last words?"

"May God forgive you," said Padre Miguel.

But that was not enough for Sergeant Garcia. He had had enough of this arrogant madman.

"Zorro will avenge us both."

"Indeed?" Morato was still smiling. "I look forward to that. Men!" he called to his firing squad. "Line up!"

The four guards turned toward the prisoners. Sergeant Garcia looked up at the sun.

A great booming noise came from the far side of the compound. A dozen horses cried out in fear.

"The stables!" someone called. "Quickly!" Soldiers, guards and even some of the observers ran toward the commotion.

"What?" Morato asked. "Come back here!" He looked at Garcia and the priest, and drew his sword. "Must I do everything myself?"

"I think I can help," a man in black said as he stepped from the trees beyond the stable.

Garcia's mouth opened. It was Zorro.

"I see a suitable use for your sword right here," he added as he pulled his own blade.

"So you really do exist!" Morato said with a laugh. "I should have known these fools were not capable of plotting against me."

"On the contrary," Zorro said as he drew his sword. "I believe the whole of the Pueblo de Los Angeles is ready to plot against you. Capitán, you are not well liked."

Their swords clashed. The Blade was an excellent swordsman, fully the equal of his name. He struck again and again, driving the man in black to retreat along the wall of the stable. The sergeant feared Zorro might be overmatched.

"I seem to be out of practice," Zorro said, quickly parrying three attacks in a row. "I have not defeated anyone of your caliber in quite some time." He side-stepped the Blade's thrust, causing Morato to lose his balance. It was Zorro's turn to strike, and the Capitán barely countered his attack, retreating back along the wall.

Zorro smiled. "I think, my Capitán, that you are losing your command."

Morato was breathing hard. "I will not have everything taken away from me!" He looked at the crowd, which had fallen back a short distance to allow the two men to fight.

He took a quick step to his right, and grabbed Juanita! She shrieked as he spun her around to use her as a shield.

"You will let me go, and I will take that wagon." He nodded to the cart so recently returned. His sword point pricked at Juanita's throat. "Otherwise, this woman is dead."

"Mi amor," the sergeant whispered. Juanita did not look afraid and her strength emboldened him.

Zorro shook his head, his smile gone. "I do not think you will be taking any more victims."

Juanita bit Morato's hand.

The Blade screamed, pushing her away, shaking her so as to remove her teeth.

Zorro's sword slipped past the stumbling woman and found its target in the shoulder of Morato's sword arm.

The Capitán gasped and fell to the ground. Zorro knelt beside the fallen woman. "Are you hurt, señora?"

Juanita shook her head fiercely. "I could not let him hurt my soldier!"

Zorro stood, looking at the sergeant. "Your wife is a treasure."

Garcia fumbled for words to explain his actions. "Zorro!" he began. "I—"

"I understand that today we are working on the same side," Zorro replied before Garcia could go any farther. "If you do not speak of this again, sergeant, neither will I." He freed both prisoners with two swipes of his sword.

And then, as quickly as he came, he was gone.

Garcia helped his wife regain her feet.

Juanita. If anything had happened ..."

"Hush, my little soldier."

"Ah," another voice called. "The very man I want to see."

The sergeant turned to see Don Diego striding across the plaza. "I understand you may have need of me. And I certainly have news for you."

He looked down at the wounded Morato. "I fear I have come too late." He cleared his throat and looked up at the crowd as he removed an envelope from his pocket. "I discovered something while I was away. It seems our Capitán Morato's papers were forged. He was nothing more than a mercenary." He looked to the cart laden with silver. "And a very greedy one at that."

So he was even more of a scoundrel than Garcia had thought. He grinned at Don Diego, then turned to the priest, and Padre Miguel smiled back at him. With the help of Zorro, they had saved the day.

Juanita leaned against him. "My soldier! My brave little soldier!" Garcia took her in his arms. Perhaps he would get some sleep after all.

"I must rest," he said to the crowd.

"I'm sure the town will at least allow you that," Diego agreed. "And I trust we have had the last of all this excitement."

Sergeant Garcia could certainly agree with that. He headed toward home, his wife by his side. Tomorrow, he would go back to being sergeant of the guard, and Zorro would once again be an outlaw. But for this new, dawning day, Garcia was glad to have had Zorro by his side.

Surely, the new commander would be a far fairer man than the one his soldiers now dragged away. And Sergeant Garcia would never speak of this day again.

THE SILENCE
OF THE
NIGHT

BY TIMOTHY ZAHN

It was still an hour before noon in the Pueblo de Los Angeles, but the blazing sun had already turned a warm day uncomfortably hot. Strolling through the marketplace, pretending not to hear the babble of conversation filling the air around him, Bernardo loosened his hat a little and wondered how long he should wait until it would be proper to join Don Diego in the cool of the *taberna*.

The question was a delicate one. Though Bernardo was Diego's close friend, he was also technically the don's manservant. Diego himself didn't care what Bernardo did with his free time, especially considering the long hours Bernardo put in after dark assisting Zorro. But some of the townspeople, the older caballeros in particular, had very definite ideas as to how hard a servant should be worked. Sometimes Bernardo could feel their eyes on the back of his neck when he wandered along with apparently nothing to do.

Of course, since everyone thought he was deaf as well as mute, most of them weren't shy about putting their disapproval into words among themselves, as well.

On the one hand Bernardo had his pride. On the other hand, anything that helped Diego's reputation as a poetic dreamer was ultimately to the good. A delicate question, indeed.

He was studying a display of saddles when he spotted the young couple across the plaza.

At first it wasn't clear that they were a couple. The woman was standing beside a display of scarves, while the man was fifty paces away talking to one of the sellers of imported metalwork. But the woman's eyes were on the man, not the scarves, and her hands were trembling as she restlessly fingered the material. As for the young man, his left hand was gripping the pommel of his sword as he spoke to the vendor.

Part of Bernardo's job, though it was a part the disapproving caballeros would never know, was to be curious. Giving the saddles a final look, he headed leisurely toward the line of scarves. Diego's friend Isabel de Romeu liked such things, and it might be that Bernardo would find something his master could give her.

The young man had finished his conversation and was heading toward the woman. Bernardo picked up his pace, hoping to cross the man's path first.

He succeeded, passing the other about five steps in front of the woman and smiling genially at him. The other didn't seem to notice, his eyes on the woman, his face troubled. Bernardo tried the smile again, this time also giving the man a little wave of his hand.

The troubled eyes snapped to Bernardo like the flick of a bullwhip. "What is it?" he demanded. "What do you want?"

Bernardo let some puzzlement touch his smile, waving his hand around him in a gesture of welcome.

"I said what do you want?" the stranger bit out, his right hand shifting to a grip on his sword.

Bernardo took a hasty step backward, shaking his head as he waved at his ear and his mouth. "I said what—?" the man began again.

And broke off as the woman slipped past Bernardo and caught his arm, her face rigid, her hands fluttering against his. She pointed to Bernardo, at her own ear, and shook her head. "You mean he's—?" The man looked at Bernardo again. "He's deaf?"

The woman nodded. "Are you sure?" the man asked. "What if he's—?"

She reached up and touched his lips, and once more he fell silent. She looked at Bernardo and gave him a strained smile. Bernardo smiled in return, nodded again to the man, and turned his back on them as he pretended to study the scarves.

And listened carefully.

"He said there's a ship docked right now in San Pedro, but it won't be sailing for two more days," the man murmured as they headed away. "I don't know if we can…"

Bernardo strained his ears, hoping to hear the rest of the sentence. But the voice had already faded away into the background of marketplace noises.

But Bernardo had seen and heard enough. Picking out a red and blue scarf Isabel might like, he paid for it and folded it carefully away inside his jacket.

It was time to get out of the heat.

Z

Isabel de Romeu shook her head firmly, her proper eye focused on Diego's face, her stray eye focused somewhere else. "No," she said firmly. "They were experienced bandidos. They had to be."

"I didn't say they weren't experienced at thievery," Diego said mildly. "I merely said they weren't experienced at stealing the King's gold."

"They took on six of the King's lancers," Isabel countered hotly. "Three against six, and they prevailed. And don't forget, the Alcalde himself saw their sword work before they fled. They knew what they were doing."

"Then, yes, but what about now?" Diego persisted. "Do they have a plan for safely disposing of the gold? You know as well as I do that a fresh minting is very hard to disguise."

Behind Isabel the *taberna* door opened, and Diego looked up to see Bernardo hurry in. He glanced around, spotted Diego and Isabel, and maneuvered his way through the tables toward them. Diego gestured to an empty chair and Bernardo dropped into it, his hands already weaving rapidly through the air.

"Wait a moment, slow down," Isabel protested. "I can't understand a word he's saying."

"He met a young man and woman in the plaza," Diego said, translating Bernardo's sometimes obscure signs. "Strangers. They seem very nervous, and are hoping to take the ship at San Pedro. They wear peón clothing, yet the man wears both a sword and a heavy money pouch on his sash. The woman's scarf has spots of dried blood on it." He raised his eyebrows slightly as Bernardo touched his throat and shook his head. "She also appears to be mute."

"Are you certain?" Isabel asked, frowning.

As he always did in public, Bernardo was careful to wait until Diego had signed the question before replying in kind. "He thinks so, yes," Diego said. "Yet her throat did not appear injured."

"Something terrible must have happened to her," Isabel murmured, her proper eye filled with sympathy as she looked at Bernardo. "We should try to find them."

Behind Bernardo, the door opened again. "I don't think that will be a problem," Diego said as a young couple came furtively into the *taberna*. They glanced around, then headed toward the bar and the innkeeper cleaning glasses there.

Bernardo glanced over his shoulder and then turned back, nodding confirmation. "Perhaps one of us should bid them welcome to the Pueblo de Los Angeles," Diego suggested.

"I'll do it," Isabel said. Standing up, she headed across the room.

She was nearly to the bar when the door again opened and Sergeant Garcia stepped wearily inside. "Sergeant Garcia," Diego called, lifting a hand. "Come—join us."

"Gracias, Don Diego," Garcia said, maneuvering his vast bulk through the room toward him. The patrons along his path grabbed for their mugs, lest the living earthquake jostling past their tables knock them over. "It is very thirsty duty today," the sergeant added as he sank into the seat Isabel had just vacated. "Hello, little one," he added, waving at Bernardo. Bernardo, smiling genially, waved back.

"The Capitán is working you hard?" Diego asked, gesturing to the server for another mug.

"The Capitán and the Alcalde both," Garcia said with a sigh. "It is these bandidos, the ones who stole the gold coming from Monterey." He leaned closer to Diego. "I think, Don Diego, that the Alcalde is taking it personally. He was right there, you know, coming to meet the wagon when they attacked it."

"But was too far away to interfere before they escaped," Diego reminded him. The server set a mug down on the table, and Diego poured it half full. "It is hardly his fault."

"I know," Garcia said. "But try telling the Alcalde that." He took a long drink of the wine, and suddenly brightened. "*Would* you try telling the Alcalde that?" he asked eagerly. "Please? If we don't find the bandidos today, tomorrow we're to be sent out into the Topanga Canyon. We will be searching all day."

"And with nothing to drink but water," Diego commiserated. "I wish I could do something, Sergeant, but I very much doubt the Alcalde would listen to me."

"Si," Garcia conceded. "Besides, he may be right. The canyons are where *I* would go if I had stolen all that gold."

"A soldier's life is not an easy one, eh?" Diego slapped Garcia's arm lightly with the back of his fingers. "I tell you what, Sergeant. Tomorrow evening, when you return from Topanga, bring your lancers here. I will leave word that you are all to have a glass of wine on me."

Garcia's downcast face brightened. "Gracias, Don Diego," he said. "That will give us something to look forward to."

He downed the rest of his wine and hauled himself to his feet. "And now, I must return to duty. Adiós." He started to go, hesitated, then poured a little more wine into his glass and drank it. "Adiós," he said again, and made his way back through the crowd.

The door had barely closed behind him when Isabel was back in her seat. "Their names are Lucio and Morena Borjia," she said. "They've taken a room for two nights."

Diego glanced at Bernardo, who nodded slightly. "So, they *are* taking the ship."

"So it would seem," Isabel said, reaching her cupped hand over the center of the table. "And Lucio tried to pay with this." She opened her hand just far enough for Diego and Bernardo to see inside.

Diego felt his eyes widen. The gloss of a freshly minted gold coin was impossible to mistake. "Alfonse saw this, and yet didn't call the lancers?"

"Alfonse didn't see it," Isabel said, smiling slyly. "I distracted them all, and replaced it with one of my own." She leaned a little closer. "Lucio also asked about a doctor. Alfonse gave him directions to Doctor Lozada."

"They will have a long wait," Diego said, still gazing at the piece of stolen gold. "I understand that the good doctor left early this morning to treat someone at one of the northern haciendas. I doubt he'll be back before nightfall."

Bernardo tapped Diego's arm and began signing. "Bernardo doesn't think they're the robbers," Diego continued, making a few random signs back for the benefit of anyone who might be watching. "I have to agree."

"Not unless they're foolish enough to try spending their money less than ten miles from where they stole it," Isabel agreed. "But then where did they get the coin?"

"That is indeed the mystery," Diego agreed. Draining his glass, he stood up. "If you'll excuse me?"

"Where are you going?" Isabel asked.

"Sergeant Garcia wanted me to speak to Alcalde de Soto," Diego said. "I think I'll do just that."

Ignacio de Soto, Alcalde of the Pueblo de Los Angeles, was in a foul mood. It was not in any way helped by his guard's announcement that Diego de la Vega wished to see him.

His first impulse was to send the young fool away. Diego was full of idealistic thinking and high-minded talk, but he had no comprehension of how things worked in the real world. No doubt he had heard of some injustice done to some peón and wanted de Soto to personally attend to it.

But he was a de la Vega, and de Soto couldn't simply refuse to see him. "Send him in," he said.

De la Vega strode in, his face alight with eagerness. "Alcade de Soto," he said in greeting. "I have just had a thought."

"I cannot wait to hear it, Señor de la Vega," de Soto said with only a hint of sarcasm.

He gestured toward a chair, but de la Vega remained standing, apparently too excited by his midday revelation to sit down. "I suddenly realized who the bandidos were who robbed the Monterey gold five days ago," he said. "I believe it was Zorro and two of his accomplices."

De Soto sighed. He'd interrupted his work for *this*? "No," he said flatly.

"What do you mean, no?" de la Vega demanded. "These were bandidos. Zorro is a bandido." He held out his hands, palms upward, as if it should be obvious to the furniture itself.

"I saw them fight," de Soto said patiently. "I've seen Zorro fight."

A frown creased de la Vega's forehead. "I don't follow."

De Soto took a deep breath, holding onto his temper with sheer will power. "Zorro fights in a style taught in Barcelona, a style you would have seen at the university. Had you paid attention to such things," he couldn't resist adding. "The bandidos used a style taught in Madrid. There is a clear difference."

De la Vega's face fell. "You're certain?"

"Very," de Soto assured him. He gestured again, this time to the door. "Was there anything else?"

De la Vega grimaced and shook his head. "No, Señor Alcalde," he said. "My apologies for wasting your time."

"My door is always open, Señor de la Vega," de Soto said dryly. "If you have any further revelations, feel free to bring them to the Capitán."

"I shall do so," de la Vega promised. "Adiós."

De Soto shook his head as he returned to his chair. And here he'd thought de la Vega had already found all possible ways to annoy him.

The sun had set, and the cool of the night had once again returned to the pueblo, when the young strangers finally emerged from Doctor Lozada's home and began the short journey through the deserted streets toward the *taberna*. Waiting in the shadows, Zorro watched as they approached, noting the way Lucio cradled his wife in his arm as they walked, the way one would a child or someone ill or injured.

He also noted that the young man held her with his left arm, thereby trapping his sword between them. It was a thing no seasoned fighter would likely do.

Still, it was not proof. But he would soon have that.

He waited until the couple was five paces away. Then, stepping from concealment, he lifted his hand to them. "Buenos noches, amigos," he said sociably. "Welcome to the Pueblo de Los Angeles."

For a moment both man and woman froze. Then, abruptly, Lucio leaped forward away from his wife, his hand fumbling for his sword. "Away, bandido!" he snarled as he pulled the weapon awkwardly from its sheath. "Or I will run you through."

"You have courage, amigo," Zorro said, as his own rapier flashed in the moonlight. "Have you skill to match?"

Lucio's tongue flicked across his upper lip. "Step closer and find out."

"As you wish," Zorro said, and strode forward.

Lucio made the first move, lunging almost before his opponent was in range. Zorro parried the attack easily, countering with a short jab toward the young man's face. Lucio twitched violently away from the feint, swinging his sword desperately across the rapier's blade and knocking it aside. But instead of following through with an attack of his own, he merely swung the blade back again, as if trying to block a thrust that wasn't even there.

The man didn't fight in the Madrid style that Alcalde de Soto had described. In fact, he fought in no style whatsoever. He was a peón, pure and simple, whose ability with a sword had probably been learned entirely by watching others.

Zorro gave it two more exchanges, just to be certain. Then, he knocked Lucio's blade aside one final time, and in the same smooth motion returned his rapier to its sheath. "Enough," he said calmly. "I am convinced—you are not the ones I seek. Tell me of your troubles, amigo. Perhaps I can help."

For a long moment Lucio just stood there, his chest heaving with his exertion, his sword still held uncertainly. Zorro waited, and slowly the sword tip lowered. "Who are you?" the young man asked.

"I am called Zorro," the masked man said. "I am a champion of the oppressed, and of those to whom justice has been denied." He cocked his head. "Also a seeker after truth. Tell me, where did you obtain the coin you used to hire your room at the *taberna*?"

The sword tip abruptly came up again. "Are you from Andrés and Enrique?" he demanded.

"I know neither man," Zorro said, leaving his own sword in its sheath. "Did the coin come from them?"

Lucio sighed, and once again his sword tip dipped. "No," he said. "It was from their friend, Vittorio. They are evil men, Señor, very evil men. Three days ago I returned from the fields—" He broke off, looking over his shoulder at Morena, standing silently in the middle of the street. "Could we perhaps not speak of this, Señor?" he asked, turning back again. "It is…my wife has been hurt. Very badly hurt."

"Then speak softly," Zorro said. "I must know all."

Lucio grimaced. "I returned from the fields to find Vittorio in my home," he said, his voice barely above a whisper. "He was—" Even in the faint moonlight Zorro could see the young man's lips compress into a bloodless line. "He was trying to…he was holding Morena's arms…"

"He was trying to take advantage of her?" Zorro suggested quietly.

Lucio nodded, a quick jerk of his head. "His pistol was on the table," he said, the words tumbling out now like stones in a landslide. "He tried to take it, but I reached it first. We struggled…" He shivered. "There was blood all over, Señor. All over."

"And you say he had two friends?"

Again, Lucio nodded. "I knew that someone would have heard the shot, and that eventually they would come. I had no choice. I took Vittorio's sword and his money pouch—we have none of our own—and fled."

He closed his eyes. "We were well on our way before I realized Morena had lost the ability to speak."

Zorro looked at the young woman. Her face was tight, her eyes haunted, her fingers rubbing restlessly against the edge of her scarf. It was a similar event early in Bernardo's life, Zorro knew, that had exacted the same price from his faithful friend. "I understand, perhaps better than you know," he told Lucio. "Did the doctor offer any hope?"

Lucio snorted. "Doctors always offer hope," he said. "But little else."

Zorro nodded. The doctors had been equally helpless with Bernardo's condition. "Yet hope is not to be lightly dismissed," he said. "What do you do now?"

"We hoped Vittorio's money might buy us escape from California," Lucio said. "But I fear it may already be too late. The ship doesn't sail for another two days, and Andrés and Enrique will surely guess that we have come this way. If they find us here…" He looked down at the sword still gripped in his hand. "I'm not a swordsman, Señor."

"Then we will make certain that you do not need to be," Zorro said. "But first, we must assure your safety. Behind the doctor's home is a creek. Two miles upstream is an abandoned miner's shack. It will be safe for you to stay there for the night."

"What about our things?" Lucio asked. "Everything we own is still in the *taberna*."

"The value of possessions pales before the value of life," Zorro said pointedly. "But I understand. Tomorrow at this time you may return to the *taberna* to retrieve your belongings. When you do so, you should leave Morena at the shack."

"What, alone?" Lucio demanded.

"Don't worry, she will be safe there," Zorro assured him. "Once you have your belongings, I will meet you again at this spot and provide you with the details of your departure from the pueblo."

Lucio's eyes widened. "You will help us escape, Señor?" He shifted his sword to his left hand and fumbled for his money pouch. "Whatever you wish in payment—"

"Not now," Zorro said, waving the pouch away. "But bring the money with you tomorrow."

"Si, Señor, I will do so," Lucio promised.

"Good," Zorro said. "Then go at once to the miner's shack. There will be food and water waiting there for you. And remember: collect your belongings tomorrow night, then meet me here."

"I will," Lucio promised. He looked at the sword in his hand, as if suddenly remembering he was holding it, and slipped it back into its sheath. "Until tomorrow, Señor."

"Adiós," Zorro said.

Lucio had his arm around Morena, and they were heading for the creek, when Zorro slipped away into the night.

Z

They spent a long, nervous night in the miner's shack, and a longer and even more nervous day afterward. Lucio spent most of the sunlight hours moving from window to window, praying desperately that he would not see Andrés and Enrique riding toward them with swords in their hands and blood in their eyes.

Morena spent most of the day gazing out at nothing, or fingering the scarf that still held bits of Vittorio's blood, and not speaking.

Finally, it was time. Lucio bid Morena farewell, promised to return as quickly as possible, and headed back along the creek toward the pueblo. With each step the money pouch slapped silently but accusingly against his hip.

The streets weren't as empty as they'd been the previous night, with a number of citizens walking or riding along on various errands. Lucio reached the *taberna*, took a careful breath, and stepped inside.

And froze. Seated among the other patrons were no less than five tables' worth of soldiers.

He stared at them, his heart thudding suddenly in his chest. So Zorro had betrayed him. The minute the soldiers spotted him—

"It's all right," a voice murmured in his ear.

He turned. A woman stood behind him, young and dark, with an odd eye that seemed to look off to the side. "They're not here for you," the woman continued. "Go and get your things."

Lucio looked back at the soldiers. "Go on," the woman said again.

Taking a deep breath, Lucio headed across the noisy room, slipping gingerly between the tables as he headed for the stairway. No one shouted or made a move against him. He reached the stairs and, forcing himself not to hurry, walked up to the second-floor rooms.

A moment later he was in the upper hallway, safely out of sight of the soldiers below. Letting out his breath in a quiet sigh, he headed toward his room.

And stopped short as something hard jabbed into his back. "What have we here?" Enrique's voice asked sarcastically.

Lucio felt the blood drain from his face. He opened his mouth, but nothing came out. "Andrés?" Enrique called softly. "Andrés, he's here."

A door five paces away opened, and Andrés stepped out into the corridor, another pistol gripped in his hand. "I told you he would be," he said, his voice dark and mocking. He shifted his glare to Lucio. "Where's our gold?"

With an effort, Lucio found his voice. "In my pouch," he said.

There was a sudden wrench at his waist, and the weight was gone. "Where's the rest of it?" Andrés demanded as Enrique secured the pouch to his own sash.

Lucio shook his head. "That's all of it."

"You lie," Enrique said, jabbing his pistol hard into Lucio's back. "Vittorio's share of the robbery would have filled a small chest."

Lucio felt his throat tighten. The money had come from a *robbery*? "I swear this was all he had," he pleaded. Had Señor Zorro known he was carrying blood money? "I swear by all the saints."

"We waste time," Enrique growled. "Perhaps a bullet in the leg will make him talk."

"With all those soldiers down there?" Andrés countered, tucking his pistol into his sash and drawing his sword. "We do this with swords. And we do it inside." He gestured with his blade toward the line of doors. "Which is yours, peón?"

Lucio knew in that moment that he was going to die. But at least Morena would not die with him. Perhaps Zorro, once he heard of this, could find someone to take care of her.

Unless once inside the room he could find a way to signal to the masked man waiting down the street. It was a small hope, but he had to try. For Morena's sake. "That one," he said, pointing to the door beside the one Andrés had been hiding behind.

"Bring him," Andrés ordered. Turning, his sword hanging loosely from his hand, he stepped to the door and threw it open.

And jumped back with a strangled cry, whipping his sword up in front of him.

And to Lucio's astonishment, Zorro stepped out into the hallway.

The first man—Andrés—was quick, bringing his sword up into defense position the moment he caught sight of the masked man before him. But he was still moving forward, and his feet tangled with each other as he desperately tried to reverse direction.

Zorro didn't give him the chance. He slashed with his rapier, keeping the man off balance, pushing him backward across the hallway. The bandido's back slammed hard against the wall—

"Señor!" Lucio barked.

Zorro looked in that direction. The second man, Enrique, had shoved Lucio to the side and hauled a pistol from his sash. Lucio spun back around, making a desperate grab for the bandido's arm, but Enrique dodged his hand with ease. He brought up the weapon.

And with a flick of his wrist, Zorro sent his sword spinning around and flying straight up to lodge point-first in the low ceiling.

Automatically, Enrique's eyes went to the weapon, gazing in astonishment and confusion at the rapier swaying gently as it hung from the darkened wood. The spell lasted only an instant, and then he lowered his eyes once again to the man standing before him.

Just as Zorro, his right hand no longer burdened by his sword, swung the bullwhip free of his cloak and snapped it in an underhanded motion toward Enrique's hand.

There was very little power in a whip handled that way. But very little power was needed. The end of the whip stung against the bandido's hand, sending the pistol flying through the air. Dropping the whip, Zorro grabbed his rapier and pulled it free, bringing it around just as Andrés regained his balance and lunged again to the attack.

Again, the bandido was too late. Zorro parried the thrust, stepping wide to put Andrés's back to Enrique and the stairs at the end of the hallway. "To your room, amigo," Zorro called, gesturing to Lucio with his free hand.

Lucio hesitated, his eyes still on Enrique. But the other's hand had recovered from the bullwhip's tingle and he now had his sword out. "Go," Zorro ordered. "Retrieve the coil of rope from beneath the bed and wait. I will be there soon."

Lucio leaped backward as Enrique swung his sword viciously, then ran past the whirling blades of Andrés and Zorro. Andrés took his own useless stab at the young man, and then Lucio was safely out of his reach and in the room.

"You are good, Señor," Andrés spat. "But let us now see how you do against two of us."

"Yes, let us," Zorro agreed.

The two bandidos were well schooled, and schooled in the Madrid style Alcalde de Soto had described. But they were no match for Zorro. Slowly but steadily he pushed them back toward the stairs and the room full of soldiers below.

They were nearly there when Andrés seemed to awaken to what was happening. "Wait, Señor," he pleaded as the swords continued to ring together. "We have gold. We can make a deal."

Zorro didn't answer. He continued the attack, blocking and parrying and thrusting, using the tight quarters and his own footwork to force his opponents into each other's way, thwarting their advantage of numbers.

They reached the top of the stairs, moving around the wall onto the landing, and beneath the sound of clanging steel Zorro heard the conversations below vanish like morning dew as the patrons caught sight of the drama taking place above them. He glanced down, confirmed by the size of Garcia's eyes and mouth that the big sergeant was watching.

And with a final parry of his opponents' swords, he deftly slashed the tip of his rapier across the pouch of gold Enrique had taken from Lucio, sending coins flying through the air in all directions. Before either bandido could react, Zorro ducked beneath their blades and shouldered Andrés backwards, shoving him into Enrique and sending both men tumbling down the stairs.

"Adiós, *muchachos*," Zorro said, giving them a quick salute and ducking back out of sight around the wall. Once again, it was time for him to disappear.

But first, there was one other small chore he needed to perform.

"Help them up," Sergeant Garcia called across the sudden pandemonium that had erupted across the *taberna*. "Lancers—help them up."

"Do we go after Zorro?" someone called as a pair of soldiers went to the strangers' aid.

"Do not bother," Garcia said, feeling disgusted as he started pushing his way through the crowd toward the stairway. Once again, Zorro—and the reward for his capture—had been so close, yet so far. "By now he will be miles away."

The two strangers were on their feet when Garcia reached them. "What was that all about, Señores?" he asked.

"Do you just stand there?" one of them snapped. "A bandido tries to rob us, and you just stand and watch?"

"That bandido, as you call him, is called Zorro," Garcia rumbled. "And he does not draw his sword without cause."

"His cause was to rob us," the second man snarled. "If you will not give chase, then allow us to do so."

Garcia sighed. "If you insist," he said, stepping out of their way. "But I assure you it will be a waste of time."

Neither man answered. Pushing their way through the crowd, they headed for the door.

Garcia frowned as the oddness of that suddenly struck him. They were leaving *now*, with their lost money still scattered across the *taberna*'s floor and stairs?

There was a tug at his sleeve. Isabel de Romeu was standing at his side, one of the coins in her hand and a puzzled look on her face. "Sergeant, look at the money that was in the pouch Zorro cut open," she said, handing him the coin. "Do I imagine things? Or could it be—"

Garcia took a huge lungful of air. "Lancers!" he bellowed. "Stop them!"

The two solders nearest the door reacted instantly, stepping together in front of the two strangers, their muskets held warningly. "What are you doing?" one of the men demanded. "We need to stop that bandido."

"No, you need to explain where you found gold that was stolen less than a week ago," Garcia said darkly, holding up the coin.

"It was him," the second man said, pointing to the top of the stairs. "The man Lucio Borjia. He paid us this money to settle a debt. He is your robber, not us."

"We shall see," Garcia said, pointing at one of the soldiers. "You— go find this Lucio Borjia and bring him to me."

"No use," the second stranger snarled. "He will be long gone by now. No doubt with your good friend Zorro."

"Perhaps," Garcia said. "We shall see."

Z

Zorro was waiting at the agreed-upon spot when Lucio finally emerged from the *taberna*, a small tattered bag in his hand.

"Well, amigo?" the masked man asked as he stepped from the shadows.

"It was exactly as you said, Señor Zorro," Lucio said. "When the lancers untied me from the bed, I told them Andrés and Enrique had attacked me and tried to rob me, and that it was only through your fortunate appearance that I was saved."

"And the good sergeant looked inside the pouch I left you?" Zorro asked.

Lucio nodded. "At the others' insistence, yes. But the few coins inside gave lie to their claim that I was a bandido as well. Especially when they then found more of the stolen gold in the others' own room."

"Then all is at an end," Zorro said. "The bandidos are either captured or dead, and there is no longer any need for you to leave California. Return to your home, and care for your wife."

"I will do so," Lucio said. Reaching down, he untied the pouch from his sash. "I must now give this back to you."

"I trade you," Zorro offered. Taking the small bag, he handed Lucio a much heavier one. "For travel, and for her care."

Lucio hefted the bag, his face tortured with indecision. Then, reluctantly, he offered it back. "No, Señor," he said. "I cannot take blood money."

"There is no blood on this money," Zorro assured him. "You may take it in peace."

Lucio hesitated again, then nodded. "I am forever in your debt, Señor Zorro," he said, bowing low. "Gracias."

"One more thing," Zorro said. "There is no blood on this money, but there is blood on Morena's scarf. It is not good for her to keep such a memory of her terrible experience."

"I know," Lucio said with a sigh. "But it is the only scarf she has."

"Not any more." Reaching into his tunic, Zorro pulled out a red and blue scarf. "This is for her."

Lucio took the scarf, his eyes wide in amazement. "From you, Señor?"

"From another friend," Zorro told him. "He very much wanted Morena to have it."

"Gracias, Señor," Lucio said. Even in the faint moonlight, Zorro could see that his eyes were shiny with tears. "We are honored to have such friends. You will thank him for us?"

"I will," Zorro promised. "Let us pray that Morena's memories will fade, and that she will one day speak again."

"She will," Lucio said firmly. "If love and devotion can heal her, then she will be healed."

"Then you had best be on your way," Zorro said. "Morena awaits you, and you will have a long journey home in the morning."

"Not so long as the journey here, Señor Zorro," Lucio said. "Adiós."

"Adiós." Zorro said.

He watched as Lucio hurried off into the night, and it seemed to him that the peón's step was springier and his back straighter than he had seen it before.

He shook his head. Love and devotion, the young man had said.

If only it was that easy.

Stepping back into the shadows, Zorro gave a soft whistle, and with a gentle snort the great black stallion Toronado trotted out of concealment. "Come, Toronado," Zorro said as he swung himself into the saddle. "A good night's work. Let us go home."

THE WRATH OF GRAPES

BY JOHN PEEL

The mule train was barely an hour from the Mission when it was attacked. The journey from the port had been uneventful to this point, and neither Fray Quintero nor his Indian neophytes had any reason to suspect trouble. When the dozen masked riders rode down from the hills, their first reaction had been curiosity. Then the Indian at the head of the train gave a cry and pointed a wavering finger.

The riders had their swords drawn and raised as they raced down the slopes toward the train.

Fray Quintero did not know what to do. He was, after all, a man of peace, and no one in the train was armed with more than a machete. The approaching riders were clearly fighting men, unlike him. His Indian companions looked to the Father for guidance, and he shook his head. "Do nothing," he advised them. "Let us see what these men want." He strode forward, interposing himself between his followers and the new arrivals.

The riders encircled the mule train silently, gesturing the neophytes away with their swords. The lead rider bent from his saddle before Fray Quintero. "Tell your savages to abandon the mules," he ordered. "Or we shall kill them." His clothes were dark and simple, but clearly of rich material. His face was completely hidden by a cloth mask, save for two small holes for the eyes, and it muffled the man's voice.

"Do as they say," Fray Quintero ordered the Indians. "These are clearly brutal and unscrupulous men." Silently, the servants did as he commanded, withdrawing a short distance from the pack animals. The priest looked up at the leader of the raiders. "Why do you do this?" he asked. "These panniers do not contain money—merely clippings of vines."

"Treasure enough," the man growled. "And one destined never to reach your mission."

Fray Quintero did not understand. "You would rob the Holy Mother Church?"

"Why not?" he asked. "It would rob me. I merely return the favor. I offer you no violence, but you must be gone—and take those sorry wretches with you or I shall allow my men to slay them."

"You are a wretch!" Fray Quintero cried passionately. "To threaten unarmed men, to rob a priest of the church, to steal its property!"

"Enough!" the robber roared. "I have given you your lives—be grateful for that!"

"You must not do this thing!" Fray Quintero begged. "Those clippings are meant to improve the yield of the mission."

"I know what they are meant for, you whining cur," the man snapped. He returned his sword to its sheath. "And I have had my fill of your voice." He uncoiled the whip from his saddle. "Still your voice and be gone—or I shall drive you forth!"

Fray Quintero stood tall. He was six feet two inches of little more than skin and bones, and all of sixty years of age. But this man did not frighten him. "You are a miserable sinner!" he exclaimed. "Repent of your actions and God will forgive you."

"You weary my patience!" the robber cried. He struck out with the whip, still coiled, catching the priest a stinging blow across the face. Fray Quintero fell with a cry, his cheek burning and bloodied. "Leave now, or I promise you these swords will taste your blood!"

Two of his followers helped the priest to his feet. One of them dabbed at his cheek with a cloth, and the other offered his arm for support. The Franciscan realized that words would not help in this situation. "Come," he said, "we shall do as these men say." He turned to go, but looked back at the robbers. "You shall pay for your sins," he vowed. "Your actions will not go unpunished."

"Old man," the leader growled. "I would advise you to be silent—and be gone!"

Fray Quintero turned away again, and began walking, leaning gratefully on the arm of his companion. Silently, his small flock fell in behind him. As they headed on foot toward the Mission of San Gabriel Arcangel, he glanced back to see that the robbers had taken charge of the mules and were leading them into the hills. On the backs of the swaying beasts of burden were the panniers that held his precious clippings. Were they lost forever?

Don Diego de la Vega was seated on the veranda of his hacienda, skimming one of the books that had arrived the previous day on the latest merchant ship from Madrid. It was a fresh work on botany by the German naturalist Von Schtemper, and would certainly repay a more careful reading. But the day was hot, and Diego lacked the necessary interest at the moment to do the beautiful book justice. He was more than grateful when Bernardo appeared and indicated by gesture that Fray Felipe had arrived. He rose to his feet to greet his Franciscan friend warmly.

"And what brings you all the way out here on such a pleasant day?" he enquired, pouring the father a glass of fresh orange juice.

"A request for aid, I am afraid—as I am pressed to do all too frequently."

Diego grinned. "My aid—or that of... another?"

Filipe's lips twitched. "The other."

"Ah!" Diego nodded. "Perhaps you could tell me all about it." He gestured the Father to a seat, and took to his own once again.

Fray Felipe glanced at the book on the table. "I see you know that a shipment from Spain arrived yesterday—that is a new title. On the same vessel was a special cargo for the Mission—a hundred cuttings of vines, specially selected for Fray Quintero. You know he is the man who cultivates our vineyards?"

"Indeed," Diego said. "I purchase a number of bottles from him at every pressing. He is a skilled vintner, and his wines amongst the best in all of California."

"As you say. Fray Quintero enjoys his work and strives always to improve his crop. The money it brings in helps our mission to the Indians."

"And the product causes much pleasure amongst those who taste it," Diego said. "I take it the cuttings are intended to be grafted onto existing vines in an attempt to improve the yield?"

"That was the idea indeed, my son."

"I note the use of the word was," Diego observed. "I take it that there have been complications?"

"The mule train Fray Quintero was leading from the dock to the Mission was attacked last afternoon," Fray Filipe replied. "The robbers beat the good Father with a whip and stole all of the cuttings."

"I see." Diego's lips tightened in anger. "How is Fray Quintero?"

"He is recovering, thankfully, from his ordeal—but his cheek is likely to remain scarred from the blow."

"And you wish the robbers to be paid for the blow, and the vines recovered?"

Fray Felipe nodded. "The culprits offered an insult to the Mission by their actions, and this should not go unpunished."

"My thoughts precisely." Diego rose to his feet and started to pace as he thought about the matter. The Franciscans were gentle men, devoted to their work, and offered peace and hospitality to all. There were few enough in California who would offer them violence. "And is there any clue as to who the robbers might have been?"

"Not directly," Fray Felipe admitted. "They were all masked. But they rode fine stallions, and their leader, at least, was dressed in expensive raiment, according to Fray Quintero. He felt that the man was no peon, but a person of wealth and breeding."

"Wealth and breeding, eh?" Diego muttered. "Insufficient breeding, it would seem, if he would steal from the Mission and strike a priest. It seems to me that the man must be taught a lesson in manners."

"We must first learn who the villain is," Fray Felipe reminded him.

"Come now, my friend," Diego replied. "I feel certain that it can only be the handiwork of one man—Don Jose Castiliano. Simple thieves would have no need for vines, and there is hardly a black market for them. Don Castiliano has large vineyards, and he produces the most successful wines in the county. He would have the most to lose if the Mission improved its production and competed more strongly with him. I have never met the Don myself, but I have heard two interesting pieces of information about him. The first is that he is a man of temper and avarice. That gives him motive."

"Perhaps so," Fray Felipe agreed. "But it falls far short of proving him the guilty party."

"Indeed it does," Diego admitted. "Which is where the second fact becomes of use. I hear that he has a very beautiful daughter—and my father is constantly urging me to marry and hastily produce him a whole tribe of heirs!"

"Maria?" Fray Felipe looked shocked. "She is the most spoiled and arrogant young lady on these shores!"

"Well, then—even better!"

"Better?" Fray Felipe was clearly confused. "Why is it better that a girl you wish to woo is spoiled and arrogant?"

"Because it gives me the perfect excuse not to go through with a betrothal," Diego replied. "One even my father can hardly object to!" He called for Bernardo. "I shall write to Don Jose immediately and suggest myself as a prospective son-in-law. I am certain it will at least pique his interest..."

Diego studied the ranchero as Bernardo drove the carriage up the road toward it. It was large and lavish, rather ostentatious. The gardens about the house were immaculate and well-kept, and the house itself large and slightly vulgar. It was no one thing by itself—the design and furnishings were quite stylish and pleasant—simply the accumulation of everything. It spoke of an owner who wished everyone to understand and acknowledge that he had wealth. It was the home of an egotist. Little wonder, then, that the daughter was spoiled. Don Jose was a man who denied himself little, so she had learned her manners at his knee.

An Indian servant opened the door for him, but a Spanish footman announced him to the owner. The interior of the house was like the exterior—every item was precise and expensive, and the total sum simply too much. Don Jose himself was more of the same—his trousers and tunic were crisp, clean and with overly busy decorative stitching. His bolero shirt flared out over his ample belly, and his boots were ornately-wrought rawhide. The kerchief about his throat was of fine China silk. The man was stout, tanned and with a trim dark beard tinged with the onset of gray. His hair was slick and gleaming, with a similar hint of gray at the temples.

"Don Diego," he said in greeting. "I know your father, of course. I trust he is well?"

"Indeed he is, Don Jose," Diego replied. "You yourself appear to be in excellent health. I trust the same is true of your daughter?"

"We both are fine. Maria will join us shortly—she is eager to meet you, of course."

"And I her," Diego replied. "I have heard glowing reports of her beauty, and am quite eager to verify their accuracy."

Don Jose smiled a trifle tightly. "As her father, I am naturally not unprejudiced, but she is indeed a lovely girl. She takes after her late mother. So, you are eager to wed?"

"Not especially," Diego replied. "But my father seems to view it as my duty, and as a dutiful son I strive to please him." As he had expected, this lukewarm response did not endear him to Don Jose.

"I had rather hoped that any suitor for my daughter's hand might be a trifle more…enthusiastic."

"But I have not yet met her!" Diego protested. "I can hardly be expected to enthuse over a girl I do not know. I am sure my passions will be aroused once your daughter has joined us."

"Of course," Don Jose agreed. "In the meantime, perhaps I can offer you a little wine? It is of my own produce—you know of my vineyard perhaps?"

"Indeed," Diego informed him. "I am in the habit of purchasing a good deal of it for my table and my pleasure. Not too much, of course! But it is excellent. I should appreciate a glimpse at the fields where the grapes grow, if that is not inconvenient?"

"Not in the slightest!" Don Jose assured him with pride. "I believe I can safely claim to produce the finest wines in California."

"I am strongly inclined to agree," Diego said. "Your only true rival is that produced by the Mission. Fray Quintero is a superb vintner himself."

Don Jose scowled slightly. "I would not compare their produce to mine—they manufacture theirs for the peasants, not for men with discriminating palates such as ourselves." The Indian servant had poured two glasses of rich red wine, and Don Jose handed one to Diego. "Taste this and tell me what you think."

Diego sipped it appreciatively. "A fine wine, senor," he said. "A full, rich taste, a hint of the oak…most agreeable. Once it has aged a year or so I do believe there will be few wines this side of Madrid to match it."

"Ah." Don Jose was caught between enjoying the compliment and being pricked by the implied insult that he was serving it too soon. "You recognize it as this year's harvest, then," he finally compromised.

"Yes, indeed. It shows great hope for your future. And, speaking of which, I do believe this is your daughter now."

Don Jose bowed slightly. "It is indeed. Don Diego, may I have the honor of presenting to you my daughter Maria?"

Diego bowed. "A great pleasure, senorita," he said. "You are indeed as dazzlingly beautiful as I have heard." This was perfectly true, and Diego enjoyed the vision before him. Maria Castiliano was tall and slender, and her features delicate and excellent. Her dark hair hung in ringlets over her bare shoulders, framing her immaculate skin. Her eyes were dark and deep, with a hint of amusement. Her dress was—as he had expected—

costly, overly ornate and very, very flattering to her splendid figure.

"I am glad I do not disappoint," she said demurely, half-hiding her smile behind her fan.

"I am certain you could never do that," Diego assured her.

At this moment the servant announced dinner. Diego offered his arm, which she accepted, and they followed the servant and Don Jose into the dining room. The meal that followed was superb, and carefully matched with truly excellent wines. It wasn't difficult to see why Don Jose was stout—his cook was a master or mistress. Conversation over the meal was light and pleasant, but Diego could detect the stirrings of Maria's selfishness even in the slightest of remarks. If she was not continually flattered or attended to, her voice became a trifle sharp, and the fire in her eyes became menacing. At the end of the meal, Don Jose offered sherry, and the three of them drank it together. This was a fair breech of etiquette, as Maria should have left the men alone. But she clearly wished to be privy to the conversation and studiously ignored her father's glare of annoyance, turning instead to Diego.

"And are you pleased with what you have found here tonight?" she asked him, pointedly.

He smiled gently back. "Do you speak of the wine or yourself?" he asked, lightly.

With the slightest of frowns, she said: "Why, both, of course."

"Then in order: the wine, as I told your father, is excellent. I am rather looking forward to a tour of the vineyard here - I am certain it will prove to be interesting. Yourself…you are as pleasing to the eye as everyone says, senorita—a rare delight. I am somewhat amazed that you have not yet been snatched up before now by some eager suitor. It is my great fortune to be the first, then."

Maria smiled, but did not blush as many young women would have done in her place. "You wish to press your suit for my hand, then?" she asked, pointedly—once again ignoring the dark glance her father gave her. It was not her place to inquire.

"I rather think I had better," Diego told her. "My father would never forgive me if I allowed a beauty like you to escape me. And he is most eager that I should start a family. I do trust I would not be too forward if I were to ask if you are prepared to bear him a large number of grandchildren? I am his only child, you see, and he has always dreamed of a home filled with many children."

The frown on her brow was definitely more pronounced now—as he had hoped. "I am still quite young to be thinking of children, senor," she said. There was a touch of ice in her voice also. "I am more interested at the moment in dances and enjoyment."

"Then I envy you," Diego said. "I am afraid I do not dance well my-self—and I prefer to stay at home and read. The world is a fascinating place, and there is so much to learn—wouldn't you agree?"

"I should think you would learn more by going out than staying home," she said rather sharply.

"Ah, that is because you do not read much, I assume," he replied. "Books can be so transforming."

"Really?" The ice was chillingly thick in her voice now. The prospect of an end to amusement and the early onset of motherhood were clearly highly unappealing to Maria. "I prefer to enjoy life in its fullness."

"Perhaps, Don Diego, you would like that tour of the vineyards now?" Don Jose suggested, quickly.

Diego blinked as if caught by surprise, and then nodded. "I should enjoy it, certainly. I am most eager to see the source of such splendid wines. My servant, Bernardo, has my carriage waiting at your front door. Perhaps we can take that?"

"Of course." Don Jose turned to his daughter. "Please stay here and await our return." Diego caught the glower the father shot the daughter. She bowed her head demurely in acknowledgement.

Once he and Diego were seated in the carriage, Don Jose turned to him. "I must apologize for my daughter," he said. "Her mother died when she was quite young, and I have perhaps not been the best influence on her. She has a tendency to speak out of turn."

"I had noticed," Diego said—a remark that was just shy of insulting. "But, as you say, she is young, and it may be possible to cure her of that. But enough of her—tell me about your vineyards, Don Jose." Again, the change of subject so abruptly was almost insulting.

"Vineyards?" The other man scowled slightly. "Have your man drive around the house and you will see them—or, rather, the start of them. They extend for quite some distance."

Bernardo started the horses, and in a few moments the vines came into view. As Don Jose had said, they were quite extensive. Diego was im-pressed. Behind the house stood a secondary building.

"The press house," Don Jose explained. "We also store the casks for the wine in the cellar of that house. It is best to allow the wine to mature before I sell it."

"Of course." Diego frowned slightly. The sun would be setting shortly, but there were still several dozen workers weeding among the vines. They were all natives, most dressed only in trousers and sandals. As the carriage drew closer, Diego could see that most of the men had lash-marks across their backs. Many of these were fresh, but some were old enough to have scarred over. He could also now see that there were three overseers in the fields, keeping wary eyes on the Indians. The overseers all carried bullwhips, which clearly explained the scars.

"You allow your laborers to be beaten?" Diego asked Don Jose.

"It is the only way to encourage them to work," Don Jose snapped. "They are lazy, and would otherwise never finish their assigned chores. They will not listen to exhortations unless accompanied by the crack of a whip across their backs."

"I have never found brutality necessary," Diego said softly.

"It is not brutality, it is expediency," his host answered crossly. "You do not understand the Indians, it seems."

"I think I understand them far better than you," Diego replied. "They are human beings, not beasts to be whipped."

Don Jose glared at him in fury. "Don Diego, you are a guest at my house, otherwise I should have you whipped for criticizing me! I advise you to be very careful what you say to me, otherwise I shall be forced to issue a challenge to a duel." He thrust out his left arm and rolled the sleeve of his fancy shirt back. There was a scar across the forearm. "I received that when I was 17—and have never been touched by a blade in any fight since then. There is no man in this entire country who is my equal with a sword—unless you think yourself such an expert?"

"I use my mind, not my arms when I fight a man," Diego said calmly. "I assure you that if I wish to harm you, I am quite capable of it."

"Then you are more of a fool than I thought," Don Jose growled. "Even the Alcalde himself cannot touch me. I have powerful friends in Spain."

"Spain is a long way off, Don Jose," Diego reminded him. "And there is justice in this world that is not reliant on the Alcalde."

"Justice?" Don Jose gave a barked laugh. "My foolish friend, justice is what the weak bleat for when they are incapable of holding onto their own. I have no faith in justice—only in strength."

"Then there we differ," Diego said. "For I believe that justice will always triumph. You will surely be made to answer for your brutality—and for your thefts."

"Thefts?" Don Jose barely restrained himself from striking his companion. "You accuse me of theft?"

"I most certainly do," Diego replied. He gestured toward the vines. "I see fresh graftings on several of your growths. Since the only new vines that have arrived in this country in the past few months were those destined for the Mission, and since those were stolen before they arrived there, the conclusion is inescapable."

"Stop this carriage!" Don Jose roared. Startled, Bernardo did as he was ordered. The older man leaped down agilely. "Don Diego, you have insulted me and now accused me of theft. If we ever meet again, you had better be carrying a sword and be prepared to use it!" He turned to storm off back to his house.

"Then I take it that you look unfavorably on my courting your daughter?" Diego called after him, barely able to suppress a smile.

"To the Devil with you and your courting!"

"Father will be so disappointed," Diego murmured. "Well, Bernardo, my task here is done. I think it is time for Zorro to take a hand in matters…"

In the cave below the de la Vega hacienda, Diego gestured at a batch of small pots he had been filling. Each was the size of a soup bowl and filled with a thick, black, pungent material and a fuse. "Don Jose has about a dozen caballeros working for him," he explained. "Even Zorro might have trouble fighting all of them at once, so we need a way to remove them from the scene. These should do the trick." Bernardo raised an eyebrow in query. "These are filled with tar taken from Los Bocanes de Brea[1]," Diego said. "It will burn strongly and with smoke. You are to take them into the vineyards and start them going—but be careful not to get too close to the vines. I want them to think that the vineyards have been set ablaze but not to actually do so. Much fine wine would be lost if those vines are damaged." Bernardo nodded his comprehension. "Good. Then I think tonight Don Jose will discover that there is still justice in this world for all…"

The moon was close to full and low in the sky, casting a silvery pallor across the Castiliano Rancho. There were lights blazing in the main house, and also in the servants' quarters. The vineyards were deserted as Bernardo slipped off on his mission. Zorro watched as he set and lit the first pots, then saluted him briefly.

"On, Toronado," he urged his steed, patting his neck. The Andalusian gave a soft whicker, and then moved silently down the pathway to the hacienda. As soon as they were close to the house, Zorro slipped from the saddle, and led Toronado into the shadows beside the supply sheds. "Wait here," he murmured, and then faded into the shadows himself. He glanced back at the vineyard in time to see the first of his tar pots erupt into fire. It would be quite visible from the house if anyone were to glance in the right direction, but to be certain they would he cried: "Fire! Fire in the vineyards! Fire!'

There was a clatter at the rear door, and two of the servants looked out. Seeing a second pot burst into flames, they set up a wail of "Fire!" throughout the house. Zorro waited, patiently, as the house exploded into noise and movement. Don Jose dashed out and stood, aghast, at what he believed he was seeing.

"The vines are aflame!" he exclaimed. He cuffed the closest servant. "Rouse my caballeros!" he ordered. "Get every man into the fields and make certain the fire does not spread." As he spoke, a third and then a forth gout of fire illuminated the night. "Hurry, you fools! I shall follow!"

The servant rushed to obey, turning the caballeros out of their separate sleeping quarters. Cries and confusion filled the night as men sought buckets to carry water to the fire. Others grabbed blankets to beat back the flames. Then began a stream of would-be firefighters heading toward the fields.

Don Jose reappeared in the doorway, with his daughter in a thick robe behind him. "Stay here," he growled at her. "I must lead those fools, or the fire will spread across the rancho!" Maria gave a bleat of fear and dived back into the house. Don Jose started toward the growing fires, and then gave an abrupt curse.

From the dark shadows had stepped a darker one—a man dressed all in black, and masked... Zorro gave a swift smile. "Good evening, Don Jose," he said softly. "I have been intending to visit you for a while."

"Who are you?" Don Jose roared. "No matter—out of my way! I have work to do!"

"You have sins to answer for," Zorro informed him. "Your men will be sufficient to tend to the fields—you have a more important and urgent meeting with your fate." He drew his sword from its sheath. "I hear that you consider yourself the finest swordsman in California. Permit me to dispute that."

Don Jose was struggling to make sense of all of this. "Who are you?" he demanded. "What are you talking about?"

"I am justice," the black-clad man informed him. "I am retribution. I am—Zorro."

"Zorro?" Don Jose blinked. "I have heard of you—the Alcalde says you are a bandit and a thief!"

"And I say the same about him," Zorro replied. "And his day will come. But, tonight, it is your turn to pay."

"You would attack an unarmed man?" Don Jose spread his hands to show he carried no sword.

"Why not?" Zorro asked him. "You do not hesitate to scourge the helpless, nor to strike and rob an elderly priest." He saw Don Jose pale, and then laughed. "But I am not like you—I give you a chance." He took a spare sword from his belt and tossed it to the landowner, who caught it nimbly enough.

"It is an insult to me to fight with a criminal," Don Jose spat.

"And for me to tackle a thief," Zorro replied. "But if I am willing to overlook this, then so should you. Prepare!" He raised his sword and moved forward. "En garde!" He thrust with his weapon, and Don Jose was forced to parry and step back. There was no further complaint from him that he was fighting beneath his station, for he had no breath to spare to talk.

His claim of being a fine swordsman was no idle boast. He was indeed skillful, and Zorro found himself giving ground more than once. The man was fighting for his honor, which meant a great deal to him—but Zorro was fighting for justice, which meant more. Blow by blow, thrust by thrust, attack by attack, Zorro beat the other man back. Swords clashed and sparked, muscles strained and the two men fought with every last drop of skill and courage. But Zorro was the more skilled—not by much, but sufficient.

"You would scar a holy man," he growled. His sword flickered out, and a thin, bloody line appeared down Don Jose's left cheek. "Receive a mark in return."

Don Jose snarled, and touched his cheek. "You dare!" he snarled.

"I dare more," Zorro assured him. "You would beat your servants to teach them their place? Then learn your own!" His blade flashed again, and a second mark appeared on the same cheek, parallel to the first.

"Swine!" Don Jose snarled. "You will pay for this."

"No," Zorro answered. "It is your turn to pay." For the third time his sword flickered out, and left the third line connecting the first two. "The mark of Zorro has branded you," he said. "All who see you now shall know you for what you are." His sword was a burning instrument in his hands, and in three further blows he had sent Don Jose's sword spinning into the night. His own blade dashed out, and the tip rested at his opponent's throat. "And now—an ending."

"No!" Don Jose whispered, his eyes bulging as they stared at his death. "Spare me."

"You do not deserve it," Zorro said coldly. "But you shall be spared, to be a lesson to others of your kind. However, there is a price to pay." He reached under his cloak and pulled out a parchment he had prepared. "We shall go inside and you will sign this letter to the Alcalde. It is a full confession of your guilt for stealing from the Mission and for scarring Fray Quintero. It says that in recompense for your sins you will donate your vineyard to the church."

"You would rob me of all I own?" Don Jose asked.

"No. Only the vineyard. Perhaps this deed will do your dark soul some good. But you are to leave California and return to Spain. The supply ship the vines came in on will commence its return journey in two days. You will be on it. The letter includes instructions to the Alcalde for him to sell your hacienda and the remaining lands and to forward payment to you in Madrid." Zorro smiled. "As you have powerful friends there, I am sure he will not cheat you too much over his...commission in this matter."

"You cannot force me to do this! I shall have justice!"

"Justice?" Zorro laughed. "Justice is the bleat of the weak when faced by those stronger." Don Jose blanched. "Yes, I heard you when you spoke to Don Diego—it is only appropriate that your own words rebound on you."

"I shall not go!" Don Jose insisted. "I have men and wealth, and you are just a bandit."

"A bandit who can slip into your home when he wishes, and hear what you say and what you plot," Zorro reminded him. "Where are your men to help you now?" He shook his head. "No, they will not be able to help you and your wealth will not save you. I come and go as I wish. I have granted you two days—if you are not on that ship, then you will be in your grave before the end of the week. This I promise you, and you have my mark on your cheek to remind you every day that I keep my promises." He whistled loudly, and Toronado hurtled from the shadows to his side, rearing and snorting. Don Jose fell back with a cry. Zorro vaulted into his saddle, and pointed his sword at the cowering man. "Two days!" He whirled and rode off. Only his laugh floated in the air behind him.

Don Diego sat by the wharf watching the workers loading Maria de Castiliano's voluminous luggage aboard the supply ship. Her father had vanished below deck as soon as he had arrived, his face heavily bandaged. He sipped at his wine and smiled across the table at Fray Felipe. "I hear that scoundrel Zorro had a hand in your latest land grant," he murmured.

"Indeed," the priest agreed. "He seemed to think it an appropriate penance."

Diego laughed gently. "Perhaps he is a padre at heart," he suggested.

"It is perhaps a good thing he never took holy orders," Fray Felipe replied. "I would think even the Holy Father in Rome might be dismayed by some of the penances he imposes."

"And you?" Diego asked more seriously. "Do you disapprove?"

"No, my son," his friend replied. "I think the payment...most appropriate."

"Then I suspect Zorro will sleep without regrets," Diego said. He raised his glass and smiled. "I can hardly wait to taste the new wines that Frey Quintero may now produce!"

1 The then-current name for the Rancho la Brea, where the La Brea Tar Pits stand in the present day.

JUST LIKE MAGIC

By Richard Dean Star and Matthew Baugh

"Magic," said Garcia with a shake of his head. "Please, do not talk to me of magic. I cannot stand to think of such things."

The rotund Sergeant picked up his beer and drained the tankard in a single gulp. Slamming it down on the table, he belched loudly and then glanced around *La Taberna* in sudden embarrassment.

Ignoring his friend's indelicate flatulence, Don Diego de la Vega continued to play idly with a short length of hemp rope no bigger around than a child's drawing stick.

"How can you not love magic, my friend?" said Diego. "It is one of the few things that remind us of the wonders of childhood."

"Maybe," said Garcia, his voice suddenly glum, "unless you were the victim of a rope trick as a child and found yourself tied to a tree. Then you might not feel so good about such things, eh?"

Diego smiled gently. "Ah, but that is why you have friends to help you out of such situations, Demetrio."

A rueful smile flitted across Garcia's face as he remembered Diego coming to his rescue all those years ago. It was one event of many that became the basis for their lifelong friendship.

"Maybe true," he said, "but even so, I dislike not understanding what makes such tricks work. It's a bit too much like…like…"

He struggled to find the right word for a moment before Diego, his grin widening, said, "…like magic?"

"Exactly!" Garcia said triumphantly, and then waved over Victoria Escalante, the tavern's owner.

"Good afternoon, Sergeant," she said, smiling mischievously. "I'm assuming that you are waving to me, rather than simply calling my name for a very good reason, no?"

Garcia flushed bright red and began to mumble, but Victoria waved away his apologies with an even bigger smile and a friendly pat on his shoulder.

"Relax, Sergeant," she said. "I was only joking. I did not mean to upset you."

It was obvious to Diego that Sergeant Garcia and the lovely tavern owner were fond of each other. That hadn't always been the case; Victoria didn't like Alcalde Ramon's repressive use of the army. It had taken Garcia time and effort to win her friendship.

"Please, I would like another drink," Garcia said, smiling with uncharacteristic shyness, "if it will not be too much trouble."

"It is no trouble at all," she said with a laugh.

She glanced quizzically at Diego, who shook his head and smiled before turning his gaze back to the rope. He tried, with apparent difficulty, to twist the strand into a series of seemingly impossible knots and found that they refused to fall apart easily no matter how hard he pulled and tugged.

"You seem to be caught up in your magic trick," she said. "I wish you would take that much interest in poor Don Guillermo when he is scheduled to be taken to El Diablo Prison tomorrow morning."

"What can I do?" Diego said, his attention focused on the stubborn rope. "You and I know that he is innocent, but he has been convicted of sedition."

"I suppose I expect too much of you," Victoria said. With a sigh she moved away to get Garcia's drink.

The sergeant watched Diego struggle a moment longer. "I will never understand why you spend so much time trying to achieve something so pointless," he said.

"Because I have seen others perform such tricks with ease," Diego said with sigh, "and because it is a challenge. At the very least, it would be entertaining at parties."

He dropped the rope onto the table and leaned back, a small frown crossing his handsome face.

"Don Diego!"

Diego de la Vega looked up from the uncommonly elaborate hat he was studying. He knew that voice. Glancing over the vendor's cart, he was able to confirm his worst fear: that young Marisol Torres had spotted him and was winding her way through the crowded marketplace in his direction.

He waved half-heartedly and forced a smile. Bernardo smirked but Diego chose to ignore it; he had learned long ago that acknowledging his old friend's gentle ribbing would only encourage him to do more of it later. He knew how uncomfortable it made Diego when one of the señoritas of the pueblo set her sights on him.

Not that Marisol wasn't pretty enough, or lacked any of the charms of a well-brought up young woman. She was just so...so girlish. He found that he was more attracted to a woman of spirit and intelligence, a woman who cared about the struggles of the people with a passion that matched his own.

If he was perfectly honest with himself, he was more attracted to a woman very much like Victoria Escalante.

"Diego, what a wonderful surprise," Marisol exclaimed, moving deftly around the cart and pressing herself uncomfortably close to him. "Perhaps you can help me with my shopping." She had pitched her voice to sound even younger than her nineteen years, which did not escape Diego's notice. "After all," she added, "you do have exquisite taste."

"A thousand apologies, Marisol," Diego said, taking a step back from her. "I am afraid that I have only enough time for this one purchase, then I am needed back at the hacienda."

He spread his hands in a 'what-can-I-do?' gesture.

Marisol pouted, then her eyes brightened as they saw the wide-brimmed Andalusian hat he was holding.

"How lovely," she said, yanking it from his grasp. "I'm glad you've chosen something simple. Solid black is too severe, of course, but some gold stitching should set it off nicely. Let me see how it looks on you."

Before Diego could protest or move further away from her, she stood on tip-toes and placed the hat on his head, where it perched like an awkward bird. Marisol took one look at him and then hid her face—and her giggles—behind a lace fan that she seemed to materialize out of thin air.

"Diego, you are so silly," she said, folding the fan away from her mouth. "That hat is much too small for you."

"You are as perceptive as ever," he said, doffing the hat with a faint smile. "I am buying this as a present for a friend."

"For me, perhaps?"

"Alas, no."

The pout returned. "I hope it is not for some other woman. I would be very jealous."

"There is no need for that," he said. "I'm buying the hat for Bernardo, actually. Which is for the best, I think. I believe it would be...overly masculine, for a woman as attractive as yourself."

"You're buying it for...for your servant?" Marisol looked stunned.

"Bernardo is much more than that," Diego said, struggling to suppress his irritation. "He has been my friend since the cradle. In fact, as babies we shared the same mother's milk."

"Yes, but he is still only a servant, an Indian."

Diego did not care for the negative emphasis she placed on the word Indian. After a moment Marisol's disapproving expression gave way to a sly grin.

"You are such a tease," she said. "I almost believed you. Don't tell me who the hat is for, but if I see it on the head of some pretty girl, I shall be very cross with you."

"I promise you, Marisol," Diego said, "that will not happen."

They said their goodbyes and Diego watched her go, feeling both a strong sense of relief and a sudden resurgence of irritability. Although he and his father were among the pueblo's elite, he nonetheless held little patience for the dismissive and condescending attitudes of his peers toward the native population.

Not for the first time, Diego realized that Marisol's beauty could easily be supplanted by the ugliness of her views. He turned to his friend, who was practically falling down with silent laughter.

"It's times like this I am almost glad you cannot speak," he said, handing Bernardo the hat. "Here, try this on."

Bernardo accepted the hat with a grin and placed it on his head.

It fit perfectly.

Z

"Pardon me, Alcalde," Diego said, as he stepped into Luis Ramon's study. "I wonder if I could have a moment of your time?"

Ramon looked up from the papers he was signing, a look of impatience crossing his handsome features. Then he forced a smile and gestured Diego to the comfortable, leather-bound chair opposite him.

"Please," Ramon said, running a free hand through his luxurious mane of hair, his tone gracious, "be seated, Don Diego. I am always happy to have you as my guest."

"Many thanks, Don Luis," Diego said, sinking into the chair.

"How can I be of service?"

"I'm terribly sorry to be a bother about this," Diego said, "but it's about your prisoner. As it happens, I've come to beg clemency for Don Guillermo."

Ramon looked surprised. "And why would you do that? He is a traitor."

"Surely not." Diego spoke mildly, with just a touch of reproof. "Don Guillermo comes from an old and noble family, one that has known my own for more than three generations. It is hard to believe that a caballero such as he would be capable of behavior even remotely like you describe."

"He is guilty, I can assure you of that," the Alcalde said. "Don Diego, your loyalty does you credit, but this man's offenses are a threat to the public order and the authority of His Catholic Majesty, Ferdinand VII."

"Forgive me for saying so," Diego said, "but is it possible it is because he spoke out against you and not so much His Majesty?"

Diego was careful to keep his tone neutral and not antagonistic. He knew all too well that it took very little to arouse Ramon's wrath. To do so now would not be to his advantage...or to Don Guillermo's.

"Just so." Ramon folded his black-gloved hands and glowered at the younger man. "I am the duly appointed representative of the Spanish throne. To plot against me is to plot against His Majesty. As I'm sure you are aware, Don Diego, no man's blood is blue enough to excuse that."

"I do agree with you, in principle," Diego said with a gentle smile. "In fact, I admire your sentiment of justice without partiality for rank or class."

A puzzled frown appeared on Ramon's face. "I'm not sure what you're getting at," he said.

"The equality of all men under the law," Diego clarified. "I had had no idea you favored such liberal ideas. Have you read the writings of the Englishman, Locke? He has the most fascinating—"

"Excuse me, Señor Alcalde?"

Diego turned in his seat to see Ramon's adjutant standing in the doorway.

"What is it, Juan?" Ramon said, sounding relieved at the interruption.

"Capitán Vasquez from the merchant ship is here to see you, Señor. He says it is most urgent."

"Ah." Ramon stood and straightened his lace cuffs with a flourish. "You must forgive me, Don Diego, but my responsibilities call me away from this fascinating discussion."

"Your devotion to civic duty is inspiring," Diego said. "Are you certain you won't reconsider Don Guillermo's case?"

"I'm afraid not. However, I appreciate your concern."

Ramon strode out of his office, his adjutant following along behind. As Diego left the outer office he passed the ship's Capitán. He paused outside for a moment as the door closed, listening to their raised voices.

"Alcalde! Someone has robbed my ship!"

"Robbed? Surely you must be joking, Capitán. No one would dare to do such a thing while in my port. What did they take?"

"A block and tackle and a hundred yards of rope."

"What?" Ramon sounded confused. "I fail to see the profit in that, Captain."

"Nor do I!" the Captain said, sounding more frustrated than angry. "I might have attributed it to stray children, but for one very particular thing: whoever stole the items left a small bag of pesos in their place!"

It was all Diego could do to keep from laughing as he strode away from the building.

It was early in the evening and the setting sun had begun to paint the walls of the Mission of San Gabriel Arcangel a soft, mellow orange. The scene might have been peaceful except for the fact that two robed frailes were standing near the center of the wall, engaged in a heated argument.

As Diego trotted his horse closer, the taller of the two—a gaunt, older man whose weathered face appeared to have been baked into a permanently severe scowl—turned and stalked away, his sandals kicking up small plumes of dust.

The other man-middle-aged, with the shoulders of a blacksmith—watched him go. Then his face lit up as he turned and saw Diego.

"Welcome, my son," he called out. "What brings you to our Mission this fine evening?"

Diego dismounted and grinned affectionately.

"I'm afraid I've been on a fool's errand today, Fray Felipe," he said. "Victoria talked me into pleading with the alcalde for Don Guillermo's freedom. It was, however, as hopeless as I feared."

He spread his hands in a gesture of helplessness.

"The bright side, however," he added, "is that I at least managed to perfect a magic trick I've been working on."

Felipe cocked an eyebrow at the young caballero as they entered the mission church. The bell for matins prayer had not yet sounded and they were alone in the large room.

"With something as important as Don Guillermo's freedom at stake," Felipe said gently, "magic seems a rather frivolous thing for you to be concerned with, don't you think?"

Diego shrugged at the gentle rebuke. "There is only so much one man can do," he replied. "In this case, silly things such as ropes and knots help to clear my mind." Diego waved his hands dismissively. "Perhaps I'll show you the trick sometime; you might be amused."

Felipe sighed heavily. "If it could take my mind off the injustice of tomorrow, then perhaps."

"Speaking of that," Diego said, "wasn't that Fray Umberto I saw you talking to?"

"It was. I can't stand that man." Felipe glanced heaven-ward and crossed himself. "May God forgive me, but it's true."

Diego stifled a smile. "He is the one who built the new prison cart for Ramon, is he not?"

"Yes, and he is the one who will be driving it tomorrow when they take poor Don Guillermo to prison. I've been telling him that this is an unjust and un-Christian thing he is doing, but he won't listen."

"From what I've heard of the man," Diego said, "that is not uncommon for him."

Felipe rolled his eyes. "You have no idea! He had the audacity—the audacity!—to quote the Epistles at me. He actually believes that since God appoints rulers over us it must be God's will to help the alcalde! Have you ever heard of such a thing?"

Before Diego could speak, Felipe threw his hands up in the air and strode back-and-forth across the tiled floor.

"I tell you," Felipe exclaimed, "that man is just trying to curry favor in the hope of having the archbishop replace me with him!"

"Well..." Diego began, and then Felipe slapped his hands together suddenly, causing Diego to start in surprise.

225

"Bah!" Felipe cried. "I've been dealing with church politics for half my life!"

He stopped pacing and took several, deep breaths.

"Ah, Diego" he said, much calmer this time, "despite how it sounds, I'm not particularly worried about Fray Umberto. My soul grieves, however, to see a member of my order hauling an innocent man off to prison."

"Perhaps we should pray for a miracle," Diego said.

Felipe's dark eyes, which up to now had appeared downcast, seemed to twinkle. "Maybe," he said, "we should pray that Zorro will rescue Don Guillermo."

"That would take something of a miracle," Diego said. "Did Fray Umberto happen to tell you anything else about tomorrow?"

"Alcalde Ramon is taking a dozen lancers along as an escort," Felipe said. "I'm not sure that 'miracle' is the correct word. However, Zorro would most assuredly need to be a magician to rescue the Don from his captivity."

Diego chuckled. "Be careful, Felipe. If Ramon hears you talking like that, you may be the next man sent to El Diablo. But enough of this, I came here because I need something from you."

"My help?" The priest's eyes brightened even more.

"Actually, I'd like you to hear my confession."

Fray Felipe looked puzzled but ushered Diego to the confessional, then settled into the booth on the other side of the screen.

"Forgive me, Father," Diego said, "for the things we are about to do."

"We?" said Felipe.

Z

"Diego," Victoria Escalante said, leaning across the table. "As much as I enjoy your company, I feel compelled to ask if you plan to be here the entire night. As you know, I cannot go to bed until you're gone home."

He smiled up at her. "Now that you mention it, if it extends my time with you, perhaps I will stay here until the sun comes up."

Victoria shrugged, her eyes dancing in the flickering candlelight. "Suit yourself. I will be asleep on the floor, which I think would make me poor company. But feel free to stay as long as you like."

Diego laughed. "I think I would grow bored hearing only the sound of my own voice. In truth, I won't be much longer. I'm just waiting for Sergeant Garcia."

"What makes you think he'll be back in tonight after—how many bottles of wine did you buy for him?"

"Four," Diego said absently. "Or five, the precise number escapes me. In his wine-induced delirium, however, it seems that the Sergeant forgot something."

He pulled a metal ring with a single large key out of his vest pocket.

"Santa Maria." Victoria's voice was a whisper. "That cannot be! Is it…?"

"The key to the prison cart?" Diego said. "I believe it is. Garcia must have dropped it as he was leaving."

"Do you know what this means, Diego? With that key we could help Don Guillermo to escape!"

"I'm afraid not," Diego replied. "Not unless you also have a plan to get past Ramon and a dozen lancers. Besides, If I don't get this back to Garcia, Ramon will have him shot for dereliction of duty."

A loud pounding at the door interrupted them. Victoria went and opened it for Garcia, who was evidently too drunk to realize it hadn't been locked. At the sight of the key on the table he beamed and stumbled forward.

"Diego, I am more grateful than I can say." Garcia picked up the key and pressed it to his lips. Then his brow puckered in confusion. "There is wax on the key," he said.

"It was lying on the floor," Diego said. "I noticed it when I accidentally knocked the candle off the table. Some of the wax must have spilled onto it."

"No matter," the Sergeant's voice was slurred by wine and happiness. "I shall polish it before I go to bed. This little key is very important." He frowned. "Even if the job it was made for is a sad one."

Garcia turned the key and the lock responded with a crisp 'click' as it snapped shut. The wooden cage, constructed of interlocking beams secured by heavy iron spikes, comprised the entire back of the small, cramped cart. Its sole occupant, Don Guillermo, glared through the bars at him. The old man looked pitiably frail, but a light of defiance seemed to burn bright in his eyes.

Garcia turned away, abruptly ashamed at the unfortunate duty he was about to perform.

I am so sorry, caballero, he thought. He managed to keep from saying anything aloud, however. Words of sympathy for a prisoner could be dangerous when the alcalde had treason on the brain.

Garcia climbed into his saddle with effort, wondering as he did so if the horse had somehow grown taller overnight. The throbbing pain that seemed to extend from one of his temples to the other didn't help.

It almost made him regret his time spent at the taberna.

On the other hand, the wine had been so good, and Don Diego so generous...

Garcia shook his head, then wheeled his horse to face Juan Ramon. The Alcalde was, as always, immaculately dressed and had chosen for his mount a magnificent chestnut gelding. Garcia's hand snapped to his forehead in a military salute.

"The prisoner is secure, Señor Alcalde!"

Ramon smiled thinly. "Just to be certain, give me the key, Sergeant."

"Sí, Señor." Garcia moved closer and placed the ring in Ramon's black-gloved hand.

"Very good Sergeant," the Alcalde said. "I'd just like to see Zorro try to interfere this time."

"So would I, Señor," Garcia said, innocently.

Ramon's expression was unreadable. The Sergeant hoped that he hadn't revealed his sympathy for the prisoner, or his grudging admiration for the masked outlaw. He glanced at the cart driver, but the tall fray, whose name was Umberto, Garcia recalled, appeared too sullen to meet his gaze. The man sat hunched in his seat, a cowl drawn up over his head.

"Lancers," Garcia bellowed, "forward!"

They rode through the gates of the presidio into the plaza. A great crowd had gathered to watch the procession and Garcia found himself noticing a familiar face here and there.

The first one he recognized was the captain of the trading ship. From the pale, somewhat pained expression on the captain's face, it appeared that he also was nursing the effects of too much merriment from the night before.

The procession passed a crowd of pretty señoritas, and Garcia recognized Marisol Torres and Victoria Escalante among them. He suspected that the young women must feel some sympathy for their imprisoned neighbor. However, it was hard to tell from their excited chatter.

Victoria Escalante's concern, by contrast, was easy to see. Garcia has to avert his eyes from the combination of grief, anger, and disappointment on her lovely face.

As the procession left the pueblo, Garcia noticed that one face was missing from the crowd.

It's just as well, he thought. Diego is a sensitive man. Undoubtedly, he could not bear the thought of seeing Don Guillermo spend his final days in such a terrible place.

The massive fortress known as El Diablo, which clung to the coastal cliffs like some dark and malevolent creature, did not sit far from the Pueblo de Los Angeles. However, with the slow cart setting the pace, Garcia knew that it would take them until at least noon to arrive with their prisoner.

It was less than an hour into the journey, and Garcia had settled into the comfortable rhythm of the ride, when he heard a cry echo across the low, rolling hills:

"Zorro!"

One of the lancers was pointing frantically toward a hilltop several hundred yards in the distance. Garcia could see that a masked rider, dressed from head to toe entirely in black, was sitting astride a magnificent ebony stallion.

Until that moment, Garcia had only seen Zorro in full daylight on a couple of occasions, as the Fox preferred to work under the cover of darkness. He was, Garcia had to admit, an impressive sight.

"Lancers—" he began.

"No, Garcia," the Alcalde interrupted. "He is mine! Lancers, with me. Garcia, you remain with the prisoner."

"By myself? But, Señor Alcalde, what if—"

"Very well." Ramon pointed to two of the men. "You and you, remain here. The rest with me!"

On the hill, the great horse reared and its rider waved insolently. Then he wheeled and rode off as Ramon and his men galloped in pursuit. Garcia watched until they were out of sight before turning back to the cart.

"Come along, Fray Umberto," he said. "We have a long road ahead of us and there's no use waiting here."

Z

It was only a short time later that the heavy cart lurched to a stop, tipping forward onto its tongue. The robed driver stepped down and looked perplexedly at the hitch for a moment.

"You men," Garcia said to the lancers, "what happened?"

One of the solders dismounted and the fray stepped aside to let them inspect the cart.

"The rope on the coupling has come loose, Sergeant," one of the soldiers replied.

"Then fix it, baboso." Garcia frowned, "I wonder how—"

He paused as he felt a gentle tap on his shoulder. He turned and saw that it had been caused by the tip of an elegant rapier held by the robed fray. The man had thrown his cowl back to reveal a masked face and a dazzling grin.

"Zorro!" Garcia cried.

"At your service, Sergeant," said the outlaw. "Now, if you will be so good as to dismount, and while you're at it, have your men throw their weapons into those bushes on the other side of the path."

Garcia swallowed hard. "Do as Zorro says," he ordered.

He climbed down from his horse, wincing as his head began to throb anew. The masked man stripped off his disguise, never letting the point of the sword waver from the sergeant's throat. Garcia waved the soldiers ahead of him as Zorro forced them all to the back of the cart.

"Please convey my sincere apologies to Fray Umberto," the masked man said, "who happens to be tied up at the moment. I deeply regret that I had to borrow his habit, which he doesn't have much use for right now, just as I will have to borrow your horses."

"Of course, Señor Zorro." Garcia frowned. "But your plan, it cannot work."

"Oh?" Zorro rolled up the habit and tossed it into the bushes.

"There is only one key that will free Don Guillermo, and the Alcalde has it."

The masked man's grin broadened even more and he produced a key with a conjurer's flourish. Moving to the cart, he unlocked the door and helped Don Guillermo step out onto the dusty path. The old man seemed unsteady, his legs weak from being bent inside the tiny cage.

"Do you enjoy a puzzle, Sergeant?" Zorro asked as he helped Don Guillermo climb onto one of the horses.

"I suppose I do," Garcia said, unsure where the outlaw was going with such questions.

"Very good. Then tell me, how many men do you think would fit inside this cage, eh? One? Two? Perhaps three?"

Garcia eyed the tiny compartment and tried to envision himself inside of it. The image was not an appealing one. And adding another man to such a small space? Impossible.

"I would say one," Garcia said. "Maybe two. But no more."

"Ah," Zorro said, and then his playful grin disappeared. "Well, I shall counter your theory with one of my own. I think that three men will fit nicely in there. What do you say, Sergeant?"

Garcia swallowed uncomfortably. Zorro, seeing his unease, grinned again. "Order your men inside, Sergeant. And you needn't worry—I have no intention of trying to put all four of you in there together. Although I must admit, making the effort might have proven amusing."

He pressed the tip of his rapier against Garcia's neck.

"I trust you will not abandon your men to try and pursue me?"

"No, Señor Zorro," Garcia said, relieved that he wouldn't be confined to the cage.

"And I'm certain you won't mind if we take your horses," Zorro added.

"Of course not, Señor Zorro," Garcia said, and his shoulders slumped in defeat.

As Zorro and the old Don rode away in the distance, Garcia turned and looked at the three lancers. Their faces were pressed between the bars and one man was slowly turning as red as a fresh-grown tomato.

Garcia sighed. He was not looking forward to the Alcalde's return.

Juan Ramon glared at nothing as he rode. He had chased his enemy, Zorro, for half an hour before he had disappeared so completely, it was as if he had never existed at all. The situation was frustratingly familiar: the man seemed to have an endless supply of the Devil's own tricks, and his horse could outrun the very wind.

But why? Ramon thought angrily. What was the point of baiting us into a futile chase?

In point of fact, he had been wondering this all the way back to where Garcia and the lancers were waiting with the prisoner. But now, as he rounded a bend in the road, the answer became painfully clear. The prison cart sat just off the trail with his men locked inside it—rather uncomfortably, it appeared—and Sergeant Garcia was leaning against the side, apparently dozing.

"Sergeant!"

The portly man's eyes shot open and he snapped to attention–saluting, Ramon noted, rather sleepily.

"What happened here, Garcia?"

"It was Zorro, Señor Alcalde. He was disguised as the driver and—"

"Never mind that," Ramon snapped. "How long ago did they leave?"

"Only a few moments ago, Señor. I—"

Ramon ignored the rest of what Garcia had to say.

"Lancers," he cried. "With me!"

It must have been an impostor, Ramon thought as he galloped at the head of the column. Zorro tricked us again, but this time that Fox has outfoxed himself!

Ramon knew that if the impostor was riding that black devil-horse, then that meant Zorro was on a lesser mount. And with Don Guillermo too weak to ride fast, that meant the odds of catching them on the trail were better than average.

After a few moments riding, he felt a sense of impending victory rising inside him. On the road ahead he could make out two tiny figures, one dressed all in black. A moment later the two riders broke into a gallop.

But not fast enough, Ramon thought triumphantly. Zorro, I have you now!

He wished that he could force his horse to full speed, but he dared not outdistance his men. Still, each time he caught sight of the fugitives they were a little closer. Then, the two horses broke from the trail and headed into the mouth of a deep gulley.

"They're trying to lose us in the ravines," Ramon shouted. "Hurry!"

"It won't work, Señor," a lancer called back. "I know this place; it is a box-canyon."

He has trapped himself!

Ramon grinned. He could have howled with laughter, but he knew that he must remain focused. He led his men down the twisting path at a dizzying pace, the high stone walls looming on either side of them. Finally they emerged at the canyon's end to see...

Two horses grazing at the foot of a cliff.

Ramon turned his gaze upward and saw Zorro and Don Guillermo seated comfortably in two, large loops at the end of a rope. They were being drawn swiftly upward to the rim of the canyon by what appeared to be...a ship's block and tackle.

The Alcalde stifled a groan, remembering his recent conversation with the captain about items that had been stolen from his ship.

His mind raced, calculating how long it would take to get out of the canyon, how complicated it would be to find their way to the rim of the canyon and then pick up the trail again. And Zorro certainly had fresh horses waiting for him.

"Lancers," Ramon screamed. "Dismount and ready muskets. Shoot them! Shoot them down!"

The men moved to comply, but the Alcalde knew it was already too late.

Zorro had won again.

"I tell you, Don Diego, the man has the Devil himself helping him... or perhaps an angel."

Garcia gazed at his old friend over the top of a half-empty wine cup, his expression a mixture of frustration and childlike wonder.

"Perhaps," Diego said with a smile, "he simply had a good plan."

"A good plan?" Garcia snorted, then took another drink of his wine. "I do not see how any man, even Zorro, could plan for so many coincidences. It was just like...just like..."

"Like magic?" Diego said, masking his laughter behind a draught of wine.

"Magic," said Garcia with a shake of his head. "Perhaps so, but please, do not talk to me of such things, Diego. Every time I hear that word, trouble seems to follow!"

ABOUT THE CONTRIBUTORS

Keith R.A. DeCandido is the internationally best-selling author of more than 40 novels, as well as a whole mess of comic books, short stories, novellas, eBooks, and nonfiction. His most recent work includes *Star Trek* fiction in novel (*A Singular Destiny*), novella ("The Unhappy Ones" in *Seven Deadly Sins*), short story ("Family Matters" in *Mirror Universe: Shards and Shadows*), and comic book (*Captain's Log: Jellico*) form; the monthly *Farscape* comic book from BOOM! Studios; novels based on *Supernatural* (*Bone Key*) and *Dungeons & Dragons* (*Under a Crimson Sun*); comic books based on *Cars* (*The Adventures of Tow Mater: Rust Bucket Rally*) and *StarCraft* (*Ghost Academy*); and lots more. Besides the above, he's also written in the universes of *Buffy the Vampire Slayer, Command and Conquer, CSI: NY, Doctor Who, Gene Roddenberry's Andromeda,* Marvel Comics, *Resident Evil, Serenity,* and *World of Warcraft,* among others. In 2009, Keith was inexplicably granted a Lifetime Achievement Award by the International Association of Media Tie-in Writers, which means he never needs to accomplish anything ever again. Like Charlie Brown, he's always wondered how the other side felt, which was what led him to pitch a story from the perspective of Zorro's arch-enemy, Capitán Monastario and he is grateful to editor Richard and the good folks at Zorro Productions for letting him do it. Keith lives in New York City where, when he isn't writing, he's following his beloved Yankees, doing work for the U.S. Census Bureau, blogging (kradical.livejournal.com), podcasting (www.chronicrift.com and www.goodmorningsurvivors.com), Twittering (KRADeC), or practicing karate (he's currently a first-degree black belt in *Kenshikai*). You can e-mail him your comments, critiques, and raspberries to keith@decandido.net.

The 2011 Guest of Honor at Malice Domestic mystery convention, **Carole Nelson Douglas** (www.carolenelsondouglas.com) is the author of 55 novels in multiple genres but thinks of them all mostly as "adventures." She writes the award-winning, alphabetically titled Midnight Louie feline PI contemporary mystery series (*Cat in a Topaz Tango*) and was the first novelist to make a woman from the Sherlock Holmes Canon, Irene Adler, a series protagonist. The first of eight Adler novels, *Good Night, Mr. Holmes*, a *New York Times* Notable Book of the Year and received mystery and romance awards. She also writes the bestselling Delilah Street, Paranormal Investigator, noir urban fantasies, with the fourth book *Silver Zombie* out in 2010.

Carole received a "Pioneer of the Publishing Industry" award from *RT BOOK Reviews* magazine for her genre-blending and bending fiction. She's written many short stories in various genres, with eight appearing in Year's Best Mystery collections. Her work has been short-listed for or won more than 50 writing awards.

Carole and her husband, Sam Douglas, are kept as pets in Fort Worth by several formerly homeless quadrupeds.

Rubén Procopio is a multi-tasking artist with more than 25 years of experience. Rubén is a credited animation artist on dozens of Disney feature films, including ***The Little Mermaid, Beauty and the Beast, Aladdin*** and ***The Lion King***. In 2003 Rubén founded Masked Avenger Studios, reflecting his lifelong love for the masked heroes of yesteryear and providing animation, sculpting, comics and illustration services to many entertainment clients. Highlights include Rubén's sculpts of such legendary characters as Zorro, The Lone Ranger, The Phantom and The Green Hornet & Kato for Electric Tiki's Classic Heroes Line and the publication of Rubén's original character Chameleon Man™ stories. Other Moonstone Books projects include illustrating ***Tales of Zorro, The Phantom Chronicles anthology*** and its accompanying ***Artist's Annex***, ***Captain Action*** books and collaborating with Doug Klauba on the ***Phantom Generations*** covers.

See more of Rubén's work at:
http://www.maskedavenger.com
http://www.maskedavengerstudios.blogspot.com

Matthew Baugh's first encounters with Zorro came at a young age. He remembers seeing a little of an episode of the Disney TV series. He also owned a Little Golden Book titled *Zorro and the Secret Plan*, and a copy of *Walt Disney's Stories From Other Land*s which featured a Zorro story. From that point he was hooked and has been devouring movies, TV shows, and other stories about the hero ever since. He assisted Richard Dean Starr with Moonstone's *Tales of Zorro* and is excited to have his very own story in *More Tales of Zorro*. When not writing tales of adventure, fantasy, horror and mystery, Matthew is the pastor of a church in the greater Chicago area.

Z

Johnny D. Boggs–who once got a Zorro action figure from Santa Claus and whose 8-year-old son can sing the theme song from the 1950s Disney TV series–has been praised by *Booklist* magazine as "among the best western writers at work today." He is one of the few authors to have won both the Western Heritage Wrangler Award and Spur Award for his fiction. He has four Spur Awards, and *True West* magazine has named him the Best Living Fiction Writer in its Best of the West Awards. A native of South Carolina and a former newspaper journalist in Dallas and Fort Worth, Boggs has written more than 30 novels and books, several short stories and hundreds of magazine articles. He is a frequent contributor to *Boys' Life, New Mexico Magazine, Persimmon Hill, True West, Western Art and Architecture* and *Wild West*. His novels include *The Killing Shot, Hard Winter, Northfield, Doubtful Cañon* and *Camp Ford*. He lives in Santa Fe, New Mexico.
His website is www.johnnydboggs.com.

Joe Gentile keeps pretty busy running a publishing company, but in his spare moments he has managed to write graphic novels and short fiction stories: *Buckaroo Banzai, Kolchak the Night Stalker, Sherlock Holmes, Werewolf the Apocalypse, The Phantom, The Spider, The Avenger,* and many more! His latest was the critically acclaimed graphic novel "*Sherlock Holmes/Kolchak: Cry for Thunder*", which will soon be expanded into a novel. When he's not writing, editing, publishing, or trying to find time to sleep, Joe plays the bass guitar and enjoys a good life with his wife Kathy and their pack of personality-ridden dogs.

Z

Steve Rasnic Tem is a past winner of the World Fantasy, British Fantasy, and Bram Stoker awards. He has recent and upcoming stories in *Asimov's, Postscripts,* and the anthologies *Werewolves and Shape Shifters, Visitants, Mountain Magic and Spectres in Coal Dust.* A collection of all his story collaborations with wife Melanie Tem, In Concert, recently came out from Centipede Press. Also, Speaking Volumes (www.speakingvolumes.us) has brought out Invisible, a six CD audio and downloadable MP3 collection of some of his relatively recent stories, most previously uncollected. His first two novels have just been re-released as ebooks from crossroadpress.com. You can visit the Tem home on the web at www.mstem.com.

Z

Joe R. Lansdale Texas-born Mojo storyteller and scriptwriter Joe R. Lansdale is the author of more than thirty novels in all genres, including crime, Western, horror and pulp adventure. The author of *Act Of Love, Dead In The West, The Nightrunners, Cold In July, The Bottoms, Lost Echoes* and *The Drive-In* series, he is also known for his seven novels about two unlikely friends, Hap Collins and Leonard Pine, who live in a town in East Texas and find themselves solving a variety of often violent or macabre mysteries. The series began with *Savage Season* in 1990 and has continued through *Mucho Mojo, Two-Bear Mambo, Bad Chili, Rumble Tumble, Veil's Visit* and *Captains Outrageous*

Win Scott Eckert holds a B.A. in Anthropology and a Juris Doctorate. He is the editor of and contributor to *Myths for the Modern Age: Philip José Farmer's Wold Newton Universe* (MonkeyBrain Books, 2005), a 2007 Locus Awards finalist. He has contributed to seven volumes (and counting) of Black Coat Press' annual pulp anthology, *Tales of the Shadowmen*, writing about adventurous characters such as the Scarlet Pimpernel, Hareton Ironcastle, and Doc Ardan, the "French Doc Savage." His other Moonstone credits include yarns in *The Avenger Chronicles*, *The Captain Midnight Chronicles*, *The Phantom Chronicles 2*, and *The Green Hornet Chronicles*, which he co-edited. He also is writing (along with co-author Eric Fein) the Green Ghost for Moonstone's Originals comic pulp project. Win contributed the Foreword to the latest edition of Philip José Farmer's *Tarzan Alive: A Definitive Biography of Lord Greystoke* (Bison Books, 2006), and is currently writing a series of interconnected "regencypunk" stories covering the secret origins of Farmer's Wold Newton Family, the first of which appeared in the just-released *The Worlds of Philip José Farmer 1: Protean Dimensions* (Meteor House, 2010). Win's latest books are the encyclopedic two-volume *Crossovers: A Secret Chronology of the World* (Black Coat Press, 2010) and the Wold Newton novel *The Evil in Pemberley House* (Subterranean Press, 2009), co-authored with Philip José Farmer, featuring Patricia Wildman, the daughter of a certain bronze-skinned pulp hero. Win is thrilled beyond belief to contribute to Zorro's ongoing mythos. Find him on the web at www.winscotteckert.com.

Timothy Zahn has been writing science fiction for over thirty years. In that time he has published thirty-nine novels, nearly ninety short stories and novelettes, and four collections of short fiction. Best known for his eight *Star Wars* novels, he is also the author of the Quadrail series, the Cobra series, and the young-adult Dragonback series. Recent books include *Terminator Salvation: Trial by Fire*, a sequel to the movie, and *The Domino Pattern*, the fourth Quadrail book. Upcoming projects include *Cobra Guardian*, the second of the Cobra War Trilogy, *Star Wars: Choices of One*, and *Judgment at Proteus*, the final book of the Quadrail series. Also scheduled for 2011 is a 20th Anniversary edition of his first

Star Wars book, *Heir to the Empire*. As a boy, he was a huge fan of the Disney Zorro TV series. It was an immense honor and delight to be asked to write a story about his first hero.

Z

Kage Baker was born in Hollywood, California in 1952. She was an artist, actor, and director at the Living History Centre, and taught Elizabethan English as a Second Language. In addition, she won the Nebula Award for best novella, for *The Women of Nell Gwynne*, in 2010. A lifelong resident of Pismo Beach, California, she passed away from cancer in early 2010.

Z

John Peel was born in Nottingham, England, home of another adventure hero–Robin Hood. He grew up watching more TV than was good for him and has subsequently written novels based on *"Doctor Who"*, *"Star Trek"*, *"The Avengers"*, *"The Outer Limits"* and *"Star Wars"*. He's also created his own worlds with the *"Diadem"* and *"2099"* series, along with *"The Secret of Dragonhome"* and other original novels. He currently lives on Long Island, New York, with his wife and a pack of miniature pinschers. He can be found at: www.john-peel.com.

Z

Jennifer Fallon is the author of the hugely successful *Tide Lords* series, *The Hythrun Chronicles, the Demon Child trilogy* and the *Seconds Sons Trilogy*, with bestselling books published in the Australia, the US, the UK and a number of foreign language editions. Jennifer also has co-authored a *Stargate SG1* tie-in novel, has published horror and science fiction short stories in a number of publications, including the official Stargate magazine, and is currently working on new series *The Rift Runners* (Book 1 – *The Undivided* will be published in 2011 in Australia). Her novella,(*The Magic Word*, was included in Jack Dann's 2010 anthology, *Legends of Australian Fantasy*. In her spare time, Jennifer has recently created a superhero (for the *Chicks in Capes* anthology), and is currently in the process of setting up the Reynox International Writers Centre in New Zealand. Jennifer mentors up to 10 other writers a year. She has twice been short listed for an Aurealis Award for Medalon and The Gods of Amyrantha, has been nominated for the Australian Prime Minister's Literary Award and the World Fantasy Awards (several times), short listed for the US Romantic Times Epic Fantasy Award (The Immortal Prince) and was shortlisted in the UK for the inaugural David Gemmel Legend Award (Wolfblade).

Z

Richard Dean Starr is the author of more than two-hundred articles, columns, stories, books, and graphic novels. His work has been published in magazines and newspapers as diverse as *Starlog, Twilight Zone, Science Fiction Chronicle*, and the *Tribune-Georgian*, just to name a few. His publications include *Hellboy: Odder Jobs, Kolchak: the Night Stalker Chronicles, Kolchak: The Night Stalker Case Book, The Phantom Chronicles, The Green Hornet Chronicles and Tales of Zorro*, as well as a notable appearance in the 2005 Stephen King Halloween issue of *Cemetery Dance* magazine. In addition, he is the author of the graphic novels, *Wyatt Earp: The Justice Riders* and *The Spider: Exit Screaming-A Tale of the Black Dahlia*, and the editor of *Tales of Zorro*, the first anthology of original Zorro fiction in the eighty-five year history of the character. With Joe Gentile, he also edited *Sex, Lies and Private Eyes*, a collection of noir mystery fiction. Starr is currently at work on *Captain Action: Classified*, the first prose anthology based in part upon the classic 1960's toy line and DC comic book series created by Jim Shooter and Gil Kane.

JUL -- 2011